EVERYTHING HAPPENS TODAY

Jesse Browner

EVERYTHING HAPPENS TODAY

Europa
editions

Europa Editions
116 East 16th Street
New York, N.Y. 10003
www.europaeditions.com
info@europaeditions.com

Copyright © 2011 by Jesse Browner
First Publication 2011 by Europa Editions

Library of Congress Cataloging in Publication Data is available
ISBN 978-1-60945-051-9

Browner, Jesse
Everything Happens Today

Book design by Emanuele Ragnisco
www.mekkanografici.com
Cover illustration © Image Zoo/Corbis

Prepress by Grafica Punto Print – Rome

Printed in Canada

For Sophie and Cora

Seize the moments of happiness, love and be loved!
That is the only reality in the world, all else is folly.
It is the one thing we are interested in here.
—LEO TOLSTOY, *War and Peace*

EVERYTHING HAPPENS TODAY

When you've walked all the way from the Upper East Side to Greenwich Village in the middle of the night, the first sight of home should be an occasion for joy. Wes felt anything but joyful as he climbed the stoop. He had hoped that a long walk through the dark and quiet city would give him some perspective, but it hadn't worked out that way. In other circumstances, it might have been an adventure but it was all nothing but a blur, thoughts as flimsy and disposable as plastic bags. If he had been a character in a book—Prince André in *War and Peace*, say—he would have seized the opportunity for a round of rough, candid soul-searching that would inevitably have led to some brilliant new insight into human nature in general and his own moral frailty in particular. But he wasn't Prince André—he was just Wes, idiot Wes, the guy who'd just ruined his life forever and forever, and he was as confused and miserable now as he'd been when he'd set out from Lucy's apartment two hours earlier. He stood at the threshold and took a deep breath, but it didn't help: the sadness didn't go away. In fact, he felt a tear welling, and he leaned forward to rest his forehead on the cold, damp lacquer of the front door.

Wes knew it was a terrible thing for someone so young to feel so sad in this particular way. It seemed to combine elements of exhaustion, shame, hopelessness and loss. A teenager had no business feeling this way. He didn't have a lot of experience in these things, but he felt instinctively that this was a much older person's kind of sadness, informed by regrets, nostalgia, a sense of half a lifetime's squandered opportunities. It was the sort of feeling a middle-aged loser might have when he realizes that he made a bad choice twenty years earlier, and can trace everything that's gone wrong ever since back to that one moment. It was the sort of feeling that Wes could easily imagine his dad feeling. Another tear squeezed itself from his eye and was caught on his eyelash, blurring his vision. With the key in the lock, Wes changed his mind and turned to sit on the top step of the stoop.

Wes felt paralyzed by indecision and weariness. He'd been up practically the entire night, but he wasn't physically tired. He could push on to the river, only five minutes away; letting the sun rise upon him and the fresh winds wash over him might be a cleansing, healing balm. It seemed unlikely, somehow. Wes doubted that he would ever feel clean again. This was usually his favorite time of day; he was often out walking Crispy in the dark before the dawn. He loved the streets of the Village when there was no one around, when it felt like being on an empty stage that belonged to no one but him, but now it was spoiled. The coming of the daylight seemed ominous and bleak, as if the new day would set the night's events in stone— as if, should the night go on forever, there was still a chance that they could be undone. So long as he lingered out here in the night, somehow they would remain confined to the world of dream; if he entered the house and closed the door behind him, he would cut them adrift and give them their own independent life, where he would be helpless to direct a new outcome. Either way, he was fucked.

During the week, even at this hour, commuters often slowly prowled these blocks in their cars looking for free parking, but on a Saturday morning the streets of the neighborhood were deserted. A distant rumble of trucks from the avenue; the wind rising off the river rattled the few dry leaves still clinging to the ginkgos, which hissed and groaned with a sound of shale in the tide. A few late autumn clouds, underlit by the city, stood out against the magenta sky, and even as Wes watched began to turn from yellow-white to pink. A guy in a hoodie, shoulders hunched and hands in pockets, glanced up at Wes without breaking stride and was gone. Wes wondered what he himself would look like to a passer-by who knew nothing about him. Would he be mistaken for a junkie, a spurned lover, a home-less mental case? Wes generally spent a lot of time imagining what he looked like to other people, friends and strangers alike; he sometimes stood before a mirror and tried to see him-self as others might, but it was useless. He was altogether invis-ible to himself, and he wondered briefly if this is what it felt like to be a vampire—dead to all hope, all eternity stretching out before him like a lifeless, frozen sea. All the girls he knew were reading *Twilight;* Wes would never go near a book like that, but he bet he could teach them a thing or two about lone-liness and hopelessness. Wes moaned and dragged his palm across his face. One thing was certain: no stranger hurrying by at the foot of the stoop would be likely to take him for what he really was—a seventeen-year old boy who had just lost his vir-ginity. He stood up, turned once more to the black, gleaming front door, fumbled in his coat for the keys, and let himself into the house.

No one had waited up for him, of course. All was dark in the front hall, except for the faint blue glow of a cabinet light in the kitchen and a splash of pre-dawn luminosity through the lead-paned fanlight. No sound but the slow settling of floor-boards—too early, even, for the boiler to wake up in the base-ment—and the refrigerator humming to itself. Wes was home. Now the night was truly over; there was no turning back from its truths, or evading its consequences, because it no longer belonged to him. What he had done, the mistakes he had made, belonged forever now to the petrified past, the past of textbooks and Wikipedia entries and Twitter logs. Wes could not pretend it had not happened; the whole school would know about it by Monday morning, and never, ever again—no matter how long he lived, no matter what he did or where he fled, until the day he died—would he be the person he had been on Friday morning, someone with a choice between two futures, bright with justified hope. Almost anyone Wes knew or could imagine in his position would be celebrating right now. How many fucking movies had he seen about desperate nerds with hearts of gold trying to get their dicks wet for the first time? And when they did—they always did, of course—everything changed for them. Everything changed for the better, naturally. Everybody Wes knew took their cues from movies like that—horny and pimply before, manly and reticent after. And the sorriest part about all this mess was that Wes had bought into the whole rite-of-passage thing too—a bold expression of self-confidence, a source of pleasurable memories from the very fountainhead of youth. I mean, he said to himself, have I or have I not just spent the night in bed with a beautiful, willing girl who chose me, and whose scent clings to me still? Am I or am I not a virgin anymore, and will I or will I not be a virgin ever again for as long as I live? Did it really matter all that much that she happened to be the totally wrong girl?

But it was no good, and Wes knew it. The more he struggled against the feeling that he had destroyed every prospect he'd ever had for happiness and moral bearing, the tighter it compressed his heart—a Chinese handcuff, only not one that can be released by relaxing. He pulled off his sneakers and placed them gingerly on the floor beside the coat rack. He already had his tiptoe on the first riser when he heard a sound, a rustle of paper, from the kitchen.

He found his father, barefoot in sweatpants and T-shirt, leaning on both hands over the counter. The bluish light of the cabinet fixture picked up the incipient bald spot beneath the thinning hair on the crown of his head, and illuminated the architectural blueprints spread out between his hands. Wes had seen these blueprints before—they'd been drawn up for a gut renovation of the kitchen that had been put on indefinite hold by his mother's illness. Poring over them in the fish-tank glow of the cabinet light, his father looked like a hapless criminal caught in the act, especially when, startled by Wes's sudden appearance, he hastily folded them up and pushed them aside.

"Hey kid, you're up early."

"You too."

"Couldn't sleep. Guilty conscience, I guess." The joke fell flat, for obvious reasons.

"Me neither."

"Are you coming or going?"

"I just got in."

"Don't you have a curfew?"

"No."

His father nodded and took a long draw on a glass of water, tipping his head back, to cover the awkward silence. It was odd: his dad was a perfectly healthy guy, as far as Wes knew, not otherwise nervous or clumsy, but his hand always shook visibly when he drank, which made him look like an alcoholic, or at least much older than he really was. Wes imagined that, in some other distant world, if he remembered nothing else about his father, he would remember that his hand trembled when he drank water. That, or the fact that his eyes teared up whenever he heard "Brown-eyed Girl" on the radio.

"How was it?"

"How was what?"

"Your party, or whatever."

"Uh, you know."

A porcelainy sound, like a teacup shifting in a saucer, rose from the garden parlor downstairs where Wes's father kept his apartment, and they both turned to the half-open door, through which Wes glimpsed, or thought he glimpsed, a shadow glide across the stairwell wall. He locked eyes with his dad for the briefest moment, but it was a pointless exercise and they both knew it. Nobody was going to be making any confessions tonight.

"Must be Crispy."

"I'll walk her when I get up. 'Night."

"'Night Wes."

On the second floor landing, Wes paused to listen for sounds of wayward wakefulness. His mother was a fitful sleeper, easily awakened by little noises or her own discomforts, and even at this hour she was capable of making demands if disturbed. Wes himself was an early riser, but on a weekday he often heard her summoning Narita with her little glass bell even before he was out of bed. Narita wouldn't mind—that's what she was paid for—and in theory Wes didn't mind either. It wasn't such a big deal, having to take care of your mom once a week, fixing her meal or whatever, but still. He knew it wasn't true, but sometimes it seemed that his mom woke up especially early on Saturdays, when Narita stayed with her family in Ozone Park and the glass bell rang not for her but for Wes. As he stood there in the loosening dark, it was not difficult to imagine her on the other side of her bedroom door, staring at the ceiling, sending out waves of probing consciousness into every corner of the house. Not now, though; her door was ajar, and from deep inside he could hear her regular, sinus-heavy breathing. Even so, it would not be long before she needed him. Wes moved on past Narita's room and up the stairs towards his own.

The top-floor landing, with its little bell-jar skylight, was the brightest area of the house, but the glass had not been cleaned in so many years that even on the brightest summer's day the light that made it through was pallid and compromised. Now, the grayish smudge that heralded the dawn perfectly complemented Wes's mood, as if he were not going to bed after a long, trying night in New York City but waking up to a day of hopeless drudgery in a coal mine in Siberia. He staggered into his room and threw himself on his bed, determined to sleep, but almost immediately became aware of his clothes clinging to him in a way that made him feel unclean; he got up and stripped down to his underwear and lay down on top of his bedclothes. But even his boxers, slipped on warm from the dryer and fragrant as fresh-baked bread only twelve hours earlier, felt damaging and polluted, so Wes wriggled out of them and squirmed naked beneath the blankets. But now it was his body that seemed to pulse with foul emissions, his own skin coated in a film of rancid oil overlaid with a dusting of grit, cigarette smoke, stale vodka and organic decay. With an inward sigh, Wes recognized that it would be pointless trying to get to sleep feeling so soiled; he rolled off the bed and padded across the landing to the bathroom. Stepping over the sill of the ancient claw-foot tub, he grabbed a tube of Nora's lavender bodywash, positioned himself beneath the showerhead and turned on the water. As he scrubbed himself from neck to toes, then shampooed and conditioned his hair, he tried to will his mind to go blank, and to convince himself that all his troubles were simply the accumulated sweat of an eventful day that could be sloughed off and washed down the drain. But that was no good, either, because when you betray yourself and your deepest-held convictions you become a different person forever, and no bodywash ever invented can bleach out that stain, and even washing your hair becomes an act of consummate hypocrisy. Add hypocrisy to the list of his failings. He returned to his room, dropped the towel on the floor, climbed into bed, pulled the blankets over his shoulder, turned to face the wall and went to sleep.

He dreamed that he was sitting at a long gleaming table in the Rose Reading Room of the public library. Before him was a yellow legal pad with many pages rolled up and tucked under the top of the pad. The page open before him was covered in meticulously calligraphed mathematical equations and diagrams that he could not remember having written, and so exquisitely drawn that he could hardly believe they were his. He was a member of a team of efficiency experts that had been tasked with calculating the number of light bulbs hanging in the chandeliers overhead. At the same time, looking around the room, he realized that it was the physical embodiment of someone else's Facebook homepage, and that a related task was to identify the person to whom the page belonged by triangulating the hundreds of people sitting at his and the other tables. By calculating which were friends in common with each other and with the unknown subscriber, he would be able to find the subscriber himself, and thus determine the number of light bulbs. He was working under the assumption that the subscriber was Barack Obama, but as he glanced out of one of the enormous arched windows to see a jetliner angled nose down and speeding silently towards the western façade of the library, he suddenly understood that the Facebook page was none other than Prince André's, and that he would therefore never be able to calculate the light bulbs. He woke up to find himself on his back, and from the angle of the light streaming in from the yard he knew that he had only slept a few hours. The night was over, it had really happened, and suddenly this new day was at the beginning. He began to cry again, only silently and without tears. It felt like dry heaving of the eyes.

The boiler had kicked in since he'd fallen asleep; the ancient radiator hissed and clanked, and the room felt close and too hot. He rose abruptly and opened the window at the foot of his bed. He leaned his palms on the sill and stuck his entire upper body out the casement. It was a crisp late autumn day, with just a hint of wood smoke and woodlands pulling through the air. The sky, cloudless now, retained the promise of magenta it had shown before sunrise, and the sun hung coolly in the naked branches. From here he could see the backyards of just about every house on the block and the jumbled rooftops, chimneypots and water towers of half of Greenwich Village. Some were shabby, unkempt and cankered with ancient wooden sheds, cracked paving of brick or slate, tangles of skeletal briar and vigorous ivy, angled limestone lintels and crumbling mortar. These belonged to the long-term, pre-gentrification residents, like Wes and his family. Others had been remodeled, sporting new rear walls made of thick glass and heavy pivoting doors of brushed steel, stucco additions and terraces lined with cedar planters and expensive garden furniture, Japanese rock gardens or hedges of well-trimmed heritage hydrangeas. These belonged to bankers, hedge fund managers and media moguls.

Wes looked down into his own yard. Nothing grew under the ancient sycamore at the far end; it was just dirt, a farmyard where the dog peed when no one could be bothered to walk her. There was an old, warped wooden school desk and chair where his father sat on sunny days, and a white extension chord running into the basement window. Over the years the yard had been the scene of a number of utopian construction projects: a tree house, chicken coops and rabbit hutches, a wood-fired bread oven. All had reached various stages of completion before being abandoned and cannibalized. Now there was nothing but some unhappy shade borders of variegated hostas and ghost ferns, an outdoor dining set of green rubberized iron and an old kettle grill that was barely able to stand on its tripod. And there, too, was Nora, sitting on the bench that circled the foot of the sycamore, knees up to her chin, a teen magazine in her left hand, her right thumb in her mouth. She rocked as she read—in an absorbed way, not a crazy way.

Wes called down. "Hey cookie!"

Nora looked up and smiled. "Hiya daddy-o."

"Watcha doing'?"

"Memorizing slang from the old days."

"Mom up?"

"Uh-huh."

"She get breakfast?"

"Uh-huh."

"Dog walked?"

"Climb it, Tarzan."

He smiled at her again and blew her a kiss. Wes couldn't help himself. Every time he saw his sister he was filled with love for her. She was the most delightful, easy, dependable, kind and intelligent child on the planet, and all he wanted to do was to protect her from all this, have her call him "daddy-o" forever and make sure that she didn't grow up too fast or around the wrong sort of people. But then Wes remembered that he himself had become the wrong sort of person, precisely the kind of person that little sisters need protecting from, and maybe she needed protecting from him, too. He withdrew from the window and returned to the bed. He slid beneath the covers, lying on his back and cradling his head in his palms, and looked up at the cracked plaster overhead.

"I'm fixing a hole where the rain gets in and stops my mind from wandering." When he was little, Wes had never understood this line. Why would a hole *stop* his mind from wandering? Surely, his mind required a hole to escape *through* into the outside world. But now that he was older, and had a crack in the ceiling of his own, he thought he understood better. His crack did not let any rain get in, but it had a way of focusing the mind that was not helpful or conducive to unfettered daydreaming. If it should also let rain in, that would be particularly focusing and unhelpful. What a mind needed, if it was to roam freely, and especially if it was to roam productively, was a sealed space in which it was safe, contained and undistracted. That is why Wes had always thought it a mistake for Paul

McCartney to paint his room in a colorful way as an encouragement to his wandering mind, because surely plain white walls were a better inducement? Maybe it was a generational thing with color. One thing that Wes and the Beatles had in common, however, was their agreement that his room was right where he belonged. Wes felt that he could live here forever and never grow bored, no matter how faithless and shallow he might be.

Wes thought about his dream; it was not like any other he could remember, and he didn't understand anything about it. It was true that Prince André had been much on his mind lately, but it would be a challenge to figure out how he or any of the rest of it related to Wes's current circumstances. He tried to break it down to its references. Barack Obama—okay, he was on everyone's minds these days. Facebook—same. He'd spent a good deal of time in the Rose Reading Room, maybe his favorite place in the world, so that was explainable. But light bulbs, calligraphy? And what did the airplane mean? Why should a perfectly curious and enigmatic dream suddenly become a nightmare?

Wes had had a genuine nightmare not long before. An atomic war had broken out, and a bomb exploded over New York. Wes found himself in some sort of bleak, cinderblock dormitory, and he knew that he had died and gone to hell. It was explained to the newcomers that they were free to roam the city, but that they absolutely must be back at the dorm by six. The punishment for non-compliance was left to their imagination. Wes didn't remember much of the dream after that, except that his new home was a small rust-belt city under a perpetually overcast sky the color of liver, and that at some point he had found himself on a bus, looking at his watch. It was ten to six, and he had suddenly realized that he was on the wrong bus, had no idea where he was, and that it would be impossible to reach the dorm by six. Wes had woken up with a start, his heart racing. The point, he had figured out later, is that there's a very fine line between real life and hell, just the matter of a missed deadline, and you won't know you've crossed it until it's too late. All you have to do is make one mistake, and for all eternity you will be wandering aimlessly in a desolate landscape, friendless and desperate. Now that was a message he could understand.

And then he remembered that, in his dream this morning, the Rose Reading Room had been not at all like it is in real life; its distant vaulted ceilings with their multiple chandeliers seemed to leap on forever and in all directions above the gleaming tables. It had been a little like the Library of Babel in the short story. That was an interesting twist. Borges described the Library as infinite, which meant it contained not only every book ever written, but every book that could be written, past and future. Wes thought this was interesting because it meant that infinity was a concept where the difference between space and time becomes meaningless. There is no difference between something that is infinitely big and something that is infinitely old, and no difference between something that had existed forever and something that would exist forever. Wes had often daydreamed about walking through the Library, which was made up of an infinite number of hexagonal units, connected horizontally by corridors and vertically by open shafts. In each corridor there was a spiral staircase leading up and down to the adjacent level, and a bathroom facility for the "librarians," who seemed to be simply the Library's inhabitants, since there was no mention of patrons who might borrow or study the books, which would then require reshelving by the "librarians." Borges didn't say anything about what the librarians ate or where they slept or their other physical needs. Presumably they were able to wash their clothes in the bathrooms, and hang them out to dry on the railings lining the shafts, but one would imagine that there were considerable winds in the shafts—maybe even entire weather systems—so the librarians would need clothes pegs to secure their laundry, not to mention soap to wash it, and where did those things come from? Some librarians seemed to be territorial, while others were nomadic, spending their entire lives searching for a particular book. How did they replace their shoes when they wore out? Were there male and female librarians, and if so, did they have sex with each other when they met? Did they mate for life, or just hook up? What happened when the lady librarians got pregnant? Were the male librarians steadfast and faithful, or were they weak and unprincipled, and easily led to betray the ones they loved? Borges said nothing about baby librarians, or librarian obstetricians, or about librarian schools. Wes knew this was silly speculation, but it irritated him that Borges had thought to provide the librarians with toilets in every corridor, but with nothing else they would need to get by in their infinite time-space continuum.

Wes had spent a lot of time thinking about the story since he had first read it three years earlier. He had read it many times since and had not tired of it yet. He had always suspected that the endless library was a metaphor for the imagination, for the mind's infinite creative and intuitive power. The story was probably where Wes had first got the idea of his own mind as an infinite—or almost infinite—source of ideas and understanding. The mind was its own ecosystem, creating its own internal weather, like the library, and since it was the exclusive creator of all problems and all solutions, it was very possible that it had, in fact, created the universe itself. And that was precisely why it made no difference at all where it was located in the "real" world—in a sealed room all by itself, in a vast library with infinite chambers and corridors, it all came to the same thing. Wes had always imagined that he could be very happy as a monk. He almost never felt lonely.

But how could any of this help him today? This was a real problem, maybe even a tragedy, not some pseudo-mystical sci-fi conundrum. Wes had betrayed the woman he loved by sleeping with someone he didn't care about or even like very much. Wes's mind hadn't created this problem; it was not something he'd stumbled upon in his wanderings through the labyrinth of his imagination; it was not a metaphysical exercise. It was real—*real* real, as opposed to fixing-a-hole real. What did that mean? It meant it involved other people and their feelings. It meant it involved actions that could not be revoked. It meant consequences that could not be evaded by shaking the world like a Magic Eight Ball until it gave you the answer you wanted. No matter how much you might want it, life is not a Library of Babel—you can't just wander off down a hallway in search of some elusive intellectual prize. You've got to find somewhere to do your laundry, to repair the holes in your shoes. That was what his father had been doing for decades, and what he had sworn to himself that he would never do. It was what Wes had to look forward to for the rest of his life. Never, ever again—not when he went off to college, not when he figured out how to make a living, not when he wrote the novels he was destined to write, not if he got married and had children of his own—would he be able to say to himself that at least he was better than what his father had been.

Wes shook his head, trying to clear it of all these extraneous thoughts and tangents that were preventing him from examining the problem at hand. He didn't need to be thinking about dreams or libraries, and he especially did not need to be thinking about his father right now. He needed to figure out how he had gotten himself into this terrible situation and what, if anything, he could do about it. He decided that he needed to go over it methodically, step by step, try to remember exactly how it had all gone down, where he had gone wrong, what were the insuperable character flaws that had allowed him to make such an awful mistake. It was too late to take any of it back, and he doubted that he would ever find a way to forgive himself, but he had a vague idea that the fallen can be ennobled, in a pathetic sort of way, by the effort to salvage some trinket of redemption from the wreckage of their moral failure. He needed to start from the beginning.

To say that Friday had dawned full of hope would have been an exaggeration, but there had certainly been nothing to suggest that it would be a day out of the ordinary. He had an advisory with Mrs. Fielding at 7:50, so all his usual morning chores had to be done twenty minutes earlier, but that wasn't difficult for Wes. Unlike almost everyone he knew, he was an early morning person, able to leap from bed in the dark, his mind fully logged on, his thoughts warmed up and flexible before his feet hit the floor. Morning was when Wes did his best thinking, and whenever he found himself gnawing late at night on an instransigeant bone of homework, he knew enough to leave it for the morning, when it would seem more digestible. Sometimes, when he was particularly enjoying a book, he would put it down at midnight, close his eyes, then pick it up again at four as if it were five minutes later. His father had told him once, with his usual wistful bitterness, that you never again read books with the passion and intensity you bring to them as a teenager, and that was easy to believe. And it wasn't only that Wes's mind worked well early in the morning; he also felt better—cleaner, stronger, more moral, the quivering arrow of a powerful compass. He loved to be awake alone in the world, to walk the dog on quiet streets that had not yet been invaded by the trying multitudes, where he could pretend that tourists and bankers and real estate brokers were harmless abstractions. When he was even younger, the sense of a day's untapped potential had been almost physical, it had been so delicious and irresistible Wes had wanted to throw himself into the day as if from a high dive. Now, he still felt that sense of possibility, he still jumped into the day feet first, but there was less passion behind it, it was more like the feeling you get when you climb into a bed made up with freshly laundered sheets, crisp and bleachy. Unpolluted and not yet soiled.

That was what Friday morning at 5:30 A.M. had felt like. Wes had to walk the dog, shower, wake Nora, feed her and see that she was clean and properly dressed. Narita would have done it, but Wes didn't trust Nora's welfare to anyone but himself. Then, if there was still time, he would eat and read the paper and be out of the house by 7.15. These were all things he looked forward to doing, or at least that gave him no sense of being oppressed or put upon. And the feeling only increased later in the week as the *Times* crossword puzzle grew progressively more difficult, until by Friday he sometimes had trouble completing it. Because of his appointment, he would have to put the crossword off until the evening. And there was almost always some fact to look up on Wikipedia that had come to mind in the middle of the night and disturbed his sleep. It had been one such string of searches that had first led him to *The Manual.*

He'd gone about his morning tasks on Friday with the usual bustle. He'd had an argument with his best friend James the day before about the percentage of water in the human body. James had said it was ninety percent, Wes had argued that it was much lower. He'd forgotten about it until that morning, when it took less than fifteen seconds on Google to prove Wes right: sixty percent, give or take. It was not much of a victory, but it had set the right tone for the day. On his crosstown walk to the subway at Union Square, he'd rewarded himself by listening to Belle & Sebastian's "If You're Feeling Sinister" on the iPhone. It wasn't new but it was his favorite album of the moment, and he rationed his listening so as not to wear out its pleasures too quickly.

By the time he reached school he'd all but forgotten to wonder why Mrs. Fielding had asked him in early. Wes was quite fond of Mrs. Fielding, but he was generally fond of all his teachers, having found that the unpleasant but necessary parts of school, such as science classes, were far easier to get through if you thought with pity and compassion of those teachers whom you might otherwise dislike. Wes had figured out long before that people who were mean or impatient were almost always unhappy, maybe even in direct proportion to their meanness, and he had trained himself to feel sorry for the teachers who liked him less because he was not good at the subject they taught. That was true for all the sciences and math, and increasingly so for soccer. It was not, however, even remotely true for English, a subject in which he knew himself to be widely acknowledged as one of the best in school, although Wes himself did not feel that way. He was a lover of books, certainly, and knew himself to be a charming, fluid writer, occasionally glib. The piece he had composed for Mrs. Fielding was definitely in that mold—he'd written the entire thing in bed, in one sitting. But he also knew something about himself that his facility generally concealed from all but the most astute teacher—that he was a lazy and undisciplined thinker who too often relied on the shining surface of words to mask his disdain for academic pieties. Mrs. Fielding had been showing signs of late that she was on to him. It was unlikely that she'd called him in to heap praise on his latest effort.

On Friday morning, she had been waiting for him behind her desk in room 405. She had a kindly face framed in pale blond bangs that the mean girls in class insisted was the handiwork of a superior and very expensive colorist. Wes didn't know anything about that and didn't care. As far as he was concerned, remarks about a teacher's personal appearance were simply attempts to dehumanize a person who did a very difficult job for not much money, and usually—at least at Dalton— did it very well. Wes *appreciated* his teachers, even when they didn't get it, but he was also aware of the difference between not deliberately giving someone a hard time and fawning. Wes thought he was reasonably adept at treading that line. Students who pandered were viewed with distaste by their peers and faculty alike, and generally received no reward for their efforts. But this situation with Mrs. Fielding had been unknown territory. Wes was not used to causing or getting in trouble at school, and wasn't quite sure about the protocol. Mrs. Fielding had smiled at him, openly enough; there had been a smear of pink lipstick on her front tooth and Wes had immediately looked away, only to find his eyes alight on another pink, lip-shaped stain on the rim of her coffee cup, cerulean blue with white Hellenic motifs. The paper he had handed in two days earlier sat on the desktop beside the cup, and it was ominously free of red ink. When he raised his eyes again, Mrs. Fielding had stopped smiling, though in all fairness she could hardly have been said to be frowning, either.

"Good morning, Wes," she had said, motioning to the chair across from her. "Thanks for coming in early."

Wes had sat down beside her, not certain where to rest his gaze.

Mrs. Fielding had seemed to be waiting for him to say something—he always had something to say—but when he remained silent she had reached across the desk for his paper and placed it delicately in the space between them.

"I imagine you already know why I asked you to come talk to me."

"Is there something wrong with my essay?"

Mrs. Fielding had snorted, delicately, then perhaps sensing that it was a disproportionate response, she had sighed.

"Not really, no," she had begun tentatively. "It's well-written, diligently proofread, properly formatted, thoughtful and provocative in places. But it's not the assignment, and you know it."

Again, Wes had found himself at a loss for words.

"Will you read the assignment topic for me please, Wes?"

Wes had pulled the paper forward and leaned into it, as if by earnestly focusing on the immediate task he could prove the sincerity of his intentions and thereby mitigate his sin. He had cleared his throat and in a soft, serious tone read out the assignment at the top of the first page.

"'The authors of *Candide*, *Pride and Prejudice* and *The Nose* all emphasize their social and psychological themes as much through the use of language and narrative trope as they do through plot and characterization. Discuss, using any work of literature of your choice and all the critical tools at your disposal.'"

There had been a long pause, apparently not at all uncomfortable to Mrs. Fielding.

"Get it now?"

Wes had got it—he'd gotten it, of course, before he'd sat down to write the paper, but had assumed he would get away with it—yet for form's sake he'd felt he ought to put up some semblance of defense.

"It says 'any work,'" he'd muttered lamely.

"'Any work of *literature*,' Wes. This is a class of *literature*."

Wes had chosen deliberately to misunderstand her. "I know it's not European, but . . . "

"I don't care if it's European or not. If I'd cared I'd have said 'any work of European literature of your choice.' But I did say 'literature,' and you did not choose to write about a work of literature. Therefore you have not fulfilled the assignment."

"I'd say it's a work of literature."

Mrs. Fielding had smacked the edge of the desk with the tips of all ten fingers, as Wes had seen her do a thousand times when a student failed to see the obvious. "Come on, Wes. How many classes have you and I had together over the years? Conflict, resolution, growth, self-understanding, hubris, submission, *Iliad*, *Romeo and Juliet*, *The Quiet American*. You know me better than that. *You* know better than that."

"I thought . . . a break with convention . . . "

"No, you were being smug and clever and lazy. You thought I'd be so dazzled by your iconoclasm and wit that I wouldn't notice that you'd barely gotten out of bed to write this. And that's why I'm making you write the paper again. Not because the US Army's M16 Operator's Manual is an unfit subject for an honor's class in European literature, although it is, but because you tried to get away with something that is unworthy of you."

"Okay."

"Stretch, Wes. *Stretch*. You're too young and too smart to take the easy way out. If you sit on your laurels now, at your age, you may never get up."

"Thanks, Mrs. F. I appreciate it. I really do. When do you need this by?"

She had turned to him in mock, wide-eyed astonishment and held out her hands, palms upward in the universal expression of powerlessness. Wes had thought, rather, that the palms, angled both towards each other and towards him, were reflecting mirrors, or the dishes of a radio telescope, concentrating upon him beams of energy summoned from across the universe. With her neatly plucked eyebrows raised, and her mouth open in a cannon's pucker, she'd been sending him some alien message across the generations. It was ostensibly couched in a language he understood, spoken by an intergalactic traveler who appears in human form so as not to cause panic. "I can't believe that's all you have to say to me after all this," he was supposed to read the message as saying. In fact, Wes had known that she was actually saying "Please be a good person, be as kind as you can possibly be, because I will be dead so soon, so soon." Wes had heard the message loud and clear, and had instantly regretted that his reaction to Mrs. Fielding's critique had been less than generous and grateful. Message relayed, she had lowered her eyebrows, closed her mouth and turned away.

"Monday morning will be fine, Wes."

And now it was Saturday morning, and despite the fact that the entire world had changed in the intervening twenty-four hours, Wes still had a whole paper to write from scratch. Not entirely from scratch, as he already had copious notes for *War and Peace*, but still. It wasn't precisely that Wes felt himself ill used, or that Mrs. Fielding had been unfair in her judgment of his efforts, but it now seemed kind of dismal and petty in the light of events, this quibbling over intent and mere words. If she only knew how damaged and debased Wes was feeling at the moment, he was convinced that Mrs. F. could muster the compassion and empathy to let him off the hook. But no one would ever know, or care. If only they knew the love and generosity, the open-heartedness and pity, with which he thought of them, they would consider him the greatest person in the world. But it's not something you can tell people.

Wes rolled over and retrieved his backpack from beneath the bed. From among the dog-eared sheaves of paper, heavy textbooks and loose implements he pulled the offending manual, which he had taken to carrying with him as incidental reading at moments of leisure. Wes had found the *Manual* online, following a link from the Wikipedia entry on the M16, which he'd stumbled upon at the end of a string of links that had begun with a query about the breakup of the B-52's, following a drunken boast by Wes's father that he had danced all night to "Rock Lobster" and "Private Idaho" when he was in college. It was a simple PDF file available for download and evidently photocopied directly from a yellowing copy of the 1985 edition, including a worn and fraying spine. The original had been slim and palm-sized, presumably to fit into a soldier's breast or back pocket, but Wes's printout of the file ran to almost 150 pages and was quite substantial. Wes wistfully riffled through the pages, many marked up with yellow highlighter, as if through a sheaf of old love letters or college rejections, artifacts of some earlier, more innocent interval in a life gone bitterly wrong. He stopped at his favorite passages, knowing that he was probably reading them for the last time.

The first dozen pages or so were devoted to addenda and corrigenda to earlier editions, then came a radiation hazard warning about the tritium gas sealed into the front sight post. The M16A1 weighed six and a half pounds, was 39 inches long. The only difference between the M16 and the M16A1 was that the A1 was equipped with a forward assist assembly. The manual described it as "lightweight, air cooled, gas operated, magazine fed and shoulder fired," a classic rock-and-roll song about a favorite car. Its purpose was "to provide personnel an offensive/defensive capability to engage targets in the field." Wes read it as if it were poetry—what mysterious mind had had the courage to jump the ontological chasm between "shooting at strangers" to "engaging targets in the field?" Wes felt an almost ecstatic intellectual communion with his fellow writer, very probably dead now since the M16 had entered into service in the 1960s. Even though Wes suspected that, in fact, there had never been any such person, the *Manual* having surely been written by committee, in his paper he had speculated about him at length, as one might about the writer of some ancient epic, the Bible or *Gilgamesh*, inventing a self-conscious mind behind a text accreted over centuries of oral precedent. And in creating a writer for the *Manual*, Wes had grown to love him for his lonely struggle with a resistant, intransigent vocabulary. All this he had expatiated upon at length, in keeping with the theme of language and narrative trope. He'd thought, he was sure, that he was passionate and sincere about his subject.

"When round reaches approximate end of barrel, expanding gases from burning propellant pass out through gas port and into gas tube. Gas goes into bolt carrier assembly, ejects old cartridge, and chambers a new round." "One click of elevation of windage is equal to one block change in elevation or windage." "Throw away the white gloves for rifle inspections." "Overnight while the Teflon has been forming a film for lubrication, the cleaning solvents in the CLP have been at work in the nooks and crannies (actually in the pores of the metal) seeking out carbon and firing residue." The language, Wes could not help feeling, was pure and musical, a triumph of minimalist compression on a par with anything from Carver or Beckett. Just look at the ambiguity in the use of the word "actually." It could simply mean "to be precise," as if the writer were saying under his breath: "The M16A1 is not an English muffin; it does not in fact have nooks and crannies, but microscopic pores that can be clogged with dirt and oil." Or it could be an expression of suppressed excitement, as if to suggest that an exhausted soldier could expect his dreams to be suffused with awe and wonder at the tireless industry of the lubricant that actively seeks out and never sleeps. Of course, a correct and sensitive parsing of the sentence would allow for both interpretations simultaneously, because that is what gives the sentence its resonance, as the author surely intended. Wes worshipped him for that, and the *Manual* was inseminated with such gems. In its way, the prose of the operator's manual was perfect and irresistible, and had the distinct advantage over *War and Peace* of being profusely illustrated. If the author of the operator's manual and Tolstoy were locked in a room together, and ordered to exchange writing philosophies, Wes doubted that the latter would have much to teach the former, except perhaps in the use of serial commas and in beginning sentences with conjunctions. Wes felt like a scholar who had stumbled upon a lost masterpiece and whose task was to reintroduce it to the world—gently, persuasively, lest its power be put to the wrong use or devastate precisely those whom it might, judiciously wielded, most benefit.

But *War and Peace* it would have to be. *War and Peace* had been Wes's original subject for the paper until it had fallen to him to discover the *Manual*, but he had found himself profoundly irritated by it. There it was, sitting on his desk beneath the thesaurus; where yesterday it had looked lumpen and forlorn, it now exuded an aura of smug vindication. It did not deserve, had not earned the passion that Wes had lavished on the *Manual*, but he could write that paper in his sleep. Mrs. Fielding would give him no more than a B+ for it because it would lack conviction and transcendence, but there was nothing Wes could do about that. It occurred to him that he might just be able to place "Language, Poetry and Narrative Trope in *Operator's Manual for Rifle, 5.56-MM, M16 (1005-00-856-6885) Rifle, 5.56-MM, M16A1 (1005-00-073-9421)*" in some literary magazine, which could well compensate for the damage done by a B+ to his college prospects. His dad would know the right publication to submit it to, but as Wes could not stomach the idea of turning to his father for a favor he would have to figure it out for himself. How hard could it be? *Paris Review*, *Granta*—they all had their own websites.

The iPhone chimed daintily from some pocket in one of the pieces of clothing discarded on the pile by the bedside. It was only a text message, hardly worth getting up to retrieve, but the timing was odd. Almost everyone Wes knew had been at Lucy's party, and Wes was the only freak in his acquaintance who could stay up most of the night, fall asleep half-drunk for a couple of hours, then get up and leave while it was still dark and walk home across half the city. The rest of them would sleep until way past noon. Who could possibly be texting him at this hour? Wes wondered what the time was, but he didn't own a watch and the only clock was on the iPhone. He supposed he ought to check in with his mother, but since Nora had already brought her breakfast there was no immediate hurry. The iPhone chimed again, as it would every minute until Wes read or responded to the text, but since he had chosen the tone precisely for its soothing effect—a thin metal blade being struck twice against an expensive crystal wine glass—rather than to spark any sense of urgency, as other tones seemed designed to do, he continued to stare at the ceiling.

Wes heard Nora coming up the stairs, her pace light and skipping, a large mouse. She knew he heard her; like him, she had learned from necessity how to climb the stairs in complete silence, and this was her way of announcing herself. Instead of knocking, she would stand outside his door and count to three, giving him the time to tell her not to come in if he did not wish to see her, which was rare but occasionally necessary. And here she was.

Dressed in green capris and a white, short-sleeved polo with her school crest, she flounced in and dropped herself beside him on the bed. She took his free hand in both of hers and stroked the tips of his fingers.

"I'm bored."

"Why are you wearing your school uniform?"

"I couldn't find anything else clean."

"I'll do the laundry later. Call a friend. I'll walk you over."

"Nobody's around. They're all at their country houses. In Connecticut." She pronounced it "connect-i-cut" on purpose.

"All of them?"

"I was supposed to have a playdate with Claire, but she's grounded."

"Why is she grounded?"

"She took a picture of herself in her underwear with her cell phone and sent it to Leo."

"Why would she do that?"

"She likes him."

"That's disgusting. How old is she?"

"Eleven. Leo texted her back and said he hates her and told her to fuck off, and now no one will talk to him, but I'm sure it was Katrina who told him to do it."

"Who's Katrina?"

"His sister. You know her. Do you want to see Bobby?"

"No."

"Will you play Mastermind with me?"

"I can't. I'm writing a paper."

"You're lying in bed."

"I'm writing it in my head. Where's dad?"

"Dunno."

"Find dad. He'll play with you."

"Whatever, dipstick." She got up and walked out in a huff, but she closed the door behind her so gently that it didn't even click.

He hated it when she said "whatever." On the one hand, she was quite right—dad would never play Mastermind with her, even if she could find him, and it had been a little cruel of Wes even to suggest something so ridiculous. On the other hand, until recently it would not have occurred to her to use an expression like "whatever." She was growing up; any day now she would be a teenager, no longer the sweet thoughtful child who always worried about everyone's feelings and never sulked, who was able to put an optimistic spin on any unpleasant circumstance. She would stop coming to share his bed when she couldn't sleep at night, or he would have to find a reason to send her away because she was growing boobs. Wes had always felt that she was the best part of him, that he could always find something good about himself when he looked at her, and if she stopped being that he wouldn't know where to go looking for it. She reminded him of that incredibly sad section in *Mary Poppins* where the twins outgrow their ability, shared by all babies, to speak the intimate language of nature and to communicate with all animals and even with inanimate things like the wind. Wes had read the book the previous year with the idea of writing a comparative study about childrearing in fiction, intending to match it with *Oliver Twist* and *Less*

Than Zero, but he had so embarrassed himself crying inconsolably over the fate of the twins that he'd dropped the whole idea. Now he thought that maybe he should play Mastermind with Nora, and do the laundry, and check in on his mother, before it was all too late. He began counting, and when nothing happened he started again from zero. This time, when he reached sixteen, he got up.

He sat on the edge of the bed with his hands clasped between his knees and his head hanging down, just because it seemed like a cool position and if someone interesting should happen to walk into the room at that very moment it would make him look extremely philosophical and deep. He remembered Katrina, or at least he remembered her hands because he'd spent much of the eighth grade staring at them. They were very pale and her fingers were unusually long and slim, the nails often lacquered. She was said to have given someone a handjob in the jungle gym in the playground, but no one could say precisely who it was or when the blessed event had occurred. Wes didn't remember anything else about her—not the color of her hair or her last name—or where she'd gone to high school, even though almost everyone who attended a private high school on the East Side knew each other and a girl who gave handjobs was sure to be popular. The phone chimed again, and since the pile of clothes in which it was hidden lay right between his feet he was able to justify the effort needed to locate it. The text was from Lucy. It said "Hey you."

Wes lowered the phone to the floor, nesting it among the crumpled clothing as if it were an egg or a bomb that might explode. The text window was still open, and he stared at the message. Hey you. Instead of looking up his number, she had added her message to the string of their broken conversations from the night before, her texts in white balloons, his in yellow. It was an entire history of their evening in shorthand, more terse and expressive even than the *Manual*.

Oct 31, 2008 8:16 P.M.
Yellow: "What's ur address?"
White: "623 park 11a"
Oct 31, 2008 10:16 P.M.
White: "can we talk"
Yellow: "Where r u?"
White: "behand u"
Oct 31, 2008 11:49 P.M.
White: "want 2 dance?"
Yellow: "bnkdl"
Nov 1, 2008 12:02 A.M.
Yellow: "Where r u?"
White: "bdrm"
Yellow: "Too many. Which?"
White: "find me"
Nov 1, 2008 9:28 A.M.
White: "Hey you"

As he stared at the screen, Wes was struck by the fact that
he had dutifully punctuated all his texts, whereas Lucy did not
even seem to know where to find the punctuation keys on her
Blackberry. It somehow seemed to carry a special significance
that Wes did not care to parse. Wes felt sick to his stomach and
panicky at the same time, and the iPhone screen went black.
He stared at it a while longer, willing his mind to go blank the
way he did in restaurants when he didn't know what to order,
trusting his instincts to make the right decision for him. When
the nausea and panic subsided a little, he picked the phone up
and turned it on. The wallpaper was a photo of Wes and Nora
in a swimming pool, clinging to the edge and smiling up at the
camera, their arms draped around each other's shoulders. It
had been taken six years earlier in Tuscany, on their last family
vacation. People Wes's age who had seen the photo made fun
of him for it, but he didn't care. It always made him happy to
look at it, but not this time. In fact, it made him feel infinitely sad,

which was better than panicky, but not much. Wes unlocked the phone and pressed the text button.

"Tell Bobby 2 come c me," he typed. The "send" bar had barely filled when the response came back. "K." Wes slipped back under the covers. Twenty seconds later Nora was at his door, her upper lip pulled back against her teeth in Bobby's signature grin.

"You called?" Bobby said hopefully, his voice distorted by Nora's effort to keep the lip in position while talking.

"Tell me a story, Bobby."

"'Kay. Did you know I got married again?"

"Tell me."

Wes lost the thread of the story almost as soon as it began, but it didn't matter. The sound of Bobby's voice, rasping and slurred at the same time, was the point. Bobby the bisexual mouse-boy was Nora's most popular and fully-developed character, with an entire life history behind him that included being thrown out of his parents' house at the age of three because of an incurable addiction to cheese, a stint (Wes seemed to recall) as a streetwalker in mid-town, where he met his first boyfriend Lee, a hustler who had died of AIDS, and then marriage to a cricket named Raquel; Bobby and Raquel had had several children, whose names Wes could never keep straight and who had grown up to have children of their own. When Raquel died of breast cancer, Bobby had hit the road and become involved in a series of adventures with any number of itinerant characters, which was more or less where his life's story had led him up to the present day. Wes could not remember Bobby's origins, either; he had seemed to spring to life fully formed a couple of years earlier, just as their mother's illness was beginning to bite. At first, Bobby happily monopolized entire family meals, keeping them in tears of hilarity while the food turned cold on their plates. He was always funny, always cheerful in the face of the terrible tragedies for which he seemed destined, and you never knew when to expect an appearance. But as their collective meals had gradually fallen apart and eventually disintegrated entirely, and everyone had retreated to the privacy of their own rooms, Bobby had taken on the role of family therapist, summoned whenever needed for solace and his peculiar philosophical perspective. Wes knew he wasn't the only one who relied on Bobby's advice; he could sometimes hear Bobby's patient, irreverent voice lecturing their mother in her room directly beneath his own. In fact, Nora was almost always Bobby with mom these days. Wes wasn't sure if his father ever turned to Bobby, as his moments of greatest need often coincided with his moments of greatest incoherence, but he did know that Bobby was not shy about sharing his opinions uninvited—often at times when they might be most unwelcome. In earlier days there had been other creatures, including Wes's own Enochs the spitting monster, and Enochs's best friend Sunny, a boy who lived in the Sun and who had pressed on for a while, pale and sickly, even after Wes had put aside such games. Bobby had eclipsed them all, Yahweh to their Olympus, but Wes supposed they might still be alive somewhere, waiting with pathetic and forlorn hope for their religion to be revived.

"What's a matter?" Bobby's voice broke into his thoughts as he took Wes by the hand.

"What? Nothing?" Wes turned his head away.

"Leslie's crying."

"Leslie's not crying."

"Leslie has baby jellyfish in his eyes, maybe? Leslie's crying. Bobby always knows when Leslie's sad. Don't be sad, Leslie. Life can always get so much, so much worse, and it surely will."

"I don't want to be sad, Bobby, but I can't help it."

"But why, Leslie, why?"

"Life is sad, Bobby. Life is too fucking sad."

"Bobby knows *that*. Silly Leslie. All Bobby's grandchildren are junkies, even baby Ramsey. But is Bobby sad? No sir! Life is sad but Bobby's happy. Why is Bobby happy, you ask?"

"You know, Bobby? I know I asked you to come, but I don't think I'm really up for this right now."

"Suit yourself, daddy-o. Bobby doesn't hang with losers anyhow."

The moment Bobby withdrew Nora flung her arms around Wes's neck and burst into tears. Wes hugged her to him and pressed her hot, damp face into his shoulder.

"Don't cry, Cookie. It's nothing. I'll get over it soon enough." The words were wet ashes in Wes's mouth, but he made himself say them, over and over, until one of them, anybody, would believe them. "It's all right. It'll be all right."

Nora sobbed silently. When her heaving subsided, she leaned so still against him that Wes wondered if she'd cried herself to sleep. Wes felt sick again, sick and so filled with sorrow that it seemed enough for ten, a hundred people to share. He remembered how he had felt early that morning on the stoop, that no young person should be able to feel this way because it was older people who were supposed to be grief-stricken by a sense of the futility and wastefulness of it all, not someone with everything ahead of him and a world of possibilities, which Wes knew himself to be despite it all. But he couldn't help himself. It was as if he were standing before a mirror that reflected him as he would be in ten or twenty or thirty years from now, a curse of limpid foresight that no teenager should have to endure. No one he knew, no one his age felt as he did, except maybe James in his better moments; they lived their lives like animals, unaware even of such a thing as the future, and he hated and envied them for it in equal measure, all of them dancing and drinking and texting. He'd love nothing better than to be callow and thoughtless, to be able to pump his fists and say "Fuck yeah," but it was a lost cause. He had never been one of them, could never be, but still he seemed to spend his life trying, pretending, and look at the disaster he'd gotten himself into. Everything he did, the good and the bad alike, turned to dust.

"Mom's ringing." Nora's voice was normal, serene, a little impatient even, as if she had long since recovered her equanimity and had only been waiting for the right moment to break the silence.

"I didn't hear anything."

"She's ringing. It's your turn."

"Okay, let me get dressed and tell her I'll be there in a minute."

Nora, relieved of duty, scampered from the room and bounced heavily down the stairs. Wes knew, among all his countless weaknesses, that he mustn't cry in front of Nora, or really be anything to her but the strong, optimistic big brother. What he really needed to be was the man of the house, competent and involved, forging on, a brave pioneer armored in fortitude and resilience, most especially for Nora's sake, since who was left to take care of her but him? What kind of a childhood was it for her? Wes, at least, had a handful of happy memories to fall back on. Nora had had to be the strong one, the cheerleader; fortunately she seemed to have the right stuff for it, but still it wasn't fair to her. After some jag of self-pity or weariness, Wes always felt renewed and capable, determined to relieve Nora of her burden, but it never lasted very long, and soon he'd be back in his room, hiding out among his books, and Nora would be left rattling around in that decaying old house, preternaturally silent, to play computer games, videochat and do her homework alone in the dining room that no one used anymore. This time, Wes told himself as he climbed into last night's jeans and a clean T-shirt, he would do it, and do it right: he would let Nora do her homework in his room when she asked; he would help her with her math and science; let her read a story to him out loud instead of making her feel like a baby; make sure she always had clean clothes to wear to school; not make fun of her for talking too loud and too fast and losing her train of thought in mid-sentence; accompany her on her walk to school sometimes; have a serious talk with dad about the need to be a more conscientious parent to his preteen daughter. Barefoot, Wes padded across the hall to splash some water on his face in the bathroom. Staring at himself in the mirror, trying on a smile that only made his pale blue eyes look watery and weak, Wes thought that even if he couldn't be strong enough to be a good person, he really might have it in him to be a better brother. As he looked at himself, he suddenly thought of Lucy and how horrified she would be to see how he lived, even for five minutes, and as he pictured that pretty face of hers distorted in disgust and incomprehension, with its Mustique tan and ski-jump nose and thick, dark scimitar eyebrows, he felt a mild twinge of triumph, as if he already were the good brother he aspired to be. She probably wouldn't even like Nora.

Wes dried his face and went downstairs and stood before the door to his mother's room, its surface creamy and rippled with generations of white gloss enamel. He hesitated only a moment before rapping gently and pushing inwards, the door whispering benignly against the thick burgundy pile.

He stood in the doorway, allowing his eyes to adjust to the dark, mitigated by the wan glow of the television. The new flat-screen LCD emitted a light far less lurid than that of the old cathode tube, but it was also less bright, and Wes had not yet accustomed himself to the change. It was an improvement, he thought, and the room now felt more like an aquarium for tropical fish than a laboratory in a science fiction movie, but he doubted that his mother, with her fading eyesight, had any great appreciation for the difference. The pervasive aroma of urine, buttered toast and topical antiseptic remained unchanged, and would do so as long as the windows, blinds and drapes sealed the room from the outside world. The natural reaction of anyone entering his mother's room for the first time would be to throw it all open to the light and air, but Wes no longer even raised the issue with her. The light hurt her eyes, and the fresh air brought on uncontrolled trembling, even when it was warm. This was her natural habitat now, and it was for visitors to adapt or inure themselves to it, as Wes and Nora had. Wes lifted his nose for any hint of pus or necrosis in the air, but the bedsores seemed to have healed since she had recovered limited mobility after the last attack.

"Hi, mom. How you feeling?"

"Wes? Come over here, honey."

Wes crossed the room to the side of the bed, which was adjusted to raise her upper body for ease of viewing. The bedclothes were neat and folded at the top, which Nora must have done earlier, and her arms lay on top of them at her side, sleeved in the thin cheap cotton print of a hospital gown. Her head was nestled in a cradle of newly plumped pillows, hair so thin and colorless now that the white of the pillow cases showed through it. Wes propped himself at the edge of the bed, which was so high he was almost on tiptoes, and leaned in for a closer look.

"How are you feeling?"

"I'm just dandy." Her voice was whistling and reedy, as if she had to push it through a rattan sieve to get it out; still, it was quite a bit stronger than it had been a month earlier, and no longer slurred. "How are you, honey?"

Wes was never quite sure what she meant when she asked him this. Sometimes, she was genuinely alert to what he had to say; more often, it was just the disease talking through her, as if she were a ventriloquist's dummy, and what she was really saying was "Just pretend everything will be alright." Usually these days, Wes was reluctant to test her, but now he let a note of equivocation creep into his voice.

"I'm okay mom."

"What is it, honey?"

"Oh mom, I don't know. I . . . "

"Only I'm a little hungry. Can you bring me some pudding?"

"Didn't Nora already make you breakfast?"

"No she did not, the little beast."

"She didn't make you breakfast?"

"Wes, do I have to tell you? She didn't make me breakfast, damn it."

"Okay, okay, keep yer panties on. I'll take care of it. Can I turn the light on for a minute?"

"It hurts my eyes."

"Just for a minute. You can close them. I want to check your skin."

"Go ahead."

Wes stood up and turned to the bedside lamp and walked straight into the support strut of his mother's electric lifter. It didn't hurt but Wes swore at the machine under his breath. It was a kind of swing set straddling the bed, but instead of swings it had a nylon sling, like the kind that are lowered from helicopters in rescue operations. In theory, Wes's mother could roll to the side, position the sling beneath her buttocks, press a button and rise and slide to her wheelchair besides the bed. The idea was to make her feel independent, but in fact she found it almost impossible to position the sling properly beneath her and hadn't used it for months. Wes and Nora had tried playing on it when she was in the hospital, but it had been less than fun. It was only kept around in anticipation of the day when she could no longer walk herself to the bathroom at all, even when assisted by one of her children, and that was why Wes hated it with its gunmetal finish and bright yellow warning labels ringed in orange. The insurance rep had told them, sitting around the dining room table, that it was cheaper to leave it there than to dismantle and remove it, only to have to reinstall it six months later.

Wes switched on the lamp and returned to his mother's side. Her face could be a little frightening to look at under its corona of colorless wisps, but Wes rarely noticed because it had been such a gradual decline. He had only the vaguest memories of her as a healthy woman—a beach somewhere, where she had leaned back against her elbow and he could see her eyes smiling behind her sunglasses; some walks to school, with singing and hand-holding; a bright office in midtown, where she designed book jackets on enormous computer monitors and taught him how to use the software to make digital collages. He seemed to remember that she'd been gregarious, that she'd worn colorful scarves on her head, knotted at the nape, that she cried watching E.T. That she had played show tunes on the upright downstairs. It was odd how little he remembered, given that the earliest symptoms of illness had not manifested themselves until Wes was seven or eight; he supposed his mind must have packed all those memories away somewhere. It was as if she had always been sick. Nobody ever talked about her getting better or anything like that. It was only on the rare occasion when he joined Nora in her intense scrutinies of the family photo albums, the only evidence that their mother had ever been anything but a diminished invalid, that the damage stood out in stark contrast. Deeply sunken eyes the color of aged porcelain rhimed with red, grey lips collapsed upon themselves, restless liverish tongue always licking and seeking—Wes noted it all briefly with alarm, then allowed it to fade from consciousness. Now, under the lamplight, his only interest was in the color of her skin. The optic neuritis that had recently attacked her one good eye had been treated with massive doses of steroids, which had dyed her skin yellow. It was still as dry and transparent as tracing paper, but it seemed to have purged itself of most of the toxins, although it was hard to tell in this light. Wes kissed her on the cheek, switched off the lamp and leaned back against the raised segment of the mattress.

She was watching "The Joy of Painting," and Wes sat beside her and watched for a few minutes. This obsession with "The Joy of Painting" had all started out as something of a family joke when Wes had come home from school one day to find Nora transfixed. For a while, they had made it a family tradition, poking fun at Bob Ross's afro and his obsession with woodland creatures and his catchphrases. They'd gone around saying "It's your world" and "beat the devil out of it," and Wes had even begun calling Nora his "happy little cloud." But then one day, after she'd taken to bed for good, his mother had explicitly asked Wes to find "Joy of Painting" on cable for her, and he'd tivo'd it, but by that point the show was only on once a week so he'd offered to find her some DVDs. In the end, though, it didn't make a difference as she didn't seem to mind watching the same limited number of episodes over and over again. She was often agitated, and it wasn't always clear what she was agitated about, or even if she could see the television clearly, but there was something about Bob Ross's gentle, monotonous diction that soothed her. Now it was just about the only thing she ever watched, along with "Gossip Girl," about which she was almost as passionate as Nora. As a matter of fact, Wes himself was fascinated by Bob Ross and had even considered basing the protagonist of his first novel on him, although he was worried about lawsuits and might not take the risk.

As he sat beside his mother watching Bob Ross patch together a vile Alaskan wilderness, Wes thought of the thousands of bland, cheerful housewives and retirees in their converted garage studios across the country, following Ross's every move with their own fan brushes and alizarin crimsons, and he thought of his mother's imprisonment in this room and her declining health. He was convinced that she would never have watched Bob Ross if she was healthy. It seemed so totally unfair, but then could you ever really say that one person was worth more than another, or that the people who painted along with Bob Ross were making better use of the comfort he offered than someone who lay in bed all day and watched the same 12-year-old rerun over and over again? Wes thought of that game children play with each other, maybe when they're six or seven and first become aware of mortality and the ethical dimension of decision-making. "If someone comes with a gun and says he'll kill your mother or your sister, who would you choose?" It was never about who you loved more; in fact, there was always a right answer. If the choice was between saving your mother or your sister, you saved your sister because she was younger and had more to live for; if the choice was between your mother or your sister and your dog, you saved the dog, because it was innocent and blameless, although a few forward-thinking kids saved the sister because it was a sign of mature selflessness to sacrifice your dog for a lesser, though human life. Wes had never really understood the pleasure of the game, because the real mystery, which you were supposed to ignore, was how this situation was supposed to have arisen. Wes was always distracted by the question of what kind of circumstances could drive a person to offer you such an option. Why would it ever be necessary for anyone to have to kill either your sister or your dog, and even if it were, why would they offer the choice to a six-year-old child? These side issues always spoiled whatever was supposed to be fun about the game, both for Wes and the other kid. Wes supposed that, like playing with dolls or in competitive games, children instinctively grasp the need to rehearse in safety the only dimly understood decisions they see their elders make, but it wasn't until very recently, when it seemed as if his mother had finally gone into terminal decline, that he had seen the relevance of such preparations to his own life. That held even more true for Nora. Mother or brother? Mother or dog? It was even a game you could play by yourself, if there was no one else around to play it with.

It was, by all evidence, a game adults played among them-selves, too. Wes had hazy memories of the house once having been lively with visitors, boozy dinner parties that ran late and rose muffled to his room through the floorboards and the pil-low, but the visitors had gradually stopped coming by when she could no longer walk and became moody and withdrawn. At first, Wes had assumed that they had stopped coming because they were not real friends and she was no longer any fun to be around, but then he understood that she was the one who had sent them away. Was it because she was ashamed of what she had become, or too prideful to let others see her in this condition, or perhaps even that she had never much cared for them to begin with and had seized on her aggravated infir-mity as an opportunity to let them drop? After a while, it didn't matter very much anymore. When it had become too difficult for her to negotiate the stairs to the second floor, they had considered installing an electric chair-lift, but that wouldn't have solved the problem of the stoop and her wheelchair, especially in the winter, so it had been decided to relocate her to the garden floor, where at least she had some access to the outdoors. When the weather was fine, a few friends of long standing would occasionally drop by to sit with her in the dap-pled shade and light her cigarettes. But she hadn't been kind or patient with them and they had gradually stopped coming. And it had become apparent by then, too, that Wes's father was secretly—and then not so secretly—resentful of having had to give up his study with the French doors to accommo-date his wife's illness. One summer's evening, as he and Wes had sat on the wrought-iron dining room balcony overlooking the backyard, directly above the wide-open French doors, he nursed his third scotch and complained bitterly of how restricted his private life had grown, between work and par-enting and insurance claims, that the only place he had left to call his own, where he could retreat and write and *just think*, had been his room on the garden, and now that was gone too, and then he had compared himself to Shakespeare's sister and reacted very peevishly when Wes had immediately recognized the allusion. And then he had moved out altogether for a while—Wes had almost forgotten that part—and didn't come home until it was clear that she would be bedridden for good. When he moved back in, she had returned to her bedroom on the second floor, where she had remained ever since, excepting hospitalizations, and his father had converted the garden study into an apartment, where he now slept and wrote and fucked his students.

It was his father who had destroyed the collective family pleasure of watching "The Joy of Painting" together by drunkenly denouncing Bob Ross as a sell-out.

"It just really gets to me how mediocrity is rewarded again and again in this country while true artists go hungry in the streets. I mean, this guy must be a zillionaire, and just look at the crap he's making!"

"Don't you have to have ideals before you can sell out, dad?"

"He had ideals, this fucker, don't think he didn't. Of course he did! Everybody does. And now look at him. Making it harder on the rest of us."

"How is he making it harder on *you*?"

"Think I wouldn't sell out in a second if I could? In a second! But I can't. I'm not selling widgets here. I can't just crank it out—it's got to mean something to *me*. It's got to come from *somewhere*."

"Well Bobby thinks he's a very nice man. Bob Ross likes little animals like Bobby, and Bob Ross loves everybody in America. And he's been dead for ten years."

"Let me tell you something, Bobby. I don't care if he's dead. Bob Ross is a cunt. He's a rich, pandering, talentless hack cunt."

Nobody wanted to hear him say that word again, so they all went back to watching the show in chastened silence, but after that day making fun of Bob Ross seemed to have lost some of its luster, and they'd stopped watching the show *en famille.*

Bob Ross was putting the finishing touches on his landscape, using a palette knife to scrape a layer of snow down the mountainside. Wes's mother took his hand in hers. It was always a defining moment of any show when Bob Ross applied the snow; with nothing but a knife, some white paint and a few spare sweeps of his hand, he brought the entire composition into three dimensions, creating boulders and crevasses and shadows and arcing slopes where a moment earlier there had been nothing but flat planes of color. His father was right—it was sleight of hand, nothing more—but irresistible for all that. Wes could definitely sympathize with anyone who'd rather watch and listen to Bob Ross than deal with reality. Wes's mother squeezed his hand, and he looked down at her and smiled warmly.

"Pudding."

"Oh yeah. Be right back."

Nora was in the kitchen, standing in front of the open refrigerator and peeling the plastic off a mozzarella stick. She was wearing the stringy blue wig that they had bought Crispy for Halloween, but which had made Crispy look so reduced and defeated that no one had been able to bear seeing her in it. Nora smiled at Wes shyly, to which he responded with a deliberate glare, and the smile vanished. Unlike the other rooms of the house that faced the back, the kitchen had no curtains or blinds on the window, and the light from the yard, with no leaves on the tree to filter it, was unpleasantly bright and yet dead and thin at the same time. Wes pushed past Nora and slid the lower sash open with casual brutality.

"It's too hot in here."

"What's the matter?"

"Nothing's the matter. Where's Crisp?"

"I think she's with dad. What's wrong?"

"You sure you walked her?"

"I didn't walk her. You asked, and I told you I didn't walk her."

"Anything else you didn't do?"

"What didn't I do?"

"Mom's pudding? Like you said? Is it too fucking much around here to . . . ? Oh, fuck it. Just give me a fucking pudding. I'll do it."

Nora was already crying copiously by the time she reached the sink, her eyebrows reddening as the wig slipped partially down one side of her head. She reached into the sink.

"I *did* give it to her. Here's the spoon, see? Here's the cup, see? I told you." She held up a dirty spoon, a few grains of white rice and a film of dried cream still clinging to it. "See? See? See?"

Wes's anger instantly collapsed in on itself. Nora always looked five years younger when she cried; even as a helpless baby, her eyebrows had reddened just like that when Wes startled her with a sudden noise, such as deliberately dropping a fork on the metal tray of her high chair or sneaking up and clapping his hands just behind her head of silky blonde curls. What was worse, he knew that the moment he offered her words of regret and a gesture of comfort, she would accept it gratefully, without hesitation, and with all her great heart, as she had done as a baby. This was now twice in one day—in one morning—that he had made her cry, and the second time he had had to take her in his arms to staunch her tears. She was a better person than Wes would ever be, but he wasn't sure how many more times he could get away with it before it stopped working.

"She told me you didn't, Cookie. I'm sorry."

"She doesn't remember, Wes. She forgets everything."

"I know, I know. I'm truly sorry."

"Nyeh."

"Is that 'Nyeh, I forgive you' or 'Nyeh, you're an asshole?'"
She giggled into his T-shirt but didn't answer.

"Tell you what. I know you're bored. Give me a little time—
let me take this up to mom and get started on my homework—
and I'll take you out later."

"Where will you take me?"

"Dog run?"

"Nyeh."

"Museum?"

"Nyeh."

"Movie?"

"What movie?"

"*Taxi to the Dark Side?*"

"Nyeh."

"Your choice. Nothing too girlie. And walk the dog, please."

"Nyeh."

Wes rinsed the soiled spoon in the sink, shook off the
excess water, and retrieved an individual-portion cup of rice
pudding from the fridge. He took the stairs on his tiptoes,
three steps at a time, and again paused outside his mother's door
before tapping. This time he entered without waiting. Bob
Ross had started a new painting, a subdued forest scene with a
winding path, shrubbery in full bloom, and a sunlit clearing
just around the bend, but Wes's mother seemed to have fallen
asleep. Wes was not entirely sure, as she had not moved and
she often closed her eyes even when she was awake, but there
was something about the rhythm of her breathing that told him
so. Just to be sure, he allowed the bowl of the spoon to make
a light ping as he placed it on the glass tabletop. Her eyes
opened momentarily then closed again. Wes could see them
moving beneath the pinkish lids, blindly looking for something, as she licked her lips. She looked just like a lizard lazing
on a rock, but in the darkened room the resemblance took on
a sinister cast.

Occasionally Wes stumbled into wondering what things would be like when his mother was gone. When his mother was dead. Usually, he was able to suppress these thoughts, reminding himself that her disease was not fatal in itself, and that even in her weakened state she could easily survive another bout or two of pneumonia, as she had survived the last. But every so often the doubts would sneak in when he wasn't paying attention and entertain themselves in his head, bouncing off each other and jockeying for dominance before he caught them and shut them down. And then, too, especially when he was too tired, fed up or depressed, he sometimes gave them free rein and listened, with a kind of detached, horrified fascination, to what they had to say. The first thing that would happen, without doubt, is that his father would move back into the master bedroom. All this—the sling, the carpeting, the heavy drapes, the television, the hospital bed—would go. And although his father never talked about it, Wes knew that, despite her inheritance and the medical insurance, his mother's illness weighed heavy on the family finances, so when she died there would be money to pay for the redecoration. Wes was as sure as he could be that his father would want to make a new start. The kitchen would be the first thing to go—his dad was obsessed with the plans for the new kitchen, with its under-the-counter Sub-Zero freezer and six-burner Wolf cooking range—but the bedroom would come next, and there would be nothing left to remind anyone that she had spent years as a dying prisoner here. But he also knew that whenever he passed on the landing and heard the clicking of laptop keys instead of Bob Ross's soothing murmur, it wouldn't make any difference. This room would always be haunted, even if his father never sensed it. As for Nora, his mother's death would be a disaster. Already, Nora clung to the wreckage like a ship-wreck victim hanging on to a floating timber, desperate to convince herself that it would keep her afloat indefinitely. It meant everything to Nora, being able to go to her mother, even when she was half incoherent from painkillers for her bedsores or had soiled the bed, and read to her or watch "Gossip Girl" together, or just lie by her side and suck her thumb. She treated her mother the way a lonely child treats her favorite doll, skilled at convincing herself that she was an equal partner in the conversation, that she could lift her own cup, that she could hear and respond to her worries and concerns. What would Nora do when all that was gone? What were the chances that their father would man-up and step in? Wes wanted to believe that he himself could make up some of the shortfall, at least until Nora was old enough to take responsibility for her own emotional welfare, but he knew that he would be at best a woefully inadequate substitute. And then what would happen? Would Nora just drift away? Would she start taking drugs, flunking school, sleeping around? Would she shut down, become remote and joyless and unreachable, or would she take all her wit and sparkle and use them as shields—the funny girl who always has a clever putdown for everything and a joke for every occasion, even the most intimate—so that Wes would have to stand by and watch that beautiful smile of hers stretch and twist itself into a hideous mask?

But even worse than lying around worrying about how everything would collapse after his mother's death were the moments when Wes caught himself speculating about the ways in which life would become better, easier, less encumbered. Wes always squelched these thoughts the moment he found himself entertaining them, and was left with the nauseating stench of self-loathing, but it would be too late. The images conjured up in these fantasies remained, colorful and alive, to taunt him whenever he least expected it. It was the smallest inconveniences, rather than the cosmic implications, that he imagined he would be most grateful to be rid of. No more rice pudding in the refrigerator, no more spoon feedings, no more having to watch her try to feed herself, barely able to grip the spoon as it rode trembling to her dry lips and missed, so that she would then have to scrape the food off her cheeks or chin into a mouth sucking and gaping like a sea worm. No more late-night wake-up calls, no more adult diapers, no more waiting at the bathroom door having to listen to her grunts and whimpers. No more having to roll her over and wipe the shit smears off her lower back with a wet washcloth. No more rushing home on the weekends with that sick feeling in the pit of his stomach that one of her vital supplies had run out during the day. No more sitting at her side dutifully telling her about his day when she was hardly aware of his presence, when he knew full well she was a thousand miles away. No more sneaking past her bedroom like a thief whenever he needed a moment to himself, and no more fretting, every time he took a moment for himself, that he was being selfish and inconsiderate. No more being embarrassed to bring friends home after school, and no more feeling ashamed and worthless for being embarrassed. No more hating himself for resenting her. No more being angry all the time, no more taking it out on Nora. No more feeling like a shallow, egocentric brute every time, despite all his efforts not to, he slipped into little dreams of freedom. No more pretending, to himself and to Nora, that she wasn't going to die, and that it wouldn't be a relief to everyone concerned, herself included, when she did. No More.

Wes crept from the room and closed the door with infinite care.

From the landing, Wes could hear the iPhone calling to him. He went into his room and was somehow surprised to find it just as he had left it, waiting like a faithful dog in its nest of dirty clothes. He threw himself down on the bed, intending to ignore it, but it was insistent and would not rest until he acknowledged its call. He rolled over and retrieved it from the floor. A text message, a voice message and an email. The text— "pls call"—was from Lucy. The email was from James: "Today you are a man, my son." The voice mail was from Delia; her cell number was programmed into the phone, the call-back button said "Delia." As Wes stared at the name his heart began to race and he felt his cheeks grow hot, and the letters on the display seemed to ripple and pulse. He pressed the delete button and dropped the phone to the floor.

Like the kitchen, the bedroom was now flooded with light that felt like a thin, noxious vapor. It was a wintery light, but it was a long way to winter; the days were still too long, too warm, too inviting. Wes longed for the winter, when it was safe to shut oneself away. He loved waking up and going to school and coming home in the dark, the privacy of walking alone in a twilit street in the cold, the lonely romance of winter sounds— wind whisking at the bare tree branches, dry leaves scudding along an unswept sidewalk, the muffling that descends before a snowfall. What he hated was the summer, things that were bright and open and shadowless. He hated waking up in the sunlight, the skimpy clothes, the endless hazy twilights that somehow made you feel less than wholesome if you wanted to crawl into bed with a book while there was still a warm, pastel glow in the sky. He hated the way the Village streets remained crowded deep into the evening with people wandering around aimlessly in cargo shorts and sports bras, joylessly anticipating their first drink, a walk along the river with the fam, some stupid night on the town, any number of dismal prefabricated pleasures. Summer turned every New Yorker into a Disneyland vacationer; unforgivably, it blurred the distinctions between city-dwellers and suburbanites—distinctions which Wes felt should be maintained crisp and unmistakable at all times.

Wes thought of *Brave New World*, a back-up candidate for his European lit paper, and the deep sense of kinship he'd felt with Helmholtz Watson as he rejoiced at being exiled to the Falklands. Helmholtz had been offered his choice of any island in the world—Hawaii, Tahiti, the Caribbean—but he asked to be sent somewhere with bad weather, somewhere with lots of wind and storms, just as Wes would have. Until that moment, *Brave New World*, even with its abundance of casual sex for people of all ages, had seemed to Wes to be the most idiotic of books. But it had been almost redeemed by Helmholtz's request. A place where you could spend all winter holed up with your books, your notebooks, your thoughts. Wes suspected that this was not a normal desire for a seventeen-year old, but he couldn't help himself. All he wanted was to be boxed in by howling winds and lowering skies in every shade of grey. For the same reason, whenever he played Risk with Nora he always made Kamchatka his home base and defended it to the end. It would help, he supposed, to have somebody, some body, pale-skinned and red-haired like Delia, to have sex with at odd hours, but then again that could just as easily be a liability, in the event that such a body turned out to have needs of its own. If he were ever to be a serious writer, Wes reasoned, he would have to learn to embrace solitude and silence, though he did not suppose that he would suffer from loneliness. All he'd ever wanted, as far back as he could remember, was to be left alone, like Helmholtz, where the mind can expand to fill the vast silence, where a man can find peace from chatter and temptation and opinion—a one-room stone cottage with small leaded windows and a large fireplace, glacial run-off to bathe in, unpolluted, unobstructed views for the eye to linger upon in those blank moments before inspiration strikes. In the morning, black coffee from a moka pot, and a solid wedge of black bread spread thick with creamery butter and lingonberry jam. At night, a roaring fire, a mutton chop charred in the brazier, a peaty single malt, a pipe, maybe an old radio for the dramas and sports scores. Where, Wes wondered, on that rocky volcanic plain would he find a steady supply of firewood? Or coffee, whiskey, tobacco, mutton? Helmholtz, because he was technically a ward of the state, would have all these delivered to him, free of charge, and maybe a girl every so often, because those people were so keen on the pacifying effects of extremely impersonal and uninhibited sexual encounters. But Wes would have to be realistic if he were to survive and work—after all, writers in the real world do not have the luxury of being exiled by benevolent dictatorships, they have to survive by their own wits. Either you find a way to live on the cheap, or you sell yourself into lifelong drudgery and compromise in advertising or academia. Wes planned to pull a Helmholtz, but he thought that it might be better to start off somewhere more temperate to begin with, until he had honed his survival skills. Somewhere like Newfoundland or the highlands of Scotland, maybe, where he could trap grouse and grow winter barley and drive into the village once a week for supplies and a pint of bitter, whatever that was, at the local pub. And where he could roam the scented gorse in rubber boots with a fowling piece on his hip and a brown lab at his heels. But even then, where was he to get the money for rent, the car, the dog, the shotgun, the boots? How long would he have to work in the fallen world so that he could escape it? His father, after all, had pandered his entire life to a similar dream, and just look at where that had gotten him: loveless marriage, indifferent kids, a job he hated, exile to the basement. He couldn't even afford to live in a place of his own, which would have suited everybody. It was no wonder he was such a loser. Wes was absolutely determined to avoid his dad's fate, to foreswear all the entanglements—partly because it wasn't so hard to see himself behaving exactly as his father behaved if he were in the same predicament—but it all seemed so impossibly far away, impossible to imagine maintaining the necessary purity of soul and thought while he waited and plotted his getaway.

It occurred to him that he should revisit *Brave New World* as an option for his paper, as it would be so much easier and faster than *War and Peace*, but he couldn't bear the idea that someone might consider it an obvious choice, and anyway someone else in the class was bound to choose it. In any case, Helmholtz notwithstanding, Wes had truly disliked *Brave New World* as a novel; Mrs. Fielding would not appreciate the tone of snotty disdain that was sure to come through if he wrote about it. He turned his head towards the desk as if he might will *War and Peace* to float across the room to him, but it did not. The mere thought of getting up, retrieving the monstrous book, returning to bed, propping his back with pillows and proceeding to sort through 1,200 pages of highlights was disheartening in the extreme, and reminded him of everything that was wrong with his life, but it was precisely the outrage awakened by the unfairness of it all that gave him the energy to rise and do what had to be done. A few moments later, he was back settled beneath the covers with all the necessary paraphernalia spread in an arc about his lap: book, laptop, headphones, phone, legal pad, yellow highlighter and post-its.

Wes had already done almost all the preliminary work; dozens of post-its rose like buoy flags from the pages where he had highlighted relevant passages as he had read, and several pages of crabbed notes were handwritten into the flyleaves at the back. All Wes had to do was connect the dots. The problem was, he had had some sort of thesis in mind when he was taking notes, but now he was sincerely incapable of recalling what it was. It didn't matter much; he would have no trouble coming up with a new one. As a junior, every grade he received this year would be an important part of his college transcripts, and he badly wanted to prolong his unbroken string of A's in English, but he worried as he flicked through the post-its that he had never felt the least flicker of inspiration or kinship with the characters of *War and Peace*. In fact, he recalled thinking at the time that it was little more than *Gone with the Wind* with samovars. He'd read longer books in his time—*Lord of the Rings*, for one—and books that seemed longer—*Atlas Shrugged*, for instance—but *War and Peace* felt denser, somehow, as if the words weighed more on the page, the novel burdened by the gravity of its own importance, as if the years had given it a lustrous patina that made it appear more venerable than it really was. It was easy reading enough, he supposed, and not at all slow going, but irritating and clumsy at the same time, like scaling a rock face with a partner suffering from gout.

The book fell open at page 467 and Wes began to read. Prince André was listening to Natasha sing and was evidently on the verge of falling in love with her. Typically, André was choking on his own philosophical boner. "A sudden, vivid awareness of the terrible opposition between something infinitely great and indefinable that was in him, and something narrow and fleshly that he himself, and even she, was." Wes found himself distracted almost immediately. What was that supposed to mean—that our real selves are not our bodies? The tragedy of an expansive soul confined to a fragile, decaying cage of flesh? Not exactly a shattering insight. And yet, as he forced himself to read on, Wes remembered with vivid clarity precisely what had been on his mind when he had flagged this passage. It was an idea that had much preoccupied him at the time, three weeks earlier, when he'd read the book over the course of a single weekend—that life is, or should be, a perpetual interior war between alienated factions of human nature. It was only because Tolstoy was so ham-handed with characterization that Wes had been able to recognize in his writing the cartoonish extremes of a genuinely subtle and complex problem he'd been trying to work out for himself.

What Wes had finally come to see as he watched Prince André fall in love with Natasha is that Tolstoy had divided his characters between strugglers, like André and Pierre, and accepters, like Boris and Berg, and that Tolstoy was firmly on the side of the strugglers—people who are continuously engaged in an inner battle with their own natures and received ideas of the proper way to live, even if it makes them miserable and turns every little decision into a swamp of confusion and loneliness. It was a problem that Tolstoy had illustrated as a black-and-white thing, and Wes felt that it was much more complicated than that, because he knew from personal experience that no one is purely a struggler or purely an accepter, but it was no less real and perplexing for all that. Wes felt that, like Tolstoy, he admired the strugglers, or tried to admire them, even if he couldn't always grasp their internal dilemmas. To be a struggler was to be alone, and to be confused and lonely all the time, but just because you fight the good fight, choose the high road, doesn't mean you admire yourself for it. Usually you irritate yourself to no end, because you can never find a comfortable way to be, and maybe you even end up hating yourself for having become the very person you aspired to be. You start to despise people like André and Pierre for the very things that make them admirable, and admiring dickheads like Boris and Berg for the very things that make them hateful. You ascribe qualities to them they don't have, such as the thoughtfulness that would justify their arrogance and self-confidence, even though you know in your heart that they're arrogant and self-confident precisely because they don't engage in interior struggle, and that if they did they couldn't be arrogant or self-confident. How did that work? The more you think, the more you feel you should think less, and the more you feel, the more you think you should feel less? And the worse thing about it was that those who actually did think and feel less didn't seem to suffer from a similar sense of insufficiency—the smart people wish they could be more like the stupid people, but the stupid people never seem to want to be more like the smart people. Which hardly seemed fair.

Natasha was still singing, and André was still angsting. It was kind of weird, and a little sick, that all these grown men were lusting after a teenage girl, and Tolstoy let them do it without any sense that it was inappropriate. What was André—in his late twenties, maybe? He had a moustache and whiskers, he was a soldier, a hardened veteran, rich and sophisticated. He had probably fucked lots of peasants and whores. And Natasha was only fifteen, younger than Lucy. She had thin arms and a barely-formed bosom, Tolstoy said. Wes knew what that meant—a mature Russian woman, even the most beautiful, would have shoulders and arms rounded out by a little fat, big billowy boobs that had to be strapped down, a slight tub in the gut. But Natasha was probably more like a supermodel, or the star of some teen movie, with pillowy lips, hard, perky little tits, a flat tummy, and sharp hip bones that looked great in low-slung jeans. Nowadays a guy like André would be considered a total perv just for looking at a girl like that. But André wasn't thinking about her body, probably; he wasn't there, listening to her sing, trying to make out the outline of her nipples under her dress or imagining what she'd be like in bed. He was thinking of her unwearied soul, shining through her clear eyes and her piping voice, a beacon of purity and optimism and sincerity in a fallen, cynical world. That was all well and good, but a total turn-off as far as Wes was concerned, and she was still a kid no matter what you said. A freshman, for god's sake.

Now Hélène, that was a woman in every sense of the word. If Wes were in *War and Peace*, if he were André with all his money and connections, he'd have made a play for Hélène first thing, before Pierre could get his fat, clumsy hands on her. She was the kind of woman that every man who saw her wanted. Wes had been surprised at how low-cut the aristocratic women wore their dresses in those days, how Hélène was constantly flaunting her "high, beautiful breasts." Just that word "high" had been enough to send shivers down his spine. They were probably powdered, too. That scene where she leans over Pierre and he can suddenly picture her entire naked body beneath her dress.

Wes thought of Lucy and Delia and the differences between them. Physically, no doubt about it, Lucy was all Natasha, although probably darker of complexion, but much more like Hélène in temperament—manipulative, insincere, comfortable with her power over men, haughty and dismissive towards those who had nothing to offer her. Wes was certain of one thing— that he could never fall in love with someone like Lucy. Delia, on the other hand, was a full-blown woman like Hélène; true, with her pale skin and freckles and curly red hair pulled back in a casual ponytail, she didn't look much like Hélène, but she was dignified and quietly authoritative, self-possessed and powerfully built, not at all a svelte little seduction machine like Lucy or Natasha. Wes had never seen Delia in a low-cut ball gown, but he had seen her in a bathing suit and she definitely had softly rounded shoulders and high, beautiful breasts. Still, neither Lucy nor Delia was a Marya or a Sonya, earnest and devoted, but weak and at the mercy of the whims of fate. He couldn't stand that, someone clinging to him and helpless without him, someone who would never criticize him no matter how badly he treated her, eager to please but equally ready to fade into the background; taking her own vows solemnly, but content to release the faithless from theirs; feeling that she had a spark of godhead somewhere deep inside, yet not especially surprised that no one else recognized it; yearning for romance and love, yet always half-way towards persuading herself that they did not exist. Wes definitely couldn't stand someone like that.

There was a tap at the door, and Wes's father poked his head in with a sheepish smile.

"Got five minutes?"

"I'm doing my homework, dad."

His father stepped into the room, clasping an open laptop

at his hip. "Just a quick question. I won't bother you. What's the homework?"

Wes held up *War and Peace* and waved it wearily even as he lowered his eyes to his own computer screen, which had gone dark for lack of activity. Wes punched a button on the keyboard and the screen lit up again. His father strode across the room and took the book from his hand. He was barefoot, in a white T-shirt and plaid Bermuda shorts that may or may not have been underwear. His hair was freshly washed and plastered against his head, and he smelled strongly of Monsieur Balmain.

"*War and Peace?* I was just about your age, maybe a year or two younger, when I first read this. Very powerful. A big influence on me in my formative years." He began to leaf through it, as if to revive fond memories.

"Wanna do my paper for me?"

"You have to learn to think for yourself, son." He dropped the book on the bed and opened his laptop without sitting down. Wes noticed for the first time that his father had hair growing in his ears, squiggly little grey-brown hairs like pubes, and he looked down at his own toes, which had lately begun to sprout little tufts of light brown hair of their own.

"What do you need, dad? I'm very busy."

His father turned the laptop downwards to show Wes the screen, which was opened on a Facebook page.

"What do you know about Facebook?"

"I know it's not for old guys."

"Wrong, pal. There's more of my kind on here than your kind."

"What do you want to know?"

"See, I signed on a couple of months ago, kind of by accident. And I never used it, but then people started friending me. It started slowly, but suddenly it's snowballing, dozens and dozens of people coming out of the woodwork, people I haven't spoken to in decades."

"And?"

"I guess I want to know what sort of things I can do with it."

"How do you sign on 'by accident?'"

"I don't know. Nora wanted me to look at something and her computer was broken or she couldn't find the charger. I don't remember. But see, like here, somebody tagged this picture of me from college."

The photograph showed Wes's father, aged maybe nineteen, sitting at the end of a row of students on a low wall at the edge of some sort of quad or terrace, supremely pretentious, in the pre-grunge fashion of the early eighties, in a thrift-store herringbone overcoat several sizes too big, his shoulders hunched Bob Dylan-style against a non-existent chill, as evidenced by the trees in full leaf directly behind him. Apart from the full head of thick brown curls and the blue-tinted granny glasses, he looked much as he did now. The look he had apparently been stretching for was that of a down-at-the-heels artist, a writer or a musician, in the days before he had become a household name, someone indifferent to the hunger and cold that come with the territory of being a young, unsung genius. Like many of the similarly affected students at Dalton, his father might have pulled it off had he not been studying at an elite educational institution that cost more a semester than most people earned in a year. Wes did not recognize any of the other people in the photo, all men or boys, and it was not in fact clear whether his father was part of the group or simply clinging to its periphery. Wes ran the cursor over each one; some had been tagged, some not.

"They spelled your name wrong. See the question mark? Whoever tagged you didn't know you very well."

"Yeah, I noticed that. Can I change that?"

"Just go down here to 'Tag this photo,' put the cursor on your face and click. You can put in anything you want."

"But will people know it was me who made the correction?"

"I'm not sure. I think so."

"Forget it, then. What else can I do?"

"Like what?"

"You know, post my own pictures, find friends, join groups, that sort of thing."

"Dad, I really don't have time for this. Can't you figure it out for yourself? Everybody else does."

"Sure, I just thought . . . Maybe it was something we could do together."

"Nostalgia. Wasted youth. Bitter regret. I'll pass."

"Can I friend you?"

"Parents and children cannot be friends. That would be a travesty. Now please?" The iPhone rang, and Wes made a big show of pushing his father to the side, picking it up off the floor, and raising it like a talisman between them, as if it were a silver cross and his father a vampire. The call was from Lucy. Wes had no desire to talk to her, but anything was better than helping his father make a total dick of himself on Facebook. He gave his father a dismissive glare, pointed at the door and answered the call. His father shrugged his shoulders and padded from the room.

"Wes?"

"Oh Lucy."

"Where are you?"

"At home, doing homework."

"I was worried about you, when you disappeared like that. I've been trying to reach you all morning."

"I know, I'm sorry. I've got this paper due Monday and I haven't even started it."

"Can I see you later?"

"Like I said, I've got to get to work . . . "

"I know, but it'll be, like, just for a few minutes. I really need to see you."

"Lucy, any other time."

"Please? Five minutes? I'll come downtown."

Wes was not very experienced at casual cruelty, and in fact had impressed himself by holding out as long as he already had. Now he had exhausted his entire repertory.

"What time?"

"Whenever's good for you. Some time this afternoon?"

"What time is it now?"

"I don't know. Hang on. Eleven twenty."

"Say around three? You know where I am?"

"You're in the school directory. I'll find it. I had a really fun time last night."

"So I'll see you three-ish."

"Bye?"

"See you later."

Wes didn't get it at all. Why was she calling him? Why did she want to see him? Twenty-four hours earlier she would barely have been able to identify him in a line-up, and now she . . . what? Involuntarily, Wes reviewed a mental slide show of memorable moments from the previous night—memorable for him, certainly, but he could hardly persuade himself that he had so distinguished himself among Lucy's many lovers that he had ruined her for every other man. Had he somehow, quite unknowingly, touched her in a way she had never been touched before—emotionally? The truth was, he knew her mostly by reputation, had rarely spoken to her until the day before, and was hardly in a position to pretend to know or to predict what she might be thinking on any particular subject, much less about him. Wes hoped that he was the kind of person who was able to judge people on their own merits and to rise above idle gossip and speculation, but in fact he had never had any reason to question or doubt the extent to which she had earned her reputation, simply because he had never given it a moment's consideration. Lucy was the hot sophomore with pouty lips who left herds of middle-school dweebs dry-mouthed and stricken in her wake as she floated down the halls. From everything he knew or thought he knew about the kind of guys she liked—rich, well-groomed, confident, clever but not unduly intelligent—he was well out of the running for what was said to be the best fuck in the upper school, and since his interests and desires had long lain in a very different direction, he had never considered himself to be in the running in the first place. Delia was the girl he wanted, the girl he had always wanted. And he knew in his heart of hearts that when Delia was finally his, the long, humbling wait would prove to have been more than worth it, because it would have demonstrated the primacy of love and faith and patience, and gotten him laid. The Lucies of this world were for guys who set the bar a little lower.

Wes recalled the fateful moment on Friday morning, just minutes after emerging from his meeting with Mrs. Fielding, that he had received Lucy's tweet. The school had been still largely deserted, although a few early arrivals like himself were beginning to disturb the serenity of the empty halls. Because his daily commute to school involved a long walk across town and a crowded subway ride on the local line, Wes tended to arrive at the last moment, when the lobby was most frenzied and he himself had no time to loiter. But with fifteen minutes before the bell, on Friday morning he had lingered in the lobby. He had never before noticed all the campaign posters that plastered the lobby walls, and he took a moment to appreciate them. Incongruously, someone, probably in administration, with a view to some misguided concept of political correctness or to forestall controversy, had thought to balance or neutralize them by posting almost as many for McCain as for Obama, although many of the McCain posters were defaced with mustaches and horns or, in the case of Sarah Palin, erect phalluses, usually aimed towards her mouth. Almost everybody Wes knew was for Obama and felt deeply energized by and connected to the electoral process, even though most of

them were too young to vote; the few eligible seniors had been
strutting around school for months now and making their
newly fungible opinions known to anyone who would listen.
For almost everyone, Bush had been president as long as
they had memories of politics, so the imminent upheaval felt
extremely personal in a way that very few issues could to a
group of overprivileged teenagers, and even the tweenies in
middle school acted as though they were individually respon-
sible for electing the country's first black president. But Wes's
guilty secret was that he could not play along, at least not in his
heart. He despised Bush as much as anyone, he supposed, but
he worried that, like the housing market, the hysteria sur-
rounding Obama was a big bubble bound to burst. If you're in
the opposition your whole life, and you've come to identify
yourself with the frustrated, stifled and outmaneuvered moral
minority, how do you take to victory? Republicans knew this;
they were masters at playing the victim even when in power,
they didn't own it even when they broke it, but Democrats and
these kids didn't get it and they were going to get their fingers
burned. America holding its head high once more among the
comity of nations, the dawn of a new day, everything changed
and renewed from one day to the next—Wes just couldn't buy
into it, as much as he'd have wanted to. He wished he could
just be free to enjoy the moment, but he didn't seem to have it
in him to pop a woody for new beginnings.

He supposed it must have rubbed off from his dad. A vision
of his father's face, livid and distorted with anger, superim-
posed itself upon Barack Obama's calm, forceful features in
murky red, white and blue as he gazed with visionary intensity
into a dawning future of hope. Wes's father hated Bush with an
almost erotic passion, railing savagely against the President's
every utterance and decree. He was completely addicted to this
hatred, but Wes had no idea what his father actually believed
in. The closest his father ever seemed to come to expressing

conviction in anything other than the fact that someone, somewhere, had led his life astray was when he recalled the glorious
utopia that was the Lower East Side in the early 1980s. How
repulsively he reveled in his memories of a city filled with
crime, crackheads, ageing Beatniks, $250-a-month walk-up stu-
dio apartments in Alphabet City and freewheeling artists
thronging the sidewalks of Avenue A at three in the morning,
making the world safe for something. How cruel and untrue it
had been to tell someone like his father that when you ain't
got nothing you ain't got nothing to lose. He had had nothing
and had lost everything, and had spent the rest of his life
making sure that everyone around him understood that they
were accomplices in the theft. Especially his own wife, who'd
bankrolled him through two decades of bitter disillusion,
which doesn't come cheap. Wes's father, for all his so-called lib-
eralism, was the anti-Obama, and Wes could not help wondering, as he gazed at the Senator's beautiful face, what further
price he himself would have to pay for his lifelong exposure to
that virulent strain of psychogenesis.

Lost in thought, he felt a strong hand on his left shoulder,
and turned to his right to find James, smelling organically of
coffee, smiling maniacally through his blonde bangs and thrust-
ing his Blackberry into Wes's face.

"Seen this tweet?"

"What is it?"

"Check your phone."

Wes had dutifully shucked his backpack, rummaged through
the side pockets, removed his phone, turned it on and opened
Twitterific. There was a new tweet from PrincessLucy. It said:
"When the cats away . . . ! Party @ my place 9 on. C U 2nite
mice!"

"Who is this?"

"It's Lucy, man. You know, hot Lucy in tenth." James snick-
ered oddly.

"So why'd it come to me? I don't subscribe to her tweet."

"You do now, my friend. I signed you up. *At her request.*"

James seemed to be perfectly serious, yet it made no sense at all to Wes.

"How, at her request? I hardly know her. It's gotta be a mistake."

"No mistake, Wes. *She likes you.* You've been summoned. You've received the call. Resistance is futile, you lucky fuck."

And now, lying on the bed with *War and Peace* resting mutely between his raised knees, Wes felt the full force of shame wash over him. His ears began to ring, his vision blurred and his skin felt hot as coals. The shame was inside him too, snaking through the corridors of his body like that archaic video game with the worm that keeps getting longer, hollowing him out to the core. Love had not won out, of course, and yet he still couldn't quite see how it had happened. For the better part of a year, ever since the moment he had allowed himself to understand that he was in love with Delia, he had prepared himself for just such a contingency. Over and over again, he had rehearsed scenes in his head in which he found himself compelled to rebuff, gently but firmly, the advances of women who approached him in the street, at the library, at the fish counter in Citarella, on the subway, on a banquette admiring the Fragonards at the Frick, on line for bagels at Russ and Daughters, in a plush Park Avenue parlor, in a darkened screening room watching "Breathless" at the Film Forum, and offered themselves to him unconditionally for an hour, an afternoon, a weekend of unbridled and possibly kinky passion. Because he was attracted to older women, a category to which Delia nominally belonged, and because he felt that his own puppyish enthusiasm and lack of experience would be irresistible to jaded housewife types, the women in these fantasies tended to resemble the young mothers who crowded the sidewalks outside Dalton every afternoon, waiting for their young ones in tight jeans and high ponytails. No celebrities, except perhaps for the actress Blake Lively or the author Marisha Pessl, whose jacket photo he had spent many hours condoling with over her hopeless infatuation for him, Wes. To those women he would say: "I'm sorry. I'm flattered. You're very attractive, really. Under different circumstances I would be happy to oblige. But you see I'm in love, and mindless, anonymous sex with beautiful strangers holds no allure for me. Haven't you ever been in love? Then you'd know how I feel. No, not even a blowjob in the back of the taxi. I'm sorry." It was true that such advances had not come his way, but Wes felt that, lit up from within as he was by the light of pure love, the way pregnant women were said to have a special glow about them, it was only a matter of time. And when it happened, he would be ready, and he would be a rock.

And then it happened. From the very moment that James had called him a lucky fuck, leaving him stunned and paralyzed in the middle of the school lobby, Wes had spent the rest of the day constructing scenario after scenario of heroic resistance. Lucy was no cougar, but she was said to be aggressive and inventive. He told himself repeatedly throughout the day, as he mentally reviewed every conceivable permutation of the seduction scene, that to be forewarned was to be forearmed. What kind of tactics and techniques could someone like Lucy deploy to weaken the resolve of her unwilling victims? Most boys, of course, would not even entertain the notion of resistance; most boys would in fact, from the very subtlest first encouragement, seek to take charge and ascribe the outcome to their own aggressive charms, so Lucy would need a minute or two simply to grasp the notion that she was being rebuffed—and not in a coy way but with profound moral determination and integrity—by a boy who gave no particular outward sign of being different from all the rest but who had actually turned out to be unlike anyone she had ever met before.

On the other hand, once she had this concept firmly fixed in her mind, it would serve only to whet her appetite and hone her hunting instincts, and then Wes would need to be on his guard. How would she go about it? Perhaps they would be talking casually in a quiet corner of her apartment with drinks in their hands—his a club soda, hers a cosmo—when she would suddenly lean in and whisper something in his ear, her breath hot and moist, and run a red fingernail down the side of his neck. Or they might be dancing when she pressed her thigh between his legs as she stared straight up into his eyes. He didn't think it would be something vulgar or less subtle; that wouldn't be her way, but he should probably be prepared for anything. And if it had somehow come to her attention that Wes was rumored to be a virgin, he would be wise to expect the challenge to send her into a frenzy of competitive predation.

In the end, all it had taken was a simple text message— "find me"—to send Wes in search of her without an instant's hesitation, and today he saw himself for what he really was. Wes did not care to attach the cliché "saving himself" to whatever it was he had been doing with respect to Delia—that would have been too saccharine even to put into words in the privacy of his own thoughts, let alone to suggest to James who, alone among the boys of his acquaintance, might be sympathetic to his motives even if he ragged him mercilessly for it. And in any case it would not have been entirely true, as Wes had pretty much done everything but "it" in the course of casual dating before Delia. Wes was no prude, either; he felt that safe sex between consenting teenagers was probably a very good and healthy thing. Even so, he knew what it meant to have done what he had done last night. He had not been unfaithful to Delia, who suspected nothing and expected nothing from him, but he had betrayed her and himself nonetheless. He couldn't quite get his mind around what, precisely, the betrayal had consisted of, but he was quite certain that he could not take it back and that it had destroyed something that he'd taken pride in. It was precisely because he had done something that almost anyone in his place would have done that he felt diminished and clownish. Maybe he'd thought he really was different from everyone else, but now he felt like a dog in a blue Halloween wig, humiliated and ridiculous. He felt like his father—the ultimate dog in a blue wig.

And none of this, of course, went any way towards explaining why Lucy now seemed so anxious to see him. He was a notch in her belt now; by Monday morning the whole school would know that she'd popped his cherry and moved on, and even those who were most jealous of him—especially those—would make a meal of it. What more did she want from him?

Wes looked down at the book in his lap, its lines swimming. It was even heavier now than it had been earlier, and Wes felt a thousand miles away from it, could barely even remember what the book was about. The diminutive forest of post-its was daunting, and Wes shook his head in dismay that he had ever imagined this to be an easy A or even a doable assignment. He turned to the back of the book, where he had scratched down some thoughts as he had read, hoping they might jog his memory, but they were less than helpful:

- "idiotic behavior of Pierre at Borodino."

- "812. Shock that André is wounded at Borodino, presumed dead. Had the idea that A's lesson in life was forgiveness, that he would get back together with Natasha. When later, that is exactly what happens, disgust that Tolstoy is so predictable."

- "Death of Petya. Manipulative to what end except pathos? Ultimately, P's death is necessary to get Natasha to focus on her mother and someone else's grief, but that is just a plot twist. Is a boy's life of so little value? Never identified with Petya, boyscout type, but angry on his behalf."

- "Everyone learns the lesson they need to learn (list)"

- "p.1071 'And there is no greatness where there is no simplicity, goodness, and truth.' Whole book in a nutshell."

Wes stared at the last entry, willing it to mean something, anything, as he thought it should, but it was as drained of emotion as a doctor's illegible scrawl on a prescription pad. Wes sighed and pushed the book to the floor, along with the pens and papers. He sat up; the laptop slid down the blanket tented against his left leg, snapped shut and fell into the crack between bed and wall. Wes balled his fists and pressed them into his cheeks, gritting his teeth, kicking his feet and vibrating his entire skull in a silent scream that caused him to feel lightheaded and pathetic, but offered no catharsis. With a grand spontaneous gesture, he swept the covers aside, swiveled his entire body on the pivot of his butt, and planted his feet firmly on the floor. Wes thought that it might be a good idea to take the dog for a walk along the river, throw her some tennis balls, do something normal to clear his mind of all this confusion.

Leaving his dirty clothes on the floor by the bed, Wes crossed the room and removed a clean pair of underwear, black jeans and a white T-shirt from his dresser. Slipping into the pants, he paused, bare-chested, before the mirror. Until last night, he had been sure that he would look different on this day. In fact, he had envisaged this very moment many times before—the moment when he first catches sight of himself in the mirror after losing his virginity. In the fantasy, the difference between before and after was subtle and hard to describe, but quite irrefutable and as evident to everyone, friends and strangers alike, as it was to himself. Obviously, it was not physical—he was still five foot eleven and one hundred and thirty-five pounds, all protruding ribs and narrow shoulders, but well-formed arms that girls and gay men often commented on and asked to touch. Shaggy brown hair, hippies' delight, rather attractive large blue eyes and high flat cheekbones that conveyed, in general, the impression of someone two years' younger than he was, a flaw that he had always played to advantage by adopting a social persona that was both endearingly bashful and aggressively intellectual yet accessible and ecumenically open to less evolved points of view. But he would carry himself differently, he had imagined; no swagger, of course, and only occasionally aware of the change, but with less apology for taking up space, allowing his arms to swing in uninhibited arcs, fingers lightly curled, his stride easier, swaying, not on the balls of his feet but on his heels like a character from R. Crumb. Mostly, though, the change would be visible in his face, in the steadiness of his gaze and the serene settledness of his features. He would smile less often and less broadly, but from a deeper and less perturbable foundation of confidence. He would be like a Tibetan monk, able to slow the beating of his heart and abide fools without getting upset, and without quite understanding why people, women and men, would respond to him with correspondingly greater respect, admiration and desire.

But Wes could see now from his reflection that none of this had come to pass. His shoulders were not thrown back; his bony chest, hairless but for two ridiculous tufts of hair around his tiny brown nipples, was not swollen with a new inviolable mystery; his lips were deflated and colorless and his cheekbones eroded. His eyes seemed to have taken on the lifeless, green-gray pall of a winter's day far out to sea in the North Atlantic. What was there here that could possibly have attracted the interest of one of the hottest chicks at school? Wes scowled at himself and pulled the T-shirt over his head. He then applied deodorant to his underarms—it was original-scent Old Spice, the smell of which had given him much secret delight over the years, although it afforded him little pleasure now.

He looked in on his mother on his way downstairs. She was awake with the light on, looking perkier than he had seen her in some time, sitting almost upright, her eyes shining in a way that, if she had been a healthy person, would have made her look as if she had recently been crying. In her case, it simply meant that she was alert and functioning. Her hair had recently been washed and combed, but as usual this somehow had the effect of making her look worse rather than better. A speck of rice pudding clung to the down above her upper lip. Nora lay curled up at her side, like a toddler, her knees almost to her chin, reading aloud from a book propped against a pillow.

"I'm walking the dog. Do you need anything before I go?"

"No thanks, Leslie honey."

"Movie!"

"What are you doing there?"

"Bobby's reading to momma." Wes looked at her helplessly. Was she there on a selfless mission to keep their mother company, or was she so bored that she would do absolutely anything for entertainment? She popped her thumb into her mouth, and in the dim light it was impossible to read her impression.

"Let me walk Crisp, then we'll go, I promise."

Wes turned to leave.

"Wait, Leslie."

"Mom!"

"*Wes*. There is something I'd like, *Wes*, if you don't mind."

"Name it."

"Sweetbreads."

"What?"

"Sweetbreads."

"You mean, like, pastry?"

"Look it up. You asked what I want. I want sweetbreads."

"Do we have any in the house?"

"I don't think so, honey. You may have to go the store."

Wes thundered down the stairs, calling for the dog, who appeared from somewhere on the garden level, wagging her tail and laying her ears back submissively. He slipped into a worn gray hoodie that hung from the coat rack by the front door, and scratched the dog above the tail as he pulled the phone from his back pocket, opened the iPedia app and typed in "sweet bread." He took the leash down from the coat rack and hooked it to Crispy's collar while he waited for the query to load. He had opened the door, with Crispy straining on the leash, when his query came up, redirected to "Sweetbreads." Above the text was the photo of something brown, bulbous and glistening on a bed of creamy rice.

"Sweetbreads are the thymus glands and pancreas glands of lamb, beef, or pork. There are two different connected parts to the thymus gland, both set in the neck. The 'heart' sweetbreads are more spherical in shape, and surrounded symmetrically by the 'throat' sweetbreads, which are more cylindrical in shape. Although both are edible, the heart thymus gland is generally favored because of its delicate flavor and texture, and is thus more expensive.

"The etymology of the word 'sweetbread' is thought to be of Old English origin. 'Sweet' is probably used since the thymus and pancreas are sweet and rich tasting, as opposed to savory tasting muscle flesh. In Old English, sweet was written 'swete' or 'sweete.' 'Bread' probably comes from the Old English word 'bræd,' meaning 'flesh.'"

Wes pulled Crispy back into the house, closed the door, unhooked the dog from the leash, hung the leash back on the coat rack and returned to his mother's room. Nora was still reading, and now that she had sat up Wes could see that the book was A.J. Liebling's *Between Meals*, a book he himself had read aloud to his mother, cover to cover, twice over the past few years. She seemed to love it because it was about Paris and it was about food, but Wes could never quite figure that one out, since her diet was now basically restricted to high-fat rice pudding and the only time in her life she had been to Paris was on her honeymoon, a time he imagined she would prefer to forget. But she couldn't get enough of it. She and Nora looked up expectantly as he entered the room, holding the offending iPhone in front of him, evidence of an as-yet undiscovered crime.

"Mom! Are you kidding me?"

"What is it, Leslie? What's wrong?"

"Sweetbreads? It's disgusting!"

"I didn't know you were such a prude, honey."

"Let Bobby see!" Wes handed the phone to Nora, who peered into it as if it were an oracle or a train schedule.

"I'm not a prude, whatever that means, but I can't cook this."

"Of course you can. You're a fabulous cook. You can cook anything."

"Mom, please don't ask me . . . Anyway, I don't think it's such a good idea. All you've eaten is rice pudding for a month. It'll make you sick."

"I'll worry about that."

"Ew! This is gross! Bobby's gonna barf!"

Wes sat down at the edge of the bed and took his mother's hand, which was warm and dry.

"Mom, I don't want to . . . are you sure this is what you want? I mean, you've been kind of out of it for a while. Are you sure you're not . . . I mean, is this really what you want? Pancreas?"

"Yes, I'm sure. Please do it for me. Maybe we can even make a family meal of it. Like the old days."

"Have you ever had it before?"

"No. Never."

"Then why?"

"Bobby knows why."

"Oh yeah?"

"It's this book. It makes mommy hungry for Paris."

"Paris is where your father and I took our honeymoon. You know the story."

"I don't."

"Let Bobby tell!"

"Okay Bobby, tell."

"Momma and dada went to Paris, and they went to a romantic little restaurant with candles and red lampshades, a bis . . . a bis . . . "

"Bistro."

"A bistro. And momma couldn't understand anything on the menu 'cause it was all in French except one thing, rice and veal, so she ordered that. Only it wasn't rice and veal."

"It was *ris de veau*. Sweetbreads."

"And dada was so proud of her for ordering it 'cause it made her so so-phis-ti-cated. But when it came she almost puked. So when dada went to the bathroom she scraped the whole thing into her bag and pretended she'd eaten it. And she never told dada what she did."

Wes could see what was going on here. Whenever his mother had a momentary upswing, its effect on Nora was like a sugar rush, she became overexcited and acted silly, which his mom would egg on, thrilled to be the center of anybody's attention. That explained the sweetbreads and the baby talk. Both of them would crash soon enough, leaving Wes to clean up the mess, but he could hardly begrudge his mom for feeling frisky.

"And now you're sorry for what you did. Twenty years later."

His mother had closed her eyes, and her hand had slipped from his and was now groping, crablike, across the counterpane in a blind search for the remote. Nora turned her eyes to Wes in alarm, but his mother's face offered no sign that she had recognized the resentment in his voice.

"That's right. I'm sorry and I want to try it. How do you like them apples? It's never too late to learn something new."

"Yeah, *Leslie*. How do you like them apples?"

Nora was too young to remember a time when their mother had been in full health, but Wes was not, and he found the ups and downs disorienting. He had been through this before, periods of rapid deterioration followed by gradual recovery that never fully returned her to what she had been before the latest attack, and the pneumonias and the bed sores and the incontinence, and he knew better than to allow himself to believe that she was getting better. It almost made him angry, as if she were playing a game with them, which of course she wasn't. Even in this light he could see Nora scanning their mother's face for signs of new growth, as if the spring had come, and he wanted to shout at her, at both of them, for making things more complicated than they needed to be. For the briefest moment, he suddenly saw the image of Prince André, pale and gaunt on his death bed, with a repentant Natasha at his side, all mystically aglow with the prospects of a new life. Nora had nothing to repent, she was only twelve, but Wes knew that she was consumed with fear and guilt—she herself didn't understand what she was feeling, but Wes did—and every time his mother seemed to be improving it was as if she had been reprieved, and she was momentarily, like Natasha, filled with naïve hopes for the future and the sense that she had been absolved and redeemed. Only she had never done anything wrong. She was the only one who never did anything wrong.

"You stay there, Nora. I'll take care of it. Let me have the phone, please."

Crispy was still waiting by the front door, and wagged her tail in a despondent expression of optimism as Wes descended.

He sat on the bottom step and returned to the iPedia entry on sweetbreads. At the foot of the page was a link to a "Top Chef" recipe, but when he followed the link he found that the very first ingredient was golden raisins, and his mother hated raisins. He stood up with a sigh and a groan and went into the kitchen, where he found his father standing in front of the refrigerator, peeling slices of cheese from a package of provolone, rolling them into cylinders and sliding them into this mouth. Wes ignored him and went to the row of cookbooks lined up on a warped shelf above the counter. There were a great many of them, thirty or forty, representing every ethnic group in Queens, but he could not recall when he had last seen anyone reach for one. Wes had been the chef of record at home for some time, and it was true that he could cook just about anything from a recipe, but with homework and SAT prep he tended to keep it simple these days, sticking to the dishes that he knew Nora would eat—macaroni and cheese, spaghetti with sautéed vegetables, breaded chicken cutlets, steak, the sort of food they might eat if they lived in Indiana, he imagined. His father was the better cook, but he rarely had the energy for it these days, and refused to descend to the children's standards.

"Can I have some money? I need to go shopping for dinner."

With his free hand his father pulled his wallet from the back pocket of his shorts and handed it to Wes.

"Take what you need. What are you making?"

"Sweetbreads."

"You've gotta be kidding me."

"That's what Mom asked for."

"Count me out. I'll have cereal. Can't stand sweetbreads. Barely stand to look at them."

"Mom wants it to be a family night. You have to."

"Have my wallet back?"

His father left the room and Wes turned to the cookbooks. After coming up blank in the first half dozen, he finally found

what he was looking for in *The Union Square Cookbook*—
"seared sweetbreads with mushrooms and frisée"—although
the idea of wilted frisée struck him as excessively gallic, and he
thought he might substitute baby bok choy, if it was available.
He typed the list of ingredients into a new memo on the notepad
app of the iPhone. As he typed, his eyes wandered down the
various steps of the recipe. The sweetbreads were to be soaked
for an hour in ice water, which would have to be changed every
fifteen minutes; they were then to be poached for three minutes, drained, cooled in fresh cold water, trimmed of fat and
connective membranes, and pressed under a weighted plate for
five hours. Only then were they to be dredged in flour and
fried to a golden brown. Wes trudged back upstairs and leaned
in at his mother's door.

"Mom, it's going to take about seven hours. Are you sure
you . . . ?"

"Leslie, do I have to tell you . . . "

"Okay, okay. Where's Nora?"

"I don't know, Leslie."

Wes left the house and turned east, his hands buried deep
in the pockets of his hoodie. The streets were crowded now,
mostly with people Wes deemed to be tourists and daytrippers
from the outer boroughs and the suburbs because they walked
too slowly and did not look intelligent enough to live in
Greenwich Village. The sidewalks were narrow, and even
when the crowds were sparse they were strewn with obsta-
cles—trees and fenced beds, garbage cans, fire hydrants—that
had to be negotiated. Now they were lousy with invaders, all of
whom imagined themselves to be an integral part of the life of
the city; Wes had to turn sideways just to squeeze past them.
How he hated them, with their high-tech strollers, their pristine sneakers and shopping bags and Jersey license plates, all
converging on his neighborhood from places that no one
would ever want to visit, let alone live in. They were all so

puffed up and pleased with themselves because they had pur-
chasing power and hard-to-secure reservations, but they were
the kind of people who would never know what it's like to
belong, to truly belong to a place the way Wes belonged to the
Village. They were the kind of people who move whenever
they can afford to buy a bigger house in a richer place. They
thought of the city as a place that is impervious, a place to drive
badly and behave rudely and give vent to their most basic
acquisitive instincts; they consumed it as if it were both inex-
haustible and disposable, but they would never know how tender and fragile the city really is because they were neither tender nor fragile themselves. How could they be, living in boxes
surrounded by lawns like minefields, never rubbing shoulders,
never looking strangers in the eye, never really understanding
what it is to be living human beings? To know one small place
like this one, and to know it as few others did, and to understand one's place in it without complication and doubt, seemed
to him an almost blessed condition. Some jerk in his class had
written a pretentious, pseudo-Marxist analysis of "The Wizard
of Oz," concluding that Dorothy was a reactionary know-noth-
ing who preferred to return to the ignorance and squalor of her
Bible Belt dirt farm, with its libertarian promise of individual-
ism, than to lead the citizens of Emerald City out of the bonds
of oppression. Wes had offered a furious counterargument and
was, in turn, condemned as a reactionary, but his outrage had
had nothing whatsoever to do with politics. The fact was,
Dorothy's Kansas and Wes's Village had a great deal in common, and Dorothy's extended family had much in common
with Wes's ideal of what family life should be. The class had
taken a straw poll, and everyone but Wes had agreed that, in
Dorothy's shoes (no pun intended), they would have chosen to
remain in the land of Oz. But Wes had no patience for world
travelers, for what is there to see outside one's own internal
monologue, the infinity of one's own mind?

Wes turned right on Bleecker, encountering an even denser wave of tourists. A long line of happy people—European teenagers, Mid-Western families, Japanese tour groups—snaked from the entrance of the Magnolia Bakery and around the corner. Wes whistled the tune to "Bah Bah Black Sheep" as he sidled by them, but doubted that any of his targets would have the wit to understand they were being insulted.

Wes was put in mind of *The War Between New York and New Jersey*. About four years earlier, his father had rented a car and the entire family had taken a day trip to a no-kill shelter in southern Jersey where they hoped to adopt a dog. They had found Crispy within the first five minutes, an adorable eight-week-old white puppy with black spots and a patch over one eye—maybe a pointer mix but maybe also an Australian cattle dog, no one seemed to know which. On the way home they had stopped outside a picturesque river town for a picnic on the banks of the Delaware, and it was there that the entire plot for *The War Between New York and New Jersey* had come to Wes in a flash of inspiration. It was to be set in the midst of a civil conflict that had broken out over the secession of Staten Island, and New York's militia now occupied most of New Jersey and was closing in on the capital. The character based on Wes was a teenage volunteer from Manhattan who had been posted to a farmhouse on the banks of the river outside a pretty village just like the one where they were picnicking. His job was to monitor traffic on the river and prevent smugglers from ferrying relief supplies to besieged Trenton. The boy would be a thoughtful, intellectual type but a true believer in New York's cause—the triumph of liberal urban civilization over suburban ignorance and conformity—but then he would fall in love with the milkmaid daughter of the dairy farmer whose house he was occupying, and his certainties would be thrown into confusion. There would also be an evil realtor who had set his sights on the milkmaid, and Wes's character would have to shoot him to protect his beloved's honor, but even though his valor and courage would bring them close together, tragically he would still not get the girl because there was too much cultural distance between them. Of course, Wes had never written more than the first three pages, but it was the first time that he had ever imagined what it would be like to be a writer. The idea of the book had lingered with him long after he had dismissed it as childish and didactic, and it lingered with him still, or at least the title did, along with the feeling that there were irreconcilable differences between people who chose to live in suburbs and those who remained loyal to the city, the birthplace of civilization.

Wes raised his head to find himself on the corner of Seventh Avenue. Even here, half a mile from the entrance to the Holland Tunnel, the weekend traffic was backed up almost to a standstill. As Wes felt another wave of irritation building within him, he remembered to be mindful, as Delia had taught him, and by focusing his attention on his emotions he was able to calm them. A good Buddhist would not allow himself to be tied up in knots by negative energy. Wasn't it just possible that each of these people, as mediocre as they appeared to be, was an ocean of fear and blind suffering every bit as real and valid as Wes's own? In place of peevishness Wes now felt a welling of platonic love for all these suburbanites filling his city's streets with noise and stink, because being benighted and blinkered was a condition that called for compassion and sorrow, not impatience and disdain. As he waited for the light to change, Wes tried to reconstruct the string of thoughts that had led him to this revelation, but finding it hopeless he mentally shrugged his shoulders, quite mindful of what he was doing, and decided that it had not been a string of thoughts at all, but a moment of pure insight. He crossed the avenue and tried to keep his mind blank, but when he reached the guitar shop he stopped and felt a pang of acquisitive envy, and instead focused his mind on admiring the objective beauty of the instruments, and felt himself suffused with love for the guitars, their makers and their eventual purchasers, not despite but because of the fact that he would probably never be one of them.

He turned left on Jones Street and a minute later found himself at the butcher, a tiny wedge of a shopfront that had been there for generations and that made him feel like an insider because there were never any tourists there and it was not in any guidebook and had sawdust on the floor. When there was a line here, it was composed of locals like him who knew something other people did not and called to the butchers by name, and when you ordered something they didn't just pull it from the glass display case but cut it for you right there on heavy butcherblock pedestals that were worn and smooth with age and use. They were always busy, but you never minded waiting because the butchers at their work were something beautiful and Zen-like. If Buddhists ate meat, they would shop here, Wes thought, but then he grew nervous and shy as his turn to order came. The compact Hispanic lady in the white coat behind the counter who took the customers' orders was called Teresa. Wes knew her name but was pretty sure she didn't know his, and he could never figure out how to address her. He wasn't even convinced that she recognized him from one visit to the next. Wes wondered how the other customers had first made their names known to Teresa. He wanted her to know his name because he and his father were lifelong customers and he knew how gratifying it would feel to be welcomed personally in front of the other customers, and before coming to the store he often rehearsed scenarios in his head of ways that he could lead the conversation in a manner that would require her to ask his name, but there didn't seem to be such a way. If he simply said "Hi there, Teresa, how are you today?" she would be unlikely to respond "I'm fine, thank you, and what's your name?", even if she didn't find it impertinent that a boy his age would address her by name.

"Next," she called, and Wes shuffled forward.

"Do you have any sweetbreads?"

She narrowed her eyes and smiled conspiratorially at him, as if he had just given her a secret password.

"Veal or lamb?"

"I don't know. I never made them before. What's the best?"

"Veal is better, but lamb is good. How much do you need?"

"I don't know. For one?"

Her eyebrows lifted and her smile broadened. "I'll see what we have." She disappeared into the walk-in at the back, leaving Wes feeling very grateful that he had not introduced himself. He studied the old black-and-white photos that hung on the wall, showing the store as it had been one, two and three generations earlier, and all the dead butchers who had once worked there. There was a time, it seemed, that they had all been Italians, some of them younger than Wes, the older ones with mustaches and shiny hair and quite dark skin, but all the butchers now were Mexican. Wes wondered what all the young Italian men who might have been butchers were doing instead, and if any of them were happier than they would have been if they had been butchers. As Wes watched the Mexicans trimming the fat off great lumps of meat with long curving knives, or carving chicken breasts into cutlets, he wondered if he could be happy as a butcher. On the one hand, he thought, it would be a great job for someone who was conscientious, a perfectionist who believed that life offers never-ending opportunities for self-improvement and thoughtful application, as Wes did. Clearly, you could work an entire lifetime as a butcher and never fully satisfy yourself that you were as artful as you might be, and that was a good thing. On the other hand, Wes believed that the time would come when, as an artist focused on honing his craft and grappling with philosophical and literary conundrums, his interest in food would gradually fall away, leaving nothing but the core need to satisfy hunger as he became increasingly ascetic and otherworldly; by his early twenties at the latest, when he had stopped growing and no longer needed lots of protein, he would certainly have given up meat-eating, especially given its karmic and ecological implications. Now it would be incredibly interesting to consider the moral and ethical implications of being a vegetarian Buddhist butcher, and probably an amazingly difficult and worthy exercise in principles of self-mastery, but Wes couldn't be certain that he had it in him. What if, after decades of devoting your life to form and mindfulness, it should just turn out to be really boring? In theory, Wes didn't believe in boredom because there was always something to do with an unoccupied mind, but still.

Teresa emerged from the walk-in with a sheet of butcher's paper in one hand, on which there sat something pink and shiny and mottled, enmeshed in a network of threadlike capillaries and pocked with globules of fat. It looked perhaps like a giant embryonic mouse. Teresa tilted her hand towards Wes so that he could assess the quality, and several waiting customers leaned in simultaneously to get a better look, one even emitting a low, awestruck gasp.

"That looks fine."

"Two pounds is the smallest I have. Too much for one, okay?"

"No it's fine. I'll take it."

An old lady in a tweed overcoat and a thick grey scarf around her neck nudged Wes in the elbow, tutting. "How are you going to cook that?" she asked in an old-fashioned Little Italy accent.

"You have to soak it and poach it and press it. Then you can fry it and serve it with mushrooms or raisins."

"You're the cook?"

"It's easy. It's just complicated." The old lady nodded approvingly and gave Wes's forearm a little squeeze. It was like something out of a movie, and Wes felt a little swell of pride in his heart. He looked up to see if Teresa had noticed that something special had passed among her customers, but she was wrapping the sweetbread with her head lowered. She would remember him now, and the next time he came he would be sure to introduce himself.

Wes continued along Jones, turned east on West Fourth, then immediately north on Sixth Avenue on his way to Citarella. Although the brown paper package containing the sweetbread was light and unobtrusive, it felt heavy and conspicuous, as if it concealed the tell-tale heart and was calling out to everyone on the street. Although he planned to be a vegetarian one day, Wes was still an avid meat-eater and did not generally suffer ethical qualms about it, so he was puzzled by this creeping sense that he was doing something wrong. Unless there was something he didn't know about sweetbreads, in theory they were no different from any other cut of meat, since the animal from which they came had had to die in order to supply it. Wes thought that maybe it had something to do with Teresa's question: "Veal or lamb?" He remembered now that when she'd asked, for an instant so fleeting that he was unaware of it until it had passed, there had popped into his head the image, almost like a drawing in a children's book, of a calf and a lamb with a backslash between them and a question mark to the right. There was something about calves that upset him, even when he thought about them ever so casually, because of the way they seemed to be born to suffer. Lambs, at least, gambol and play, but calves seemed to be sad, somehow, from the moment they're born because virtually all mammal babies are cute but calves seem to be stamped with the mark of death from the very beginning, like the condemned calf in "Dona Dona." And he couldn't help but think, as he strode towards the Jefferson Market library and noted the time on the clock tower, of the very calf that had died to give Wes its one and only pancreas or thymus gland, and he saw in his mind's eye a kind of accelerated history of his sweetbread, which was really the brief and doleful biography of a living creature that had maybe never even had one sip of its mother's milk before it was carted off and kept in concrete pens and fed from stainless steel hoppers and shouted at and taunted and tolerated on this earth just long enough for some blank-eyed stranger with a knife and elbow-length plastic gloves to reach deep, deep into the recesses of its hot, frightened body for that glistening pink jewel of viscera. Of course Wes knew that the butchering process was not like that at all, that the sweetbreads would be among the last thing to be removed once the body had been dismantled, but in this montage it was the sweetbreads that had held all the other parts together, and once they had been harvested everything else—the various cuts of meat, the hide, the components of the head, the bones and the intestines—all flew apart, pieces of a puzzle or a planet exploding in outer space, and away to their appointed destinations in foam trays in supermarket coolers, tanneries or great vats of boiling water. And when you abstracted it that way, when you allowed yourself to think of the body as an assemblage or a vessel, rather than as a sodden sponge infused with sorrowful knowledge, it did help a little. You could imagine the calf's soul soaring free and exuberant from the wreckage, and that tiny interstice in which it had been entrapped in its living body as an aberration, a hiccup that the creature's spirit could look back upon later and laugh about. This was where Buddhism, even just a smattering of it, came in quite handy. Wes was quite pleased that he was on his way to becoming a Buddhist.

A year earlier, a girl had fallen or jumped in front of an oncoming train at the 77th Street station. Wes had not known her, but those who had said that she had struggled with depression for years. Even so, the school administration had taken the opportunity to organize mandatory parent-student drug-awareness events in which participants sat in safe circles and voiced their misapprehensions about each other. To encourage candor, parents were placed in separate circles from their own kids, and that was how Wes had found himself sitting besides Delia. She was a grade above him, but he'd seen her before, of course, in the hallways or on the street, and had long been attracted to her because she didn't look or act like anyone else at Dalton. Wes found her very beautiful, with her kinky red hair and pale skin, her strong nose and the womanly curve of her lips, but she was unusual enough to allow him to imagine that no one else had ever recognized her beauty as he had, and that if she were to look deep into his eyes she would be startled, then gratified and grateful, to see herself understood, appreciated and desired for the first time in her life. When you pictured some girls naked, it was all thrashing and grunting, but when you pictured Delia naked, with her round shoulders and broad hips, you thought of waking up in a feather bed in an icy cottage on the moors with one of those strong, smooth, fragrant thighs splayed across your midsection. And that was precisely the image Wes had entertained as they held hands in their circle, while even at some distance his father's voice rose above the general murmur to insist that drugs don't always pose a mortal danger to a healthy, socialized adolescent.

Wes had no reason to suspect that complaining bitterly about his father wasn't a perfectly suitable opening gambit when they broke for juice and cookies.

"What does your father do?"

"He's a failed novelist."

"That's his profession?"

"He teaches creative writing at the New School."

"What does it mean, 'failed novelist?'"

"He's published one book in 20 years."

"Then he's a published novelist, right?"

"The failure is in his heart. If you asked him, he'd say he was a failed novelist."

"Did he give up?"

"God, no."

"Then he hasn't failed. Think of Melville or Balzac."

"They all did their best work in their youth. Trust me, he's a failure."

"That's such a horrible thing to say about someone you love, and so lacking in compassion."

"He also sleeps with his students. They do it in the house."

"Then he must be a very unhappy man. You should pity him."

And that was how Wes had discovered that Delia was a Buddhist, and that he loved her hopelessly. She was less than a year older than him, but she made him feel like a cranky little child, and then and there he had vowed to become worthy of her, to close the gap between them. For the remaining minutes of their break, he limited his self-expression to sage nodding of the head as she discoursed on meditation, mindfulness and the loving-kindness that she tried to practice toward her own parents. She was calm, poised; the gentle modulation of her voice acted upon Wes like a cool hand upon a fevered brow. She was everything he wanted to be and despaired of having, and with her knowing serenity and quiet self-confidence she continued to be just that through the entire year that Wes worked to catch up with her. She was always self-contained and unhurried, as if she didn't sweat and woke up with her breath smelling of rosehips, and despite her curvy, voluptuous body, she was always somehow untouchable. It was hard to picture Delia allowing some smooth-talking jock to put his tongue down her throat or grope her tits; she just didn't seem to be made for that kind of transaction. Even in his fantasies, Wes somehow managed to skip over most of the dirty bits because it was almost impossible to imagine Delia in a state of sexual arousal. Of course, she could be the kind of girl—*woman*—

who was attracted to much older men, graduate students in philosophy or yoga instructors, but that only added a sense of urgency to Wes's project of self-improvement because it was always possible that he could get to her before she had figured out what kind of guy she was attracted to. He had decided that he would not even attempt to have sex with her until he was confident that he had become the kind of boy—*man*—that Delia could admire on an intellectual, an emotional, a spiritual plane—until such time as he could look in her eyes and see the same shock of recognition that she would see in his eyes when she looked at him, if only he could persuade her to look hard enough. If he were honest with himself, he would have to admit that it had been not so much a vow of chastity as insurance against humiliation, but it had kept him faithfully engaged in bettering himself, which must have its own rewards other than the promise of losing one's virginity to a woman one truly loved. And until his fateful encounter with Lucy the night before, Wes had sincerely believed that he had been closing the gap, despite the incontrovertible evidence that, with only seven months left to graduate, Delia had yet to lay a thigh across his midsection. And now, as he approached the gourmet market, thoughts of Delia's thigh, which remained an object of idealized, frustrated desire, and of Lucy's thigh, which smelled of grapefruit and vanilla, confused themselves in Wes's mind until in their combined carnal warmth they became a disembodied leg of lamb, rising joyously through the dimensionlessness of karmic space.

The automated glass door opened at Wes's approach, and he headed for the vegetables, losing his train of thought. Wes knew this market well because he stopped in several times a week on his way home from school to shop for supper. But as he stood before the vegetable display case with the list of ingredients open on the iPhone in his right hand and the plastic basket in his left, as he had done in virtually identical fashion countless times in the past, it occurred to him that he had been standing right on this very spot, give or take a few square inches, only eighteen hours earlier, give or take a few minutes, but that somehow, in that very brief interlude, he had become an entirely new person and the world had been entirely remade.

He remembered himself eighteen hours earlier, who he had been and what he had been thinking. After he'd read Lucy's tweet, he'd spent the rest of the day fretting about how he would defend himself against her aggressions, should they come, or speculating about the possibility that it was all just a mistake—or worse yet, a prank—and that she had absolutely no romantic interest in him whatsoever, and then he'd left school, skipping a meeting of the Lit Club, and come here to shop for dinner, and the argument had continued to rage in his head even as he had stood in this spot. Now, barely aware of the shoppers who were forced to push past him as he blocked the aisle, Wes shook his head and smiled indulgently on behalf of his previous self, whose exercise in self-delusion had been so transparent it had taken an almost miraculous act of will not to puncture the illusion. It was as if he had sequestered an entire sector of his analytical brain and given it over to alien control, the way you can allow tech support to take remote control of your laptop during a technical crisis, and suddenly some dude in Mumbai is moving the cursor across your monitor while your own keys go limp. That was how it had been all day yesterday—some avatar who didn't know anything about the real Wes controlling his thoughts—but it was only now that he could see it. It was so obvious, at least to the new person he was today, that the whole resistance-versus-misunderstanding scenario had been a total scam that he had perpetrated against himself. Of course he had not really wanted it to be a misunderstanding, and even more, of course, he had had no real intention of resisting her if she was interested in him. If he had, wouldn't he simply not have gone to her party?

Instead, he had found himself in this market after school trying to decide what he would make for dinner on the basis of how he could impress her, later that night, by describing the exotic, sophisticated supper he had prepared for his family that evening. He had entered the store intending to buy ingredients for a meal of grilled pork chops and baked potatoes, but he'd taken one look at the bin of Idahos and realized how lame it would come across if he tried to make a boast out of such a pedestrian effort. Instead, he'd ended up spending a fortune on saffron, carnaroli rice and Nantucket bay scallops to make a risotto that no one but his father had really enjoyed, and that Nora had rejected altogether in favor of a peanut butter and jelly sandwich, and all so that he might possibly be able to use it to impress a girl who might possibly but probably wasn't interested in him. And he had done all this without once admitting to himself that this was what he was doing. In the end, at some point in the evening he had told Lucy about the risotto, and she had been duly impressed. Like a jerk, he had even promised to cook it for her one day. Still, it wasn't easy to admit to yourself that you were the kind of boy who thought that bragging about your exploits in the kitchen was a good way to seduce girls. Wes wished he'd made the pork chops instead.

Wes could only marvel at his former self and his capacity for self-delusion, and maybe envy his naivety a little. How lucky he was in a way, that dopey little virgin, with his preoccupations with risotto and army manuals, so little suspecting that he would shortly be engaged in an exercise to tear down everything he believed in. Maybe, despite everything, he had done himself a favor. In fact, maybe what he had done the night before had actually been to shed the final, ragged skin of childhood—not the virginity but the capacity to see the world as you wanted to see it and not how it really was in all its hypocrisy, deception and selfishness. Surely this new clarity of vision must be the one absolute requisite of adulthood, if anything was, without which it was impossible to survive in *their* world? It was the thing that allowed his father to look his own children in the eye every morning. It was the thing that gave the calf its mournful eye and made it old even in its infancy. Tolstoy always gave it to his characters when it was too late to be of use to them, or at least he made them earn it by really running them through the ringer. Maybe, even more than having betrayed his noble love for Delia, it was the thing that had made him cry today. He wished he didn't have it; even more, he wished he didn't need it. Wes thought of Louis XVI's diary entry for July 14 1789: "*Rien.*" Nothing. Louis XVI had no clarity of vision, and that one-word diary entry was what had doomed him. Without clarity of vision, the most important moments of your life come and go without you're being aware of them. Wes had always chided himself for not keeping a journal, but for some reason—probably sheer laziness—he had never cultivated the habit. If he had, he would have been able to go back and track the heedless innocence that had led to yesterday's debacle. If he had, he knew just what he would put in today's entry. "Everything. Everything happened today." It occurred to him that he should stop in at the stationery store on his way home and pick up a blank notebook. If ever there was a good day to start a journal, this was it, but then he thought no, it would not be a diary but a novel. It would start with the words "Everything. Everything happened today," and it would be called *Everything Happened Today.*

Without quite remembering how it had happened, Wes glanced in his basket to find that he had filled it while daydreaming. He checked off its contents against the shopping list: mushrooms, bok choy, shallots, garlic, tomatoes and parsley. The only thing missing was veal stock, which was prepared fresh and kept in a refrigerated display near the front of the store, along with homemade soups, pasta sauces and guacamole in small plastic tubs. As Wes bent down for a container of stock, his eye was caught by the packages of precut crudités—carrot, celery and red pepper sticks—kept alongside the dips. The celery reminded him of the first Bloody Mary that James had had ready for him the night before when he had arrived at Lucy's at nine-thirty. It had been fresh and sludgy with horseradish and black pepper and a celery stick for a stirrer, delicate pale green leaves still attached. Earlier in the day, Wes had silently pledged to stick to sparkling water at the party so he would be sober enough to resist Lucy, but he had accepted the Bloody Mary without hesitation. They had not spoken as they clinked glasses at the threshold, and Wes's second thought had been about a story he had recently been told third hand about a party where a girl had gotten so drunk that she'd wandered off, passed out and drowned in a puddle, and every kid who had brought alcohol to the party had been arrested and charged as accessories to her death, as had the parents of the boy who'd thrown the party, even though they were away at the time and had had no idea that anything was going on in their home. And even as he raised his glass to his lips, Wes had imagined Lucy's parents at their cottage in East Hampton or wherever and how they must feel about their daughter to trust her enough to leave her alone in the city for the weekend, and all the things they didn't know about her, and how incredibly sad that was for them, and how incredibly duplicitous and manipulative Lucy must be to throw a massive blow-out behind their backs and know she could get away with it. And then as he had sipped his fiery drink, which was so strong as to be light pink and almost translucent, and James had taken him by the shoulder and led him into the party, where the Velvet Undergound was playing, Wes had scanned the room of some thirty kids, looking not for Delia but for Lucy, but then he had caught sight of Delia, standing by a pair of French windows with another senior girl and almost enveloped in the floor-to-ceiling

Venetian damask curtains, and had made directly for her. He had been about half-way across the room when Delia had looked up from her conversation and appeared to see him, but then immediately turned back to her friend. Delia usually wore long, colorful, flowing dresses that concealed her shape, along with black leggings and South Asian-type necklaces and bangles, but tonight, Wes noted, she was dressed quite uncharacteristically in tight-fitting denim capris, a sleeveless white tunic and cork-soled wedges with ribbons that ran up her calves in a crisscross pattern. Her beautiful red hair, which she usually allowed to flow freely, was done up in tight pigtails that opened a crisp white part from the top of her head to the nape of her neck, where it was lost in a mist of loose curls, a tropical waterfall seen from a great distance. Seeing her like that had immediately made Wes feel guarded and proprietary, but then almost instantly ashamed, so that he'd felt his face grow flushed and ran the cold tumbler across his forehead before he reached her. He tapped her lightly on the shoulder, and she partially turned towards him with a vague smile—just far enough to acknowledge his presence, and too briefly for someone who didn't know who it was that was standing behind her. But just as he had been preparing to move away before anyone had seen what she'd done, she'd reached out and grabbed him gently by the wrist in such a way that the girl she was talking to couldn't see, and a moment later she'd swung around and was standing very close to him and he was looking down into her eyes, which were heavily lined with kohl. It had been an odd moment for Wes, because although he knew it wasn't true, he always had this idea that she was taller than him, but even after all this time they had rarely stood close enough for it to make a difference. Now he could smell her mimosa shampoo, and it made him momentarily dizzy. Delia held on to his wrist as they talked.

"I'm so glad you're here," she'd said, almost in a whisper, and leaned in to kiss Wes on the cheek, but because Delia had very full lips that Wes often imagined kissing it felt different from a peck and sent a little electrical shock through his body.

"I'm glad I am too. I mean, I didn't expect to see you here."

"No, you didn't." She'd said this with a sly smile that, like her clothes, was so at odds with her usual manner that Wes had found himself confused and a little alarmed. Delia was not the bantering kind and was rarely coy or playful, which contributed to the awe and uninformed esteem in which she was widely held at school, and perhaps also to the failure of gossip and lack of suitors in her orbit. Wes had learned how to be around her—earnest, attentive, morally engaged and one push shy of challenging; there had been a time when he had worried about how such deference would affect their sexual compatibility, if it should ever come to that, but he had long since set such concerns aside. If she was sometimes a little intimidating or intellectually dismissive, that was part of why he loved her. But everything about her tonight—the way she was dressed, the makeup, her relaxed body language, the whispering and the mystery—was new and confounding, and left Wes feeling unprepared and unprotected. He wasn't sure he liked it.

"What do you mean, 'no, you didn't'?"

"I mean I wanted it to be a surprise. For you."

"Well, I am surprised, I guess. I didn't even think you knew Lucy."

"Seniors don't need invitations."

"What made you so sure I'd be here?"

She gave his wrist a squeeze that, if he hadn't known better, he would have interpreted as suggestive. Wes wondered if Delia had been drinking. That was not her style at all, but then again, nothing about her was quite right this evening. There was no glass in her hand, and she did not have liquor on her breath, but that didn't mean anything. Between the smell of her hair, the wrist-holding and the sting of her kiss, Wes was feeling decidedly lightheaded, and he thought that there was probably a simple explanation for her odd behavior, if only he could find a moment to breathe and get his bearings.

"I think I need a drink."

"You already have one, Wes. Come and sit with me on the couch. I don't know anyone here."

Even though it was not on his list, Wes took a package of celery sticks, which came wrapped with its own little container of French onion dip, because they were Nora's favorite snack, more even than baloney.

On his way home, Wes stuck his free left hand in the pocket of his hoodie and found an old pair of ear buds that he had thought lost long before. He stopped, placed the shopping bags gently between his feet, retrieved the iPhone from his back pocket, and plugged the ear buds in. Pressing the iPod button, he found the music paused in the middle of "Ballad of a Thin Man" where he had interrupted it while doing the previous day's crossword puzzle before getting started on the risotto. It had been a difficult puzzle, as Fridays' always were, and the music, rather than serve as a focusing medium as it usually did, had distracted him. Now, rather than search through his playlist with all these bags encumbering him, Wes merely reset it to start at the beginning of the album, and his heart did a little loving skip on the opening drumbeat of "Like a Rolling Stone." He listened to the music for a few moments before he started thinking again, and then it was only to find himself rehashing the argument he'd had so many times with his father about whether rock and roll had created a bond between the generations that had not existed prior to the 1950s. His father always pointed to the fact that he and Wes listened to a lot of the same music, mostly from the '60s and the '70s, whereas he, Wes's dad, had no feeling whatsoever for the Depression-era musicals or the swing that had been the soundtrack of his own father's youth. But Wes would argue that this so-called common ground between them was artificial, since he himself was not even born until the '90s and in his own childhood his father had listened not to Dylan or Hendrix but to crappy pop bands like the Monkees and Herman's Hermits. If anything, it served as a barrier to common understanding. His father liked to claim that his very first memory was of sitting on the porch of his family home in Flushing in 1965 and listening to the Beatles perform in Shea Stadium, but Wes had been to that house on Delaware Avenue and strongly doubted that it was close enough to hear anything from Shea. And that was so typical of him—using cultural landmarks to prove that he'd been at the center of every happening scene since the Summer of Love, like a dog pissing on every tree it passes— that Wes tended to question anything his dad might have to say with the authority of age about social, literary, artistic or political issues. Pretty much everything, in fact—it was all lies or distortions at the service of his father's fragile, loser's ego. It so happened that Wes even agreed with his father that the heyday of rock lay somewhere in the 1960s, but he couldn't very well admit it without giving him an opening to drive his poisonous truckload of self-embellishment through. So when his father had come home one day waving a copy of *Rolling Stone* magazine hysterically over his head to share with Wes the mysteries and joys of its first-ever greatest-songs-of-all-time list, with "Like a Rolling Stone" at the top, Wes had been compelled not only to shut him down (by pointing out that any greatest songs list that omitted "Spiders from Mars" wasn't worth shit), but also even to re-evaluate his own preferences. When, later that night, he had gone down the list only to find it really top-heavy with stuff from the '60s, he'd decided to disown it privately and to stop listening to "Highway 61 Revisited" for a while. It was typical of adults of his father's generation to think that everything revolved around them and to ruin it for the rest of humanity with their stupid lists.

But the fact remained that "Like a Rolling Stone" had so

faithfully followed Wes his entire life that he couldn't help feeling that it had a special, secret message for him. When he was eleven, he'd taught himself to pick out the chords on his guitar and learned the words by heart from his father's original LP, only to have his father point out that the words were not "do the bump and grind" but "threw the bums a dime." Wes had never picked up his guitar again (almost), and to this very day he believed that one of life's saddest let-downs is when you finally understand a word or a phrase in a song that you have misunderstood all your life. And then there was the time a few years later, in seventh grade, he had shared with Forrest Schaeffer his idea of writing an abstract poem using only the rhyming words from the song ("Time fine dime grind prime didn't you/ Call doll fall kidding you/ About out loud proud/ Meal feel own home unknown stone" etc), and Forrest had stolen the idea and submitted the poem for an English assignment, and the teacher had figured out what it meant and given him an extra commendation for creative appropriation. And then when Wes had transferred to Dalton and found himself among all these spoiled super-rich kids, it had been "Like a Rolling Stone" that had put words to all his confused feelings of resentment and humiliation. They went to the finest school all right, but one day they'd all be lonely because they had so few emotional resources of their own. And a lot of them did get juiced in it, but maybe one day they'd have to learn to take care of themselves like Wes had done for most of his childhood, and some of them might end up living on the street with no direction home, but not Wes, because his spiritual compass always pointed due north. And at that moment, Wes arrived at his house, where he found Nora sitting on the stoop engaged in a lively conversation with James, who sheltered two bottles of beer between his feet, very poorly concealed in paper bags. Wes pulled the buds from his ears.

"What are you doing here?"

"Nice way to greet a friend. What's up with that, Nors?"

"Bobby says 'What are *you* doing here, *Leslie*?' You think you own the place or something?"

"Is that beer for me? Shove over." Wes climbed the stairs, wrestled the shopping bags into the corner of the door jamb, and took a seat on the top step, to James's right. James lived in an apartment building—in a six-bedroom duplex between Fifth and Mad, to be sure, but an apartment nonetheless—and his favorite thing in life was to sit on Wes's stoop and drink beer, and he was right. Nothing in the world makes a man more of a king than when he sits high up on a stoop and condescends to the passers-by, most particularly in Greenwich Village. Wes sat there, knee to knee with his best friend, and felt immediately better than he had. James turned to Nora as she breathlessly pursued the story she was telling him, apparently the same story she had told Wes that morning about her friends Claire and Leo and the sexting. James seemed to be enrapt, and Wes thought that might have less to do with his affection for Nora than with a prurient interest in Katrina, whom James had never met but surely knew by reputation and online through Facebook. There was a smell of fried dough and Italian sausage in the air, and Wes supposed there must be a street fair somewhere in the neighborhood, late as it was in the year. Normally the mere thought of a street fair would bring a hot flush of indignation to Wes's face, but he was feeling too good here on the stoop with his best sister, his best friend, the dappled sunlight playing on the windows of the house across the street, a light breeze cooling his cheeks. He closed his eyes and listened to the sounds of the street. There was nowhere better in the world to be right now than exactly where he was, he thought, and offered himself modest praise for being a good apprentice Buddhist, but in the very act of praising he recalled to himself all the reasons why he might be unhappy—Lucy, Delia, his sick mother, the uncooked sweetbread, the unwritten paper, the unwalked dog, his father, his sad sister—and felt a pang of panic. Was a Buddhist supposed to empty his mind of negative thoughts and emotions or dispassionately examine each one as it emerged? He couldn't remember what he was supposed to do. And the more he tried to recall what he had read and what Delia had taught him, the more crowded and confused his mind became with thoughts that surely weren't supposed to be there, and each thought split in two and became two, which became four, until suddenly his head was filled with myriad images buzzing around each other like angry insects: Tibetan monks hooked up to fMRI machines, mandalas made of colored sand, *sukha* and *dukkha*, the emptiness of inherent existence, sub-atomic particles that cease to exist the instant they are born, "the world, Chico, and everything in it," Diogenes in a barrel, an African child crouched in the dust, the Dalai Lama's gallstone operation, Nora sucking her thumb. But then, in the midst of his confusion, Wes remembered one concrete instruction and clung to it. Someone had once explained to him that Buddhist monks memorize complex paintings and then recall them during meditation, focusing for hours on each minute detail. Delia had taught him that, contrary to popular belief, it is not necessary to make your mind go blank when you meditate; it is in fact preferable to have one image in your mind's eye to focus the thoughts and slow them down. Wes took a deep breath and turned his inner attention on his heartbeat, willing it to slow down, and as he did so he pictured all the extraneous ideas in his head as particles of sand stirred up by rough seas, and now, with the return of calm, sinking slowly back to the bottom. And as the water cleared, there arose through it the image of a calf lying on the grass, its legs tucked beneath it, its head resting on the ground. Wes saw himself approach it. Was it injured or suffering? He could not tell, but in the gaze of its eye shone a light of infinite sorrow and infinite patience. Wes saw himself sit down beside it and rest his head on its neck, feeling the rise and fall of its breath, and then from his back pocket he withdrew a little pouch and unfolded it. It was the kit of cleaning implements for the M-16, normally kept in the storage compartment on the bottom of the buttstock. From among the rods, swabs, bore brushes and pipe cleaners, Wes selected a toothbrush, then carefully refolded the pouch and returned it to his pocket. Then he began methodically brushing the calf's fur, focusing on a small patch just above its shoulder. Motes of dust rose where he brushed; they glittered in the air as they revolved in the soft sunlight, and were borne away by the breeze. Wes looked up and saw that he and the calf were near the top of a broad meadow that sloped gently downwards to a sparkling, meandering stream, and beyond it the green land rose and fell towards a great forest on the horizon, and he realized that both he and the calf were dead and that they were in heaven, and he understood that they were paired together for eternity, and that he would never have any other task than to keep brushing. He looked at the calf and smiled and said: "Good." The calf half raised its head and smiled back at him with such radiance and generous love that it was clear that the calf itself was God. The calf lowered its head back to the ground and said: "Yo dude."

"Did you fall asleep?"

"What, no?"

James had his arm around Wes's shoulder and he and Nora were shaking with laughter.

"Oh Leslie, you were so funny with your head on Jamie's shoulder, girlfriend!"

"You need to get some sleep, Wesbo. Long night?" Wes stood up, knocking the beer off the stoop. Still wrapped in its paper bag, the bottle fell one step, then a second, and stopped, unbroken and having lost almost none of its contents. Wes went down to fetch it, and looked up at James and Nora.

"I can't hang out, friendo. Way too much to do."

"Such as?"

"Paper to write, dog to walk, dinner, homework."

"Take Nora to the movies."

"Take Nora to the movies."

"Doesn't sound like so much to me. I'll make dinner."

"Wait'll you see what's for dinner. Help me with this stuff."

Together they gathered up the bags and Wes led them into the house and straight back into the kitchen, where his father was standing by the window eating a sandwich made with white bread, which Wes thought he must have his own stash of, since they never kept white bread in the house. He turned as they entered and smiled uncertainly as he chewed.

"Just dump that stuff on the counter. Dad, you know James?"

"Don't think I do." He leaned forward and shook James by the hand. Wes began to unpack the grocery bags onto the counter. There was no point in putting any of it away, since he planned to use it all. When he got to the celery sticks, he handed them to Nora, who wordlessly went to work pulling back the cellophane wrapper.

"Wes doesn't bring too many of his friends down here."

"Wes doesn't have any friends except me."

"That would explain it. You at Dalton, James?"

"Yes sir."

"Happy there?"

"Sure, why not? I've been there my whole life."

"What're you reading?"

"Come again?"

"What are you reading? What authors are they teaching in English class."

"I'm doing this American lit elective. Melville, Wharton, Fitzgerald, that sort of stuff. Not sure what's coming next."

"Oof. Heavy stuff, boy. Let me know when you get to the

Beats. Anyway, back to work. See you round, boys." He took his sandwich and returned to the basement. There was a lingering silence, which Wes clung to in a somewhat proprietary funk, punctuated only by the crunching of celery sticks. Finally, James cleared his throat.

"What's he working on, your dad?"

"A book."

"I didn't know he's a writer."

"He's not. He's a teacher."

"That's not true, Leslie. He *is* a writer. He only teaches to make money."

"No, he's a teacher who thinks he's a writer who only teaches to make money. There's a difference, cookie."

"You're mean, Leslie. He did so publish a book."

"What's it called?"

"It's called *The Breadbaking District.* It takes place in New York City a long time ago. It's a love story, and there are bread riots and barricades and stuff."

"Did you read it, Nora?"

"My dad won't let me. He say's there's too much sex in it, even though I already know everything already."

"You, Wes?"

"I'm waiting for the movie. Cookie, why don't you go upstairs and get ready for your movie? What are we going to see, anyway?"

"'Zack and Miri Make a Porno.'"

"C'mon."

"'My Best Friend's Girl.'"

"Shit man, couldn't you find anything better?"

"Bobby likes Dane Cook. Bobby lo-o-oves Dane Cook."

"Christ, all right. When and where?"

"Union Square, two-thirty."

"What time is it now?"

"Dunno. Two?"

"Okay, go go go. We leave in ten minutes." Wes began to unwrap the sweetbread as Nora pounded up the stairs to her room.

"So? Jesus fucking Christ, what the hell is that?"

"It's a sweetbread, obviously. Don't you know anything?"

"But what is it?"

"It's the thymus gland of a calf. I'm making it for dinner. Hand me that cookbook?"

"That is truly disgusting."

"Shit, I forgot. You've got to change the water every fifteen minutes."

"What are you talking about?"

"You've got to soak this for an hour to get all the blood out, but you're supposed to change the water every fifteen minutes. I've got to take Nora to the movies."

"I tell you, Wes, you soak it for a year it's not gonna be any less revolting."

"So you think it's okay if I just leave it in the same water?"

"Sure. What the fuck do I know? Now will you please stop fucking around and tell me what I came here for."

"What did you come here for?"

"The skinny. The juice. The 411. How'd it go with Lucy last night? Pop yer cherry?"

"Oh, I'm not talking about that."

"You've got to be shitting me! I set you up with babe-a-licious supreme and you're holding out on me? On me, man?"

"Why are you talking like that? Never mind, I'm just not ready to talk about it yet."

"Not ready to talk about it? What's the matter with you? You think she's not talking about it? You think half the school doesn't know by now that the last of the red-hot virgins is no more? I guarantee you everybody knows, friendo. But to me, his so-called best friend, his only friend, he's not ready to talk about it, quote unquote. You're a total douche, you know that?"

"Can you keep your voice down, please? My mom's right upstairs. I'll talk, I'll talk if it makes you happy. I'm just feeling really weird about it right now."

"Here we go. Did you fuck her?"

"Yes I did."

"Brother man!" James leaped across the kitchen and picked Wes up in a bear hug and swung him around the room, then he dropped him and held him at arms' length. "How many times?"

"I don't know. More than once. Three, maybe?"

"She hot hot hot?"

"I guess."

"Nice pussy? Juicy?"

"Gimme a break."

"So how did it go down? Where were you? What did she say?"

"She texted me."

"What do you mean she texted you? You were at the party."

"I'm in the living room or the kitchen, I get this text. 'I'm in the bedroom, come find me.'"

"Jesus, she texted you? That little slut."

"Hey Leslie, I'm ready. Let's go. Who's a little slut?"

"No one."

"Wesbo's girlfriend."

"Leslie has a girlfriend? You didn't tell me."

"There's no girlfriend, Nora. Just lemme get this thing in some water and we'll go. You guys wait for me outside."

Wes hated it that Nora was subjected to such talk. He had no idea how long she'd been standing there listening to James, but even if all she'd heard was "slut" it was bad enough. It was true that she already knew everything—a little friend of hers had once innocently referred to her synagogue, B'nai Jeshurun, by its acronym, "BJ," and Nora had sniggered like some red-neck tramp—but that didn't mean Wes couldn't do everything in his power to delay the inevitable. Nora was growing up too fast, he felt, and the kids in her grade, the girls especially, were already far more sexualized than he'd been at her age. He couldn't stand it that she might know what a slut was, or worse yet, be able to picture in her mind what a slut did, or that one day someone might call her a slut or, worst of all, that she might one day come to think of herself as a slut. He wanted her to grow up straight and tall, confident and strong, immune to the peer pressures and self-image problems that plagued him and almost everyone he knew. Most of all, it was because he knew so many guys like James, who was a truly decent and thoughtful person most of the time but typical when it came to girls, that he never wanted her to be in a position where she thought it necessary to trade sex for something else, like self-esteem or popularity. The idea of other people talking about Nora the way people talked about Lucy was almost unbearable to him, enough to make him choke up when he envisaged it. It was a bit weird being involved with your little sister's sexual education, but he didn't suppose she was getting the right guidance from her parents, and Katrina was giving out hand-jobs by the time she was thirteen, and even if she wasn't people were saying she was, and that was practically worse. Wes would be leaving for college in less than two years, and Nora would be thirteen by then, and who would look after her and tell her right from wrong?

Having dumped the sweetbread in a bowl of water, added a splash of juice from a plastic lemon, and slid it into the refrigerator, Wes found Crispy waiting by the front door. He gave her a little scratch between the ears, whispering "I'll be back," and slipped out. Nora and James were sitting on the top step, she with her hands cupped over her ears, listening to James's iPod and bobbing her head.

Wes smacked James on the back of the head and skipped down the stairs, leaving the other two to follow. The street was even more crowded with day-trippers than it had been earlier, but Wes strode purposefully forward, his hands shoved deep into the pockets of the hoodie. He found his way blocked by a slow-moving family of five, obese and oblivious, and muttered "New Yorker coming through" as he sidled around them. A moment later, he found James by his side.

"Slow down there, friendo. Your sister can't keep up." Wes slowed and turned to see Nora, some 20 feet back, happily engrossed in scrolling through James's playlist, an oversized set of noise-canceling headphones on her head.

"I wish you wouldn't talk that way, especially around Nora."

"What way?"

"'Slut' and 'pussy' and all that. That isn't you, and it's definitely not me."

"Forgive me for offending your delicate sensibilities. I'm just happy for you is all. This is a big day for you."

"Yeah, well I told you, I'm feeling kind of weirded out about the whole thing."

"Did something untoward happen last night? You didn't, like, slip her a roofie or anything?"

"For fuck sake, I'm serious. I'm just not feeling good about it, you know?"

"I don't follow you."

"I don't know. I guess . . . I guess I just wanted it to be a little more . . . special."

"Jesus, you know what you sound like right now? You gotta try to be a little more manly about this sort of stuff."

"Yeah, I know."

"Is this about Delia?"

"It must be. I mean, I've never even kissed her or asked her out or anything, but somehow I just thought . . . It's all I've thought about for a year, and now I've fucked it up before we've even got it started. You remember that time I spent the weekend at her place? I mean, I didn't even care that we slept in separate rooms or that she didn't sneak into my bed that night. I was just so happy to be around her, and her family was so cool and nice, I had this idea that there was something incredible, like we were destined for each other or something. I had this idea that I had to be extra specially something to deserve her, that if I did it differently from everybody else there would be this amazing, like, payback—no, not payback, I just wanted her to see that I wasn't like everybody else . . . I mean, what can you do?"

"You could've asked her on a date."

"But that's just it, that would've been too . . . I wanted her to see what I was doing, everything I was doing because I loved her really, like, purely. For her, for who she was. I thought, when I'm ready, when I'm transformed, when I'm not just acting it out but I really am that person I want her to think I am, she'll see it, she'll know it, she'll come to me. But she didn't do anything, I mean she didn't do anything wrong. It's not like she turned out to be some jerk who was fucking with me just because she could, and then she broke my heart and I just went out and found anyone I could. You know that Elliot Smith song—'You broke your own 'cause you can't finish what you start?' That's me exactly. I broke my own fucking heart."

They walked down West Thirteenth in silence, and James took Wes's left hand in his right and gave it a squeeze, but then he held on to it for a few seconds, and that unit of two hands hung between them like a hawser mooring a ship to its berth. Wes even lowered his gaze to look at it, its surprising substantiality, then glanced backwards to make sure Nora was still following them. At that moment, she happened to look up from the screen of James's iPod and she smiled at him shyly, a little frightened maybe, and flicked her head to disengage her bangs from her eyebrows, and Wes had a momentary vision that she was the most beautiful soul on Earth. He wanted to run to her, like in a movie, and sweep her up in his arms and tell her how much he loved her, but he didn't want to scare her and in any case he thought that maybe there had been enough melo-drama for one afternoon. James let go of his hand and they walked on.

"Can I just say one thing?" James asked as they reached the corner of Fifth Avenue.

"Yeah, of course."

"See, no offense, but it seems to me you're telling two dif-ferent stories here. There's the story you think you're telling, about how basically you're the knight in shining armor on this impossible quest to win the love of the fair maiden or whatever, and you failed because you weren't, like, pure enough of heart. And then there's the story I heard, which is that you're waiting and waiting for something that might never happen, which is that *she* asks *you* out, because you're too chickenshit to take a risk. I mean, you put it all on her, and when she doesn't come through you blame yourself? It's not her fault she doesn't love you, but it's not your fault either, Wes. You shouldn't be so hard on yourself. You should've been able to enjoy yourself last night. And now look at you. It's all fucked up in too many ways."

"No kidding."

And now Wes felt that he was back exactly where he had started that morning. Nothing had changed after all. Everything had happened, and nothing had happened. Wes wasn't a dif-ferent person; he was exactly the person he had been twenty-four hours earlier, no wiser, no smarter, no happier, no noth-ing. He thought of Elliot Smith again, "fighting problems with bigger problems." Whenever he heard that line it made him think of boxes within boxes. You have a bunch of problems and you put them in a box and they become a single problem. Then you accumulate enough of those boxes and you put them in a bigger box, and they become one problem again. Elliot Smith, for instance, had put all his problems in a box so big that ultimately it was life itself that was in the box, life had become the one and only problem, with one and only way to solve it. But life, living, wasn't a problem for Wes, he would never commit suicide no matter what, so even his biggest box would have to be smaller than Elliot's. What, then, was his own biggest box? Was Delia a small, discrete problem or did she share a box with other, similar problems, and if she did, what bigger problem did that box represent? Some problems seemed to come in different sizes, too. You could say that Wes was indecisive, fearful, a dreamer, shy, lonely, whatever, and put it all in a box called "Delia." But you could look at his love for Delia as just one little problem, along with his mother, his sister, his father, that all belonged together in a box of their own. Either way, Wes was no closer to solving any of them today than he had been the day before or would be the day after. And in any case, Elliot Smith wasn't talking about solving problems; he was talking about fighting them. Wes wouldn't know how to go about doing that.

"So what should I do?"

"I think you've already done it."

"You think I should drop this thing with Delia?"

"What thing with Delia? There is no thing with Delia. There never has been a thing with Delia. It's all in your head, like a piece of shrapnel. Look, all I'm saying is, think about it. Here, I brought you a present."

James reached into his back pocket and pulled out an overstuffed billfold, through which he rummaged with his fingertips before extracting a strip of torn scrap paper. He handed it to Wes.

"I wrote it down a couple of nights ago when I was reading *The Great Gatsby*."

Wes took the gift. On one side of the scrap, a phrase was written in blue ball-point in James's hallmark scrawl. It said: "Personality is an unbroken series of successful gestures." Wes read it through carefully several times to make sure he understood it.

"What's it supposed to mean?"

"I was hoping you could tell me. Anyway, I thought of you when I read it. Let me know when you've figured it out."

They'd reached the movie theater at Thirteenth and Broadway. The crowds flowing down from the farmer's market on Union Square made it difficult even to stand on the sidewalk and have a conversation. Wes was convinced he had something important left to say to James, but he couldn't think of what it might be. Nora disentangled herself from James's paraphernalia and handed it to him with a curtsey.

"I saw you holding hands. Are you gay lovers?"

"Wes won't have me. Says I'm too fat."

"You're not fat. You're an awesome possum. I don't know what you see in Wes, though. He's so . . . so . . . "

"I know what you mean, but he's not. He's actually a very cool dude. You should appreciate him more."

"Oh, I *appreciate* him. I appreciate him so terribly terribly. But he's still a spazz."

"I don't know. I guess I see something in him that nobody else does. Or almost nobody else. I mean, I've only known Wes three years, but we were best friends the day we met. Didn't you ever feel that way about anybody, Nors?"

"Bobby says, 'Can I get you a hankie, princess?'"

"I'll take that as a no. Too bad, we could have had a radical future together, you and me."

"You don't want to see the movie with us?"

"I'd sooner eat sweetbreads. Anyway, I have work to do. I'm serious though—you gotta tell me what that quote means, Wesbo. I've got a paper due on Wednesday. Stay beautiful, Nors."

Wes and Nora watched James disappear into the crowd, then Nora took Wes by the hand and pulled him into the movie house. He bought her some popcorn and a diet soda, and they took their seats in the half-empty theater just as the previews were coming on. Wes sank into his seat, put his feet up on the back of the seat in front of him, and lowered his chin onto his knuckles. He was still thinking about Elliot Smith.

Wes had an idea about people who had died. He had this idea that we live behind the thinnest veil that prevents us from seeing the world as it really is, and that the very moment you die the veil is stripped away and you see and understand instantly and with perfect clarity every mistake you ever made and all the unhappiness that infused your life and infuses the lives of everyone you had known, of everyone who has ever lived. And then you spin around, you want to run right back and set it all right, share the good news with everyone—you've just died that very second and you don't realize that it's already too late to make up for it. It had been so close, so tantalizingly right before your eyes your entire life, and maybe even in rare moments when you had been filled with inexplicable sadness or compassion you had even caught the briefest glimpse of it, but you had never tried, or never tried hard enough, to push through it when it might have made a difference. Elliot Smith must have felt that way right after he'd died with that kitchen knife in his chest. Wes had never known anyone who had committed suicide, but James had had an uncle who had done it and whose memory haunted his life a little. James had adored his uncle, who was his mother's youngest brother and only ten years older than James himself. They'd been incredibly close, and the uncle had even lived with James's family for several years when James was little. This uncle was passionate and unpredictable, he was always exploding in fits of rage, but James knew—because the uncle had explained it to him at great length, and also just because—that his anger was born of pure love. But because he was so demanding, and most especially of those he claimed to love, nobody was ever pure or honest enough for James's uncle, and he had ended up cutting himself off from everyone around him. It turned out, too— which James could not possibly have known as a little kid—

that his uncle was severely depressive and constantly going on and off his medication. In the end, he'd gone away to live by himself in southern France and stopped communicating with his family, and James had thought that he, too, had somehow betrayed his uncle by being dishonest or not loving enough, and when the news came that his uncle had killed himself it had been two years since James had last seen or heard from him. Wes often thought of James's uncle, because there was something in James's account of him that reminded him of his own father—certainly not the romantic idealism, and not the utter loneliness of his situation either, but the anger that, by rights, should have been expressed as love. There was hardly anything to choose between them, the love and the anger, but James's uncle and Wes's father had just missed coming down on the right side of the divide, and it had destroyed their lives. And Wes often thought of that moment when, with the gun still hot in his mouth, James's dead uncle had woken up to the truth and slapped his forehead in exasperation at his own stupidity, but it was too late, and what a mess he had left behind. Wes thought that it was probably too late for his father, too; he had invested too much already in all the paraphernalia that the blind need to get around in this world—but more than anything in the world this was what Wes hoped to avoid in his own life. Not the suicide, but that horrible, irremediable feeling that it would have been so easy to do so much better than you did, and to be kinder and more generous to those who deserved your kindness and generosity, and you hadn't done it.

Wes looked up from his knuckles to see that the movie had already begun. He had missed the first few minutes in his reveries, but it seemed to be about some irresistibly handsome and charming guy who was paid by other men to date their recalcitrant girlfriends and behave so obnoxiously that the girl-friends would go running back to their boyfriends, chastened and grateful. Within minutes Wes was able to forecast the entire plot, and also to determine that the movie was completely inappropriate for Nora. He looked around to see if there was anybody else in the audience as young as her, but there only seemed to be teenage girls in large groups and middle-aged men by themselves. On the screen, the gigolo guy was walking through a bar full of beautiful women, every one of whom turned in their seats to watch him pass and make nakedly lewd eye contact. Since the gigolo guy's best friend had already showed himself to be a well-intentioned, pure-hearted nerd, it stood to reason that he would eventually ask the gigolo to perform his services on the girl he was in love with and that the gigolo would, in turn, fall in love with the best friend's girl and experience a life-altering conversion that he would have to spend the rest of the movie extricating himself from. But why, Wes asked himself in despair, did the movies always have to hammer home the point that women are attracted to selfish, shallow dicks? It was such a bad lesson for Nora to learn, and besides it wasn't true. Even at Dalton, the jocks had to behave kindly and sensitively if they wanted a crack at the finest chicks, and plenty of brainy, bookish guys had girlfriends, even if they weren't always on the a-list. Wes didn't think Delia was attracted to bad boys, though in truth he'd never known her to date anyone and had never met anyone who had dated her. And then, look at Lucy—she could have her choice of any boy at school, and probably not a few of their dads if she wanted, and she'd chosen him, Wes.

"Shit," he muttered under his breath. "What time is it?"

"Shhh," Nora said without taking her eyes from the screen or the straw from her lips.

"I've gotta go."

Nora turned to him with a look of alarm. "You can't go! What about me?"

"I've got to meet someone. I totally forgot. I've got to do it."

"Wes!"

"You can stay. I'll meet you downstairs at the foot of the escalator when the movie's over. Just don't talk to anybody. If anyone tries to sit next to you, move over next to those girls over there, okay?"

"Wes!"

"I'm really sorry, cookie. I've got to run."

Wes was not half-way down the escalator when he felt the phone vibrating in his back pocket. Without breaking stride, he pulled it out. It was Delia calling, and it was 2:54. Wes went to push the "ignore" button but his finger changed its mind and pushed "answer" instead. He put the phone to his ear.

"Hello?"

"Hey, it's Delia."

"Oh hey."

"Did you get my message?"

"No, what message?"

"I left you a message earlier. You didn't get it?"

"What did it say?"

"Well, I was wondering if you wanted to hang out later?"

"When?"

"Like, tonight, maybe?"

"Can't do it. Too much work, and I'm making dinner for my mom."

"Oh. Did you have a good time last night?"

"Hmm."

"I missed you. I mean, we talked and everything, but you seemed a little out of it. I really wanted to talk to you. What happened to you?"

"I went home early. I wasn't feeling so good. What did you want to talk about?"

"Oh whatever. You free tomorrow?"

"Probably. Maybe. It'll depend on how my paper goes. Can I call you in the morning?"

"Yeah, sure. I'd really like to see you."

"Me too. I'll call you."

Wes had to stop to catch his breath, even though he had not been running. It was not at all like Delia to want to just "hang out." When had she ever called him just to hang out? Could it possibly be a coincidence that she had done it for the first time ever today of all days? He wondered what she knew about last night, and if she was only playing innocent. Some people might think of that as being manipulative, but Wes thought it was the considerate thing to do, and in any case as far as she was concerned he had nothing to hide. It would be surprising, a little odd even, if she hadn't caught at least a whiff of the gossip that must have been spreading all day, but then again she'd always been a little aloof from the life of the school, as if her mind were already somewhere in the future, at Yale or Brown or whatever Ivy was sure to accept her, a place where she could finally study philosophy and religion among her intellectual peers. So Wes thought it quite possible, after all, that she had not heard a thing, at least not yet. And if she had heard something, as she was eventually sure to do, how would she react? She might be happy for him, but more likely she would find it a little distasteful and sordid. She might be a little disappointed in him, and then shrug her shoulders and dismiss it as typical boyish behavior, and think that she might have been wrong about Wes, that he wasn't so different from everybody else after all. There were strictures in Buddhism for sure, the importance of self-control and resisting unhealthy distractions, but Wes was pretty sure those mostly applied to monks and nuns; even so it seemed almost impossible to imagine that she could hear of what he had done and think of him in the same way afterwards.

He remembered the weekend she had invited him to her family's house in the dunes at Napeague. Not long after they had first talked at the drug-awareness circle, she had approached him in the hallway and handed him a kind of beginner's handbook of Buddhism. He had read it straight through the night and returned it to her the next day with a request for more. After that, he had in effect become her student, ploughing through her reading lists, asking pointed questions, just skeptical enough to show that he was taking it all very seriously but careful never to come across jaded or cynical. He had even sat in on one of her classes, taught by a famous master who only came to the city from Boston once a month. Wes genuinely enjoyed the learning and tried to incorporate some of the most simple tenets of the discipline, such as mindfulness and basic meditation techniques, into his daily schedule, but always plagued by a nagging sense that he might be doing it all just to impress her or ingratiate himself. After all, he did intend to allow her to seduce and deflower him, whenever she felt the time was right.

When he was little, Wes had thought he was very rich because his family lived in a townhouse in Greenwich Village. No other pupil at his local elementary school, not one, had lived in a house. But when he went to Dalton on scholarship, he found that he was not rich at all, and that until then he hadn't even known what it meant to be rich. His father explained that when they'd bought the house with a down-payment out of his first advance, long before Wes was born, that part of the Village close to the water had still been an isolated and kind of scary neighborhood, and real estate there had been cheap. And even though Wes's mom had inherited a shitload of money when her parents died—money that made it possible for their grandchildren to attend fancy private schools and for their daughter to be attended by a live-in aide now that she was sick—they could never afford to make the same move today. So in his early days at Dalton Wes had had a bit of a chip on his shoulder about money issues and did not necessarily encourage downtown play dates or sleepovers because his home was kind of run-down and ratty compared to theirs. By the same token, he had been reluctant to accept invitations to weekend homes in the Hamptons or Litchfield County. Having grown up closely observing his father, he already knew what it felt like to be torn between contempt and envy, and he didn't necessarily need it rubbed in his face. But there was never a moment's hesitation about accepting Delia's offer.

It was a fine Indian summer Saturday morning when Wes took an early jitney to Amagansett and Delia met him in the family Mercedes station wagon. On the ten-minute drive, she was at pains to downplay the house. It was just a ramshackle old cottage, she said, bought decades earlier when Napeague was nowhere. Theodore Roosevelt had lived in it when the Rough Riders were stationed in Montauk, but then it had been picked up and transported by barge to its current location. It was really nothing, she insisted, but it was in a beautiful spot. Wes played along, sharing his own family story about living in a beautiful house they could never afford if they had to buy it today, but he knew she was snowing him, and he appreciated it. There weren't many girls at Dalton who would go to the same trouble. The car turned into a development of ugly, modern beach houses on tiny, sand-swept plots arranged in a grid. For a moment Wes wondered if Delia had actually been telling the truth about the modesty of her house, but then the road ended and she pulled into a driveway overgrown with wisteria and beach plum, and when she removed the key from the ignition the roar of the surf was the only sound to be heard.

"None of those houses were here when my parents bought ours," she said with a dismissive wave of her hand as she led him along a side path to the rear. "But you won't even know they're there."

A large deck was built onto the back of the house, with an old-fashioned cedar hot tub and a circular cast-iron picnic table with built-in benches. From here, all you could see were undulating dunes covered in beach grass, and the nearest house was hundreds of yards away at the far side of a nature preserve. You couldn't see the ocean, but you could hear it. At the end of the deck was a low gate that opened onto a sandy path that wound through the dunes and disappeared at the crest. Delia opened her arms to gather in the scene, and turned to him with a joyous smile. Wes thought that it was good that all this belonged to her, if it made her smile that way, because one day she might find that he was worth as much as all the dunes and beaches and nature preserves, and she would smile like that when she looked at him. She gave him a tour of the house; it actually was not fancy in any way, furnished haphazardly in a casual, beachy style, and had obviously been added onto more than once, as each room seemed to be on a different level, reached by steep hidden stairways of bare, worn planks. When she'd asked him to come, Delia had never mentioned sleeping arrangements, and Wes assumed that, with her parents present, this was not the moment she had chosen to upgrade their relationship; even so, when she showed him to the room that was to be his—the maid's room, down some steps from the kitchen next to the laundry room, and on the far side of the house from her own—he experienced a moment of giddy disappointment at being treated like a fond younger cousin. She went upstairs to change, and warned him to use plenty of sunblock, despite the lateness of the season. He quickly slipped into his bathing suit and pulled on a pair of cargo shorts over it, then did a dozen hasty push-ups before spraying himself with the expensive French sunblock she had left for him. She came down for him, wearing a red bikini with white polka dots and little bows at her hips, covered in some sort of gauzy, transparent caftan that emphasized the shape of her breasts. She offered to do his back, but the spray was so fine that she didn't even need to rub it in.

On the beach, she found a pair of low-slung canvas folding chairs, draped with damp towels, that she said belonged to her parents, although they were nowhere in sight. In fact, in the miles and miles of broad white strand visible in either direction, there were no more than a handful of people, strolling in pairs or with their dogs, and no one in the water. The surf was gentle and regular, producing waist-high waves delicately laced with foam. Delia assured Wes that the water still retained most of its summer warmth and that the swimming was delicious.

"Are you going in?" he asked.

"I want to warm up first," she said, stretching herself out on a striped towel with one knee slightly raised and the caftan fluttering translucently between her thighs. Wes was mildly surprised to note that she wore red nail polish on her toes. Without removing his shorts or his shirt, Wes lay down on the sand, parallel to but at a reasonable distance from Delia. The scent of the sunblock was subtly erotic, but he couldn't tell if it was her or himself that he was smelling. He took one last look at Delia on her back under the caftan, then closed his eyes and tried to make his mind go blank, though the rise and fall of her chest remained burned into the back of his eyelids. He fell into a light trance, from which he was roused by the return of Delia's parents.

The rest of the day was spent in precisely the way an idyllic interlude at the beach should be spent if you want it to remain a highlight of your memories of youth for the rest of your life. Delia's father, sporting shaggy gray hair and a modest potbelly, was a professor of philosophy at CUNY, though not a Buddhist—that was Delia's own path, he said with restrained pride—and burning with ingenuous curiosity about Wes's intellectual interests and development and his hopes for the future. It soon became clear from the tack of his questions that Delia had described Wes as a tutee of her own, rather than as a potential love interest, but Wes was happy nevertheless to bask in the sunlight of her father's approval. Her mother, a writer, was beautiful like Delia, maybe even more so, but not sculpted or even svelte like so many Park Avenue moms. Delia later suggested that all the money was on her mother's side, passed down from a famous industrial engineer grandfather. Delia had an older sister, Mariah, who was away at Rhode Island School of Design and whose lovely face, pale and freckled like Delia's but thinner and more angular, shone out from multiple instamatic snapshots magnetized to the refrigerator. When it was Wes's turn to describe his family, he shamed himself by lingering a little too long, and with a hint of self-deprecating pathos, on his mother's illness and the responsibilities it had thrust upon him, but felt that he redeemed himself with his enthusiastic renditions of Nora and her fantasy life. Of his father, he provided the minimal outline necessary, though he did acknowledge at Delia's prompting that he had written a novel long ago that had almost been made into a movie, but neither of Delia's parents had read or heard of it. Delia and Wes went for a long walk along the beach, interrupted by some splashing in the surf, after which she put her caftan back on before she was dry then removed it in one languid movement over her head when she found it chaffing, revealing the most gorgeous armpits Wes had ever seen. They talked about schoolwork, Hillary Clinton's inevitable victory in the Democratic primaries, the death of Sri Chinmoy, and Buddhism. Wes was unable to steer her in any satisfying way into a sharing of school gossip, let alone any history of boyfriends past or future. Lunch was a Caprese salad with fresh baguette and tapenade, after which her parents retired upstairs for a nap and Delia and Wes drove into East Hampton to browse the bookstore and buy fish for dinner. Delia bought Wes a book about happiness written by a French Buddhist monk who had given up a promising career in molecular genetics for life in a Tibetan monastery in Nepal. By the time they got back to Napeague her parents were awake. Wes and Delia went for another swim and a long walk, during which they twice brushed shoulders, the first time by accident, though Delia seemed not to notice either event. Dinner was a simple fillet of striped bass, drizzled with chile oil infused with garlic and grilled on a gas-fired barbecue on the deck, and served with olives, spicy chickpeas and cold, marinated asparagus. Delia, a vegetarian, passed on the fish, but she and Wes drank a Bridgehampton rosé along with the adults. They talked politics and Heidegger, of whose work Wes knew nothing but Delia's father was an expert. Before bed, Delia's mother got out the Polaroid 600 and took a picture of Wes and Delia, arm in arm leaning against the deck railing. It was the closest Wes had ever gotten to Delia and it unnerved him a good deal and made him glad they were going to bed. When the snapshot had developed they passed it around, then Delia's mother stuck it among the other pictures magnetized to the fridge. He shook Delia's father's hand and kissed her mother on both cheeks, and Delia kissed him goodnight on the lips, but Wes suspected it was just the wine and that she hadn't quite meant to do it because she turned away immediately afterwards without meeting his gaze. On his way to the maid's room, Wes stopped at the refrigerator to admire their photo; it looked very natural there among all the handsome strangers, and Wes imagined that one day somebody would have to notice it and ask Delia if that was her boyfriend.

In bed, Wes tried to read the book by the French monk, but he had a raging hard-on, which he refused to touch, first because he thought it would gross Delia out to imagine him jerking off in the maid's bed, and second because there was always the remote chance that she would come to him some time in the night. She hadn't given him the slightest cause to believe that she might, and he repeated its impossibility over and over to himself like a mantra, but he could not shake the intuition that it would happen precisely because it was so impossible. Somewhere in the house—Wes suspected the parent's bedroom—a television was playing and a conversation engaged in low, light-hearted tones. Wes strained to listen; was it two voices or three? He couldn't bear the idea that the three of them were staying up and prolonging the day without him, and perhaps even talking about him. If they were, one of the parents would surely ask Delia if she had any romantic intentions towards Wes, and then she would have to put into words what she might not have considered at all up to that moment, and that would make it real and final for her in a way it would not have been if they hadn't questioned her. It could, of course, work to his advantage if the question suddenly caused her to recognize feelings of affection that she had suppressed, either because Wes was a year younger than her or because he was supposed to be her apprentice, and then maybe she would after all decide that there was only one thing left to do to make this perfect day even more perfect. But she didn't, and Wes awoke to birdsong the next morning in exactly the same position in which he'd fallen asleep.

How could he be sure he was in love? How could he know, now that it was so important to know? Is it easier to tell that you're in love if you've never been in love before, because it's something so different from anything you've ever felt, or if you have been in love before, because you recognize the feeling? And if you can't remember the feeling, is it because you've never had it or because it's different every time? Wes groaned under the burden of these luxuriant mysteries, but they were at least very interesting to contemplate. He noted to himself, however, that he had slept quite soundly despite being in love, and that was a little worrisome. Surely you weren't supposed to be able to sleep so well if you were in love? Or eat? He realized that he was painfully hungry. Maybe it wasn't love after all, or if it was it was the kind where you can sleep and eat, and also think about sex a lot, instead of about how much pain you were in. But surely that would have to be a kind of second-rate love, and Wes didn't think he was in too much pain, and this love that he was feeling now couldn't be that kind. It would bear further thought after breakfast.

Wes didn't remember much of what had happened the following day, except that they had left for the city early and stopped for steamed lobster at a restaurant overlooking an inlet. At the table, Wes had told the story about his mother, who had been raised in a kosher household in Inwood, and the first time she had eaten lobster, thinking it was some sort of fish, and had been violently ill when told what it was she had eaten. That was supposed to lead organically to the story of her first driving lesson, when she had crashed into the only car in an otherwise empty and enormous parking lot, but instead Delia's parents had latched onto the wrong part of the first story and started questioning him about his Jewishness. Wes would be naturally reticent on this subject, and had been particularly so on this occasion, where he hoped to keep their minds on his ailing mother and build up a store of sympathy that could lead to a second invitation for the weekend.

Crossing Hudson Street, Wes realized that all this had taken place eleven months earlier, and that he never had been invited back to Napeague, although he had had several hearty chats with Delia's parents on the phone and was convinced that he'd left a good impression of himself. In fact, his relationship with Delia had not really advanced in any distinctive way since then—they did not now exchange intimacies more intimate than those they had exchanged since then, if a shared preference for Twain over Dickens could be called an intimacy; they did not speak more often now than they did then, an average of once or twice a week outside chance encounters in the hallway; they did not touch each other casually on the arm or the back of the neck in the way close friends do without noticing, although Wes surely would have noticed if they had; and Wes had not come any closer in these long eleven months to telling Delia how he felt about her than he had when "accidentally" brushed against her naked shoulder on the beach. There was something wrong in all this, something he realized probably should have disturbed him a long time ago if he had not been so fixated on his own struggle to better himself on Delia's behalf. The way he had struggled and struggled without making any headway was, in fact, perfectly Tolstoyan in its total lack of self-consciousness and, apparently, of tangible outcome. So what could she now suddenly have to tell him that was so important?

The moment he turned the corner, Wes saw Lucy sitting on the stoop of his house, halfway down the block. It was odd and a little shocking, seeing her like that because, despite everything that had happened between them, it was almost like looking at a stranger, as if he would have to walk up and introduce himself and start from zero, the way they'd done the night before. That feeling of trepidation and possibilities was what had remained with Wes most clearly, and Wes relived it now as he advanced down the block. Last night at the party, James had hunted him down and was goading him to make his move, but Wes had been deeply distracted and disturbed by his conversation with Delia.

"Delia's behaving all weird tonight. What's she doing here, anyway?"

"Weird how?"

"I don't know. She's all . . . flirty. I've never seen her like this. It's driving me nuts."

"Forget about Delia, man. Try to stay focused. You're here for Lucy, remember?"

"I know, but I haven't seen her anywhere."

"Don't look, but she's standing right there, and she's staring right at you. I'm gonna stand up and walk away, fix you another drink, then when I'm gone you look up, as if you're looking for me, and catch her eye. I'm gone."

Wes stared into his tumbler and counted to five, but when he looked up Lucy was nowhere to be seen. He stood, pushed his way through a small scrum of dancing sophomores and wandered into a hallway that seemed to lead to the rest of the apartment. At the far end, beyond a half-dozen closed doors, a brightly lit doorway evidently led into the kitchen, which even from this end Wes could see was packed to overflowing. He turned back towards the living room, but his eye was caught by a wall of family photos, primly framed and symmetrically arranged between the molding and the oak wainscot. Wes knew that nothing could more severely compromise his cool than to be caught in a lonely corridor, perusing the artwork all on his lonesome in the midst of a drinking party, but he couldn't help himself. All the pictures were essentially the same: a handsome couple with great posture and a conservative wardrobe, smiling for the camera in a variety of exotic settings with two pretty young girls, the younger of which was Lucy. Here they were on a white banquette on the deck of a yacht, probably somewhere in the Mediterranean; on horseback, in shiny black knee boots and riding helmets; an outdoor café on a piazza in Rome or Barcelona; squatting beside a tame cheetah on an African wildlife preserve. In all the pictures, the father's hair was immaculate and immobile, the mother's eyes were shaded by a broad hat brim or a hand at her brow, except in the very earliest one, in which she sat in pink satin nightgown in a luxuriant bed, propped up by fat white pillows, with a newborn baby in her arms and a look of weary apprehension. In all the pictures, Lucy's sister smiled boldly, confidently, and more radiantly as she grew older, but Lucy kept changing, and the series told the story, Wes thought, of an ever-widening gulf between her and her perfect, antiseptic family. The littlest Lucys wore a face of open joy that gradually gave way to a sad, frozen grin as she got older, and ultimately to dull resignation and withdrawal. In these photos, she didn't look duplicitous or manipulative at all; just sad. Wes was astounded that anyone should willingly choose to broadcast such a dismal narrative in a public space. How could they be unaware of the story it told? He thought of the jumbled snapshots stuck to Delia's refrigerator in Napeague, and how they too told a family story; and about Nora's beloved photo albums of happier times, warehoused under a bed somewhere, and how long it had been since anyone had bothered to update them, as if his own family history had somehow come to a premature and shameful end and were being preserved, vaulted, only because the only thing worse than having to relive it was summoning the passion to destroy it. Tolstoy had been wrong in this as in so many things—Delia's family was unique in its happiness, whereas unhappy families differed only to the extent to which they were willing to acknowledge their own failure. Lucy's parents didn't even know they had been stricken, that they carried the plague with them, whereas every single member of Wes's family slouched about the world with the mark of Cain on their foreheads. Which only made Delia's quest for spiritual enlightenment a painful, mocking indictment, like a millionaire whose judicious investments make him a billionaire, while the rest of us are still looking for loose change under the sofa cushions. The phone vibrated in Wes's rear pocket.

White: "can we talk"

Yellow: "Where r u?"

White: "behand u"

Wes turned, and there was Lucy, in tight jeans, a white tanktop and gold sandals, leaning against the jamb of a darkened doorway. Wes knew enough to recognize his immediate reaction as a sort of swoon, or what would be called a swoon in a book.

Wes recalled that swoon now as he neared the stoop, trying to recapture some of its power. Lucy had yet to notice his approach. He pictured himself as a satellite and Lucy as the Earth, because from a distance the only discernible feature of her face was her thick dark eyebrows, like the Great Wall of China. She was in a man's white oxford shirt, untucked and with sleeves rolled up to her elbows, blue jeans and the same sandals she'd worn the night before. She sat with her hands tucked beneath her thighs and her knees almost to her chin. Her blackish hair was pulled back in a simple ponytail that was draped over her right shoulder. The sight of her slim, bare neck unleashed a shockingly graphic flashback of Lucy hovering over him, that black ponytail swinging at the same rhythm as her small, pear-shaped breasts, and Wes remembered that at that moment he had thought that she looked just as Natasha would have looked if she had had sex with Prince André before she lost all her beauty to devastating grief.

Wes blushed at precisely the same moment that Lucy caught sight of him. She seemed sad and worried, which only emphasized her resemblance to Natasha. Wes stood at the bottom of the stoop and waved to her just with his hand. She waved back, and smiled forlornly.

"What's up?"

Lucy shrugged her shoulders in a way that was meaningless to Wes. He couldn't even begin to imagine what she was thinking, what she was doing here, what she might want from him, unless it was more sex, which would not be possible with two adults in the house, even if Wes were able to just set everything else aside, which he doubted he could. She would probably be wanting to talk about what had happened between them the night before, which was only reasonable and right, he supposed, but that, too, seemed like an insufferable chore that they might both easily dispense with. This was a moment, Wes considered, when it would surely be handy to have a Library of Babel to get lost in, and that led him briefly to ponder the notion that no matter what he and Lucy might say to each other this morning, they would have to say it in mutually unintelligible languages, and that when people do seem to understand one another, as he and she had the night before, it was usually a willful illusion. In the meantime, there was no Library of Babel, no infinite mansion, no countless light bulbs to be tallied, not even a room with a hole in the ceiling to be fixed; there was only the house and the street, and Wes would have to get past Lucy to get into the house, and Lucy would have to get past Wes to reach the street.

"My dad's at home. You didn't have to wait outside."

"I know, I rang. He said you'd be right back, so I figured it would be better to wait for you here." She spoke so softly that Wes could barely hear her voice.

"You want to go for a walk?"

Lucy shrugged again, and Wes thought that she might be getting ready to cry.

"You know, I've got some things to do in the house. Let's go in." Wes bounded up the stoop, two steps at a time, keys already in hand, before Lucy had even had a chance to stand. His jeans brushed against her shoulder, making a kind of whispered rasp that to Wes sounded like sandpaper on glass, but by the time he had the door open she was close behind him, like a frightened child waiting in line behind her father in an intimidating crowd. Without turning, Wes walked straight through the front hall into the kitchen and opened the refrigerator. He leaned in and retrieved the bowl, which he placed on the counter. Lucy stood right beside him, looking into the bowl. The water was pale pink, only slightly more translucent than last night's Bloody Mary.

"What is that?"

"Sweetbreads. Pretty gross, right?"

"No, I love sweetbreads."

"Really?"

"With chestnuts and port sauce. Yum."

"You know how to cook them?"

"No, but there's this restaurant in Paris . . ."

"I'm making them for my mom. I don't know if I can do it right."

"So long as they're really crispy. They don't have much flavor."

"'Kay."

Lucy watched in silence as Wes drained the bowl, rinsed the sweetbread, then placed it in a small, battered saucepan, covered it with cold water, and put it on the stove to boil. He stood over the range, glaring down intently into the pot as if it had offended him and he were giving it the evil eye, but with Lucy right beside him, they could also have been proud parents watching over their infant child asleep in a basinet.

"You should probably cover that. It won't boil otherwise."

With the pot covered, it seemed somehow more foolish to stand and stare at it, but Wes tried that anyway, and Lucy joined him. At one moment, she muttered something under her breath that sounded like "Typo."

"What?"

Lucy just shook her head and went on staring at the pot. Perhaps Wes was just imagining it, but with nothing to go on it still felt that the mood had softened a little, that a moment of crisis had passed, and that the future of the planet did not now depend on what he said next. He tried to think about some of the things they had said to each other the night before, something he knew might be of interest to her, but nothing came to mind. He knew they had spoken to each other at some length, but because of the Bloody Marys and other things, the memories would not come when summoned, so he allowed his mind to relax and wander a little, and it flitted about for a moment or two before alighting on port sauce. That had been an oddly specific thing to say, as if Lucy had been referring to her birth sign or her mother's maiden name, and it had carved out a little niche for itself, like a dog digging in the hot sand to make a cool hole in which to rest. Wes wasn't sure if he had ever tasted port sauce, or if he would recognize it if it were placed before him, and he knew that he had never been to Paris, but both sauce and city were clearly familiar territory to Lucy, something she could refer to without blushing or exaggerating. Wes thought he might ask her about Paris, but he had a feeling that it was something they had talked about the night before and that did not necessarily have positive associations for Lucy, and then he realized that it was because of one of the photos on the wall in Lucy's apartment, in which she had posed with limpid dejection against the railing of an upper level of the Eiffel Tower. That left port sauce.

"Personality is an unbroken series of successful gestures."

"Excuse me?"

"What does this mean to you: 'Personality is an unbroken series of successful gestures?'"

"Personality is an unbroken series of successful gestures?"

"F. Scott Fitzgerald wrote it in *The Great Gatsby*. Any idea what he meant?"

"I've never read *The Great Gatsby*."

"That doesn't matter. Just free associate. 'Personality is an unbroken series of successful gestures.' Top of your head."

"'Personality is . . . ' I don't know. It could mean anything, I guess."

"No it couldn't. Fitzgerald had something really particular in mind when he wrote that. It doesn't have to mean what he thought it meant when he wrote it, or what he said it meant after he wrote it, but it's got to mean something. What does it mean to you?"

"I really don't . . . " Her voice petered out in helpless bafflement.

"See, like this is what you might say. You might say 'What does he mean by "successful?"' Or, 'What does he mean by "gesture?"' Is he saying that a gesture is successful if it conveys precisely the meaning it was intended to convey? Or that any gesture that bridges the gap to the next gesture is successful? Is a gesture an act, an exertion of the will, a posture, or is it merely an attempt to communicate? Maybe our entire concep-

tion of individuality is based on how we try to describe our-
selves to others?"

There was an oven glove on the counter besides the range,
and Lucy now slipped her right hand into it and removed the
lid from the saucepan, in which the water was boiling furiously.
She returned the lid to the pot and with her left hand turned
the gas down to simmer. She pulled the glove from her hand
and redeposited it on the countertop.

"Maybe he didn't know what he was talking about. Maybe
he just wrote it to make himself sound cleverer than everyone
else, and to avoid saying what he really meant. How long does
this need to cook?"

"About three minutes, I think." Wes referred to the cookbook, which was splayed open to the appropriate page. "Three
to five minutes."

Lucy consulted her watch, a surprisingly childlike Swatch
with stars on the face and some sort of animal, a cat or a rac-
coon dressed like a superhero, on the strap. It was an ambiguous gesture that successfully suggested that she was both timing the sweetbread and running out of patience. "But what
does 'three to five minutes' really mean? Is it three minutes
that feel like five when you're bored? If there's 120 seconds
between three minutes and five minutes, does it actually have
120 different meanings?"

She was making fun of him, and Wes liked that, he liked it
a lot. Delia never made fun of him, and rarely made fun of anyone else for that matter, and Wes harbored the suspicion that
people who forebear from mocking you secretly hold you in
contempt. Of course, he understood that you can also make
fun of those whom you hold in the highest contempt, but they
are usually politicians or family members. He did not feel for
one instant that Lucy held him in any kind of contempt, but
the sensation of being caught dead in the crosshairs of someone who may be genuinely fond of you and might actually wish

you well was delicious and dizzying, and Wes paused in the midst of whatever it was that he was trying to do to fix her with a frank gaze of admiration. At the same time, he was also aware that smiling at her warmly and gazing at her were ways of masking his failure to come up with a spontaneous, witty retort. Instead, he performed a gesture in her general direction, half-nod, half-bow, that was meant to convey humble recognition of a superior intellect momentarily bested. It was one in a lexicon of semaphoric markers that he had perfected in Delia's company, and had served him well in a variety of delicate situations. They returned to watching the pot boil, and shortly thereafter Lucy looked at her watch and announced the passage of three to five minutes. Wes donned the glove and walked the saucepan to the sink, where he removed the lid and subjected the sweetbread to a stream of cold water from the faucet.

Again, Lucy stood at his side and closely followed his performance. Now, of course, her proximity had an entirely different flavor, but still she was an odd person, the way she hung about him yet forcefully resisted being patronized. Wes was tempted to feel flattered, yet he was so baffled by her that he wasn't sure that that was an appropriate reaction, and now a sort of sense memory returned to him from the evening before, when he had been equally confused by the way she had behaved aggressively at junctures where others might have demurred, and passively just when he had expected her to demonstrate leadership. Again, he could not quite fix a visual recall to it; it remained a sort of vague, free-floating insight, like a familiar quotation from a book you had forgotten that you'd read.

The sweetbread had been transformed by its poaching into a more compact, paler and altogether more rubbery version of itself, the world's ugliest dog toy. The surface had been cooled by the tap water, but Wes could still feel a weak warmth pulsing from within. The slimy, stringy parts—what the cookbook referred to as "connective membranes"—were now rubbery, amorphic appendages, while the unsightly bulges appeared to have been inflated from within, like flawed inner tubes. The whole thing had turned a kind of autopsy gray. Wes cradled the mass in his two upturned palms, holding it low in the sink as if it might try to escape.

"That doesn't look very crispy to me, Wes."

"It's not cooked yet. I still have to press it and fry it."

"That sounds like a good idea."

"Hand me those scissors, please."

Wes trimmed off the fat and membranes, and placed the sweetbread between two clean plates.

"We need something heavy to weigh them down. Try the fridge."

"How about a quart of milk?"

"Not heavy enough."

Wes scrounged through the cupboards, but the pickings were slim. There were a few cans of chickpeas, a bag of French green lentils, and a liter of extra-virgin olive oil from Sicily, which all together might just do the trick, but it would all somehow have to be balanced in a pyramid atop the wobbly organ. There was nothing else would do the trick. Wes glanced around the room helplessly. The dog staggered in, attracted by the smell of boiling offal, and Lucy squatted down and scratched her between the ears.

"Who's this?"

"That's Crispy."

"How funny. She's really sweet."

"Come with me. I've got an idea." Wes led Lucy from the kitchen, down the stairs to the garden apartment, through the French doors and out into the back yard, where his father, in shorts and sagging white tee shirt, looked up from his laptop at the old school desk under the sycamore, smiled and waved.

"Hello again. Found the Wes-man, I see."

"Yes."

"Dad, this is Lucy."

"Lucy and I already met."

"We're doing some school work together."

"Wes, I happen to know that Lucy is not in your grade."

"I'm tutoring her."

"Okay. What can I do for you two?"

"Nothing. We need some bricks."

"What for?"

"Oh for whatever. Come on, Lucy."

Wes pushed past his father and the tree to a heap of old building materials that had once been a brick oven meant for bread and pizzas, or had nearly been until family inertia and lack of interest had brought construction to a halt. The top of the dome had collapsed, and a pile of loose bricks was conveniently at hand through the arched door. Wes brushed away some cobwebs, which clung to his fingers, and reached in.

"Grab two. That should be enough."

As they turned back towards the house, burdens in hand, Wes paused at a lyrical call and chatter, and looked up through the branches of the sycamore. It took him a while, but finally he spotted the bird about half-way up the tree, on an outer bough.

"What is it?"

"An oriole, a male. See the orange belly? It's late in the year for him to be hanging around. That's global warming for you."

"You study birds?"

"Not really. I just like to know what's going on in my neighborhood."

Back in the kitchen, the bricks stacked neatly on the plate, two on two, and the sweetbread compressed with a satisfying exhalation. Wes returned them to the refrigerator and wiped his soiled hands on his jeans with a sigh. Crispy, who had stayed behind to keep guard, scrambled to her feet and wagged her tail in tentative expectation.

"I suppose I should walk her. Wanna come?"

"Honestly? I'd rather just hang, if you don't mind."

"Oh well, sure. I can walk her later. Let's go up to my room."

Lucy led the way up the stairs, and Wes found his eyes level with her ass, tightly clad and well defined by her jeans, though partially concealed by the tails of her shirt. He wondered if she could sense the delicacy with which he averted his eyes, or whether she would appreciate it if she could. Without actually looking at it, he tried to remember what it looked like, naked, but found nothing. Was it possible that he had not looked at it the night before, or even seen it? Was it possible that he had not paid it its due attention? Well, yes, he was forced to acknowledge, it was perfectly possible, given the attention he would have lavished on all those parts of her that he assumed other teenage boys would overlook and which, by making them the subject of tender caresses and light-as-air butterfly kisses, would earn him the admiration and gratitude of someone unused to such mature restraint and thoughtful generosity. He couldn't actually remember doing any of these things, but he had imagined it often enough to assume that he had, in fact, drawn concentric circles with his fingertips on her lower back, or kissed her behind the knees, or licked her armpits, or other things that girls would enjoy but never get from most boys. It was what separated boys from men, actually; Wes wouldn't have dreamed of grabbing her ass, or rubbing his face between her tits, or pounding at her like a jackhammer. Wasn't she here, now, at least in part because he had treated her like a woman, and not like an object? But still, as the tail of Lucy's shirt danced before him, he found himself wishing that he had taken a moment to explore the more obvious bits as well. It was a little like going to view the Mona Lisa and only looking at the landscape in the background. At the top of the stairs, Lucy turned and questioned Wes with a look, and he put his finger to his lips, made the universal gesture to indicate someone asleep, and pointed straight up. She tiptoed silently past his mother's door.

In Wes's room, Lucy made a beeline for the bed and flopped down onto it, her ankles dangling over the edge and back propped against the wall, as if she had been doing so her entire life. Wes went straight to his desk, where he grabbed the moleskin-bound daybook and a pen and began to enter the Fitzgerald line before he forgot it.

"What are you doing?"

"I keep my favorite quotes in here."

"Can I see it?"

"Sure." He tossed it to her across the room, and she caught it flat-handed. He watched her leaf through the notebook calmly, her eyes lowered, abstractedly twisting her ponytail around the fingers of her left hand.

"That's a lot of quotes. How long have you been doing this?"

"I don't know—four, five years?"

"I like this one: 'I cannot accept myself as I am but, ultimately, I am resigned to accepting this inability to accept myself as I am.' Is that you?"

"It's a British writer named Geoff Dyer."

"I mean, did you put it down because it reminds you of yourself?"

"I don't think so. It was a while ago, but I think I put it down as a warning to myself not to become like my dad."

"What's wrong with your dad? He seems nice to me."

"He's not cruel or anything. He's just sort of weak and . . . lost. He had this one moment of glory twenty-five years ago and he can't get over it. I guess things didn't happen the way he planned, but he can't move on. He's been working on the same book for twenty years, I think, but he'll never finish it. It's pretty pathetic actually."

"I don't know. Doesn't sound so terrible to me. Human frailty and all that."

"You sound like Delia."

"I do?"

"Anyway, he and my mom, they're not, like . . . together. He only lives here 'cause he can't afford his own place. And to 'take care' of me and my sister, quote unquote."

"That's weird."

"No kidding. Especially when he's got some grad chick staying the night to finish her homework."

"You mean . . . ?"

"Yeah. Great role model for his daughter."

"That's fucked up. It's kind of funny, you following in his footsteps and all. I'd have thought the last thing you'd want to be is a writer."

"What makes you think I'm going to be a writer?"

"Just look at these quotes. 'A writer is in the end not his books, but his myth. And that myth is in the keeping of others.' Or this one: 'Never trust the teller, trust the tale.' Practically every single one is about writing. I mean, if you're so worried about becoming like your dad, shouldn't you be a lawyer or a doctor or something?"

"Sometimes I think that's all I ever think about. Think of all the times you've heard your friends say that they never want to turn out like their parents, right? Now don't you think that must have been the same things their parents said about their own parents, and yet the world is still just as filled with people doing the same old shit? Somewhere along the line, every-where and at every moment, there must be a lot of people in the process of becoming the very thing they swore they would never become. Obviously, you think it will never happen to you, but what's the trick to it? I mean, I always wondered why some people react to their parents by becoming them, and oth-ers react by becoming the opposite."

"So all you have to do is figure out what's the exact oppo-site of your dad, and become that?"

"See, I'm not so sure anymore, it could be too late for me already. I mean, I have all these fantasies about escaping to some quiet, isolated place where I can be alone to think and write, you know? Just figure out who I am, like D.H. Lawrence or someone. But then at some point I realized that I've heard it all before. Maybe it's my father who wants to run away and not me. I think, shit, even my own feelings are borrowed from someone else. What do you do when you can't even trust your own desires? Maybe I don't want these things I think I want at all."

"'To the wise, life is a problem; to the fool, a solution.' Marcus Aurelius."

"Smart guy."

"You're a smart guy, too. You'll figure it out."

"Yeah, well."

Wes thought of *Brave New World*, of the hateful Bernard Marx and how hard he had tried to seduce Lenina Crowne, when she didn't need or want to be seduced. Bernard could have had her anytime he wished for the price of a game of obstacle golf, or less, but he had insisted on making a whole, dismal show of it, to force his dishonest morality down her throat before he fucked her just like anyone else would have. Lenina had no use for any of that—she just wanted what she wanted, for better or for worse. It occurred to Wes that Lucy was a little like that—not about sex, and certainly not stupid or conventional like Lenina, but she was someone who didn't seem to need to be seduced in any way, she would have no use for pretension and would not pander to someone's insecurities. Wes didn't know why he should sense this about her, since he barely knew her, but there was something about the way she had smiled at him when she'd called him a smart guy that was not at all about encouraging him, or bolstering a fragile ego, or flattery, but that merely urged him to acknowledge something of which he was already well aware. Well it was true, for all his faults he did know himself to be smart, sometimes, about certain things, but it was very easy for some people to make him forget that. Lucy had not as yet so much as hinted at why she'd been so insistent on seeing him, but Wes was beginning to get the idea. He heard the bell ring in his mother's room.

"That's my mom. She probably needs my help. I won't be long."

"Can I meet her?"

"You want to meet my mom?"

"Sure, why not?"

"She's pretty sick. I'm not sure it'd be much fun for you."

"To the wise, fun is a problem; to the fool, a solution."

"Okay then. Let's go."

Even as he stepped into the sick room, with Lucy close behind, Wes saw it as if for the first time, the impression it must make on a stranger—the gloom, the slightly offensive if indefinable odor, the hulking gun-metal scaffolding over the bed, the whispered intimacies of PBS, the yellow scarecrow enthroned in her sanctum—and he decided that, all in all, it wasn't actually that bad. If you described it in a book, you could amp up the hyperbole and make it pretty Dickensian, but the fact was, given his mother's dire condition and the general household dilapidation, it could be a lot worse, or so Wes thought. Maybe it was impossible for him to see it through truly fresh eyes, but it struck him now as just barely more seedy and oppressive than the rest of the house and, by extension, than Wes himself. The smell for now was balanced, precariously, in favor of bleached cotton over stale urine; the carpet was worn but neither dank nor dusty; the window treatments were closed but hardly Havershamian; the muted gargle of Bob Ross's patter settled over the furnishings like a fine mist of scented fog; and his mother herself wore a sincere if fragile attempt at a smile over the lacy collar of her housecoat. It was a place you could bring a school friend, at least a certain kind of school friend, with some confidence of eliciting pity, compassion even, without dread or revulsion. Delia had never been in this room or met his mother.

"Mom, this is my friend Lucy. Do you mind if she comes in to say hi?"

"Come in, come in Lucy. A little closer, sweetie, please."

Lucy approached the bed and without hesitation grasped Wes's mom's outstretched hand and looked her straight in the eye—her one good eye, which was no longer much good.

"You're so young, my goodness."

"Yes I am. I'm sixteen."

"I thought you were younger. Are you and Leslie classmates?"

"He's a grade above me. What are you watching?"

"Bob Ross. Have you ever seen him?"

"I've never even heard of him. Is it good?"

"I watch him all the time. I don't have much patience for anything else. Would you like to watch?"

"Sure."

Lucy sat on the edge of the bed and twisted so that she could watch Bob Ross paint a cabin in the northern woods without turning her back on Wes's mother. The two of them watched the television, during which Bob Ross proved his worth by saying "It's your world" twice in the space of three minutes. Wes watched Lucy, the way she was instantly absorbed by the show, her face twitching and scrunching in bafflement. At first, Wes thought she might be putting it on for his benefit, the way children open their eyes wide and perform surprise and delight upon opening a disappointing present, but if it was an act it was a very polished one. If there had ever been any truth to the rumors of her precocious promiscuity, she certainly wasn't living up to them tonight: Natasha at the piano could not have been more childlike and unaware. Just as this thought crossed Wes's mind, Lucy turned towards him with a vaguely wicked smile on her face and said, "What a freak."

"What did Lucy say?"

"She said Bob Ross is a freak."

"She's right. He is a total freak. But right now I need your help, Leslie."

"Okay mom. Why don't you go back to my room, Lucy? I'll be up in a sec."

Lucy stood and squeezed Wes's mom's hand. "It was very nice to meet you, ma'am. And I love Bob Ross. He could be a real cult icon."

"My name is Marion."

"Goodbye, Marion. Thanks again."

When Lucy was gone, Wes moved to the far side of the bed, pulled back the counterpane and sheets, and leaned down to squeeze his arm behind his mother's back and around her waist. The smell of urine was stronger at this proximity, but not overpowering, which meant that she had not had an accident but merely a few minor lapses, probably in her sleep. That, too, was a good sign that augured absolutely nothing. With his free hand, he pulled on her shins to pivot her body, then urged her forward until her bare feet touched the carpet.

"Ready?"

She nodded, and Wes hoisted her to her feet, keeping a firm hold around her waist. He could feel her lower back tense as she prepared to take her first step, but the muscles were so weak and fluttered a little, as if they were talking in their sleep. For the first few steps she actually lifted her feet off the floor, but she soon gave that up in favor of sliding them, like skis, across the carpet. It took a full minute to cross the room to the washroom door, during which time her breath grew labored and Wes, his face pressed against the side of her head, inhaled the subtly toxic miasma of steroids seeping through her skin. But the hardest part, as always, despite the slanted chrome bars that had been installed on opposite walls of the washroom, was simultaneously turning and lowering her to the toilet without chafing the healing bedsores on her buttocks or jarring her unpleasantly. It also had to be done with some urgency, because she never called for Wes until she really needed to go, but once she was seated she would still need to raise herself to slip the velcroed diaper around her ankles and raise her housecoat above her waist, which she did only with difficulty. The time would not be long in coming, Wes knew, when she would be incapable even of that, and it would fall to him—at least when Narita was away— to do it for her, just as the charge of escorting her to the toilet had fallen to him. It would be several years before Nora was big and strong enough to do it, but by that time who knew where any of them would be? Wes waited just outside the door for her to finish, because sitting on the toilet was painful for her, and being assisted by her teenage son a relatively new and unaccustomed humiliation, and he liked to accomplish it with as little fuss and delay as possible. He leaned against the doorjamb, closed his eyes, and let Bob Ross's voice wash over him like a cleansing stream. The feel of the cool, glossy wood against his lower back revived a sense memory from last night's party.

Wes had not wanted to return to the living room, where Delia might see them, or go to the kitchen, where it was too crowded to talk, but the rest of the apartment was dark and seemed to be widely recognized as off limits, except to the necking couples propped against the walls in the hall. Wes was not about to suggest that they go to her bedroom, and she did not offer, so somehow they ended up in the open doorway to a bathroom down a side corridor at the far end of the apartment, which was large enough that the roar of the party reached them as a distant, incoherent mumble of bass tones and shrill laughter. Wes felt sick to his stomach, and worried about controlling his voice, but otherwise felt that he was performing an adequate counterfeit of nonchalance as he leaned against the doorjamb with his hands tucked into the small of his back. Lucy settled against the opposite jamb, sufficiently upright to avoid entangling their legs. The only light came from a bluish nightlight in the bathroom, but it was enough to cast shadows across her nose and lips, and to set off her glossy black hair against the tank-top. Wes had assumed that Lucy had prepared some sort of opening remarks, a thesis statement, but she did not seem to be in any hurry to speak, and they stood in silence for what felt like a long time, each staring at the other's feet. Wes found it hard to credit that anything worthwhile could emerge from such inauspicious beginnings, and as the older party he felt that it was probably his responsibility to be collected, witty and detached, but they seemed to have set a trap for themselves by going off on their own where virtually anything either of them might say would come across as freighted. He wondered if maybe she just expected him to close the gap and kiss her without preliminaries, if that was just the way she rolled in situations like these, but such boldness was entirely beyond his capacities. Playing the awkward innocent, eager yet abashed, had sometimes worked for him in the past, yet he would feel foolish trying it on with Lucy, who was so much younger than him and at the same time, he imagined, far less burdened with romantic conceit. He realized with a momentary stab of panic that he had absolutely no idea what he was doing, and that it might have been better for all concerned had he stayed home in bed with *War and Peace*. This thought caused him to straighten up from his slouch, and the movement dislodged something in his throat.

"Your parents, what are they?"

"What?"

"I mean, they're out of town?"

"For a week."

"You're here by yourself?"

"Our housekeeper is staying, but she's away for the weekend."

"Aren't you afraid . . . ?"

"She's cool."

"Well, it's a great party. Beautiful apartment."

"Thanks."

"You want to get a drink?"

"Sure."

Wes heard the toilet flush, and a minute later his mother chirruped to him from the washroom, and he went in. No accidents this time, but she had not managed to fully lower her housedress, and her thighs were exposed, muscles hanging from the bones like pleated drapes, and before he had the presence to avert his eyes he saw the blotch of sparse, graying curls between her legs. He backed around to her side and hoisted her to her feet as she made the pretense of helping with her hands on the slanted bars. They shuffled back to the bed and he lowered her in, tucking the blankets beneath her legs.

"Lucy's waiting for me upstairs."

"She's awfully pretty. Is she your girlfriend?"

"No."

"Do you want her to be?"

"I like someone else, I think."

"That's too bad, Leslie. She's the one for you."

"You need anything else, mom?"

"I'm tired."

Wes retrieved a fresh diaper from the drawer of her side table and left it on the bedsheet beside her pillow, where it would be within easy reach. He bent over and kissed her on the forehead. Wes knew that some day soon, maybe very soon, his mother would be dead, and that just the way he was looking at her now would become a memory that would make him sad for the rest of his life. He saw adults all around him who were saddened by their memories, and he knew it would happen to him, it was inevitable. He tried to see his mother now as if she were already a memory, but even this much diminished she was far too real for that. She was alive—she was still alive. He wondered if it were possible, if he concentrated every particle of his will and his being, to transform this feeling of her realness into the memory, so that in years to come what he would experience when he thought of her would not be a memory but a reality. He pictured himself twenty or thirty years from now, standing at his mother's bedside and looking down at her. The sense of her reality would be so strong that, even at a distance of decades, it would overpower the truth that she was long gone. It would be as if she had never died. He could bend over her and hold her, he could bend over her and kiss her, he could bend over and tell her—something— and in thirty years she would be alive as she was now. Wes thought it might be possible to do something like that, but he also knew that he really didn't understand how memories worked.

Lucy had her back to the door when he entered, studying the poster of Stuart Murdoch that hung over his bed, her hands folded behind her.

"I didn't figure you for the kind of guy who puts rock stars on his wall. I thought you were more the Nietzsche type, maybe, or Sartre."

"It's Belle and Sebastian, not exactly Kiss."

"Can't stand them."

"It's pretty much all I ever listen to these days. I've got, like, four thousands songs on my iPhone, and I go through them all and I can't find anything else I want to listen to. How can you not stand them?"

"How can you? Everything's a big secret with them, like a personal joke that you have to be super cool to get, like they're daring you to say you're as smart as they are."

"Someone once said that all of Western culture is based on secrecy."

"What's that supposed to mean?"

"Well think of art, music lyrics, movies. The things you don't say are always more important than the things you do say. You couldn't write a novel at all without withholding information. Even saying 'I love you' is completely meaningless unless you save it for the end, unless you don't say it before you say it."

"That's total crap. Real love is all about honesty. If I was in love with someone I would just say it. 'I love you.'"

"But would he believe you? He has to think you don't love him first."

"What's the matter with you? Love's nothing but suffering and lies? Love's not something beautiful and fun and celebrating? I mean, I'm not sure I've ever been *in love* before, but I always thought I'd know it when I was because I'd be really, really happy—not whining and crying like a little bitch."

"I wasn't talking about love. I was talking about culture."

"Yeah, I noticed that about you."

"How's that?"

"You're never talking about what you're talking about. Now I see why you like Belle and Sebastian. It makes a lot of sense."

"Does every conversation with you end up like this?"

"Sometimes I can get a little impatient."

Lucy flopped down onto the bed in her former position, as if she owned that space. Wes noticed that the two bottom buttons of her shirt were undone, revealing the slimmest slice of her belly, and he tried to remember if it had been like that before and he hadn't noticed. Had she undone the buttons while he was gone, as a preliminary to something? He didn't think so, but then he'd also kind of given up trying to figure out what Lucy wanted from him, or even what she might say next.

"Your mom's really sweet. What's that thing over her bed?"

"It's an electric sling. She's supposed to use it to get in and out of bed, but she never does."

"What's the matter with her? Sorry, I mean, what's wrong with her?"

"She has progressive relapsing multiple sclerosis."

"What does it do to you?"

"It ruins your eyesight. Weakens all your muscles. You can't balance. Makes you tired all the time. Sometimes you can't eat, you can't talk right, can't control your bladder. Fun stuff."

"Will she get better?"

"No, she'll get worse. She's already had pneumonia twice from lying on her back all the time. Even the bedsores can kill you if you're not careful."

"Bummer."

"Mmm."

"But you're, like, a great son. Most kids would be embarrassed. I was kind of surprised, when I saw her, that you would just introduce me like that, bring me into her room. But you treat her just like a normal person."

"She is a normal person. A normal really sick person."

"You know what I mean. You're just super kind, and devoted. Why does she call you 'Leslie?'"

"Leslie is my name."

"You're kidding."

"They named me after Leslie Howard. *Of Human Bondage* is my dad's favorite movie."

"So how did you get to Wes?"

"Any idea how hard it is for a boy named Leslie? No one can spell it, everyone thinks it's a girl's name. You call yourself 'Lez' and everybody says 'Lezbo.' You call yourself 'Les' and they all say 'Les is more' or 'Never settle for Les.' So one summer I went to camp, I was maybe eleven or twelve, and somebody asks me my name and I kind of mumbled it under my breath, as I usually did. And he says 'Wes?' and I go, 'Yeah, Wes!' Everyone called me 'Wes' that summer, and I loved it. When they asked me my name, I'd kind of shout it at the top of my voice. 'Wes! My name is Wes!' It was like I was a new person. And then when I got home, I told everyone to call me Wes, and then I transferred to Dalton so it was easy. No one calls me Leslie anymore except my mom."

"Can I call you Leslie, Leslie?"

"No."

"So what's this homework you've got to finish for Monday?"

"I've got to rewrite a paper for English."

"You've got a paper due Monday and you haven't started it yet? Planning on community college when you graduate?"

"I wrote it, but Fielding wouldn't accept it."

"How come?"

"It's a little . . . eccentric."

"Can I read it?"

"No."

"Is this it here? 'Language, Poetry and Narrative Trope in *Operator's Manual for Rifle*,' etcetera? Jesus, talk about freaks. Too late, I'm reading it."

Wes could have argued with her, but what was the point? He moved over to the window and leaned against the sash, keeping one eye out for the oriole. He felt tired and depressed after seeing his mother, and then finding himself talking freely about her illness with someone who was practically a stranger, when he'd always done such a good job of keeping family matters private, even with close friends. How had she managed to get so much out of him? Was it always this way, that when you had sex with someone it weakened your resolve in every other particular? Was it a physiological trigger, like the release of some sort of hormone into the blood system? Wes hated the word "vulnerable"—as in, "it's okay to be "vulnerable"—and he hated the idea of being "vulnerable," mostly because it seemed so perfectly suited to every aspect of his being, and also because it was bandied about so freely by people who had no clue. It made him squeamish to imagine anyone lumping him into such a degraded category—like calling *The Master and Margarita* a clever book. But there was no doubt about it—Lucy was behaving as if she were his girlfriend, with certain rights to

his privacy, and he seemed to have ceded those rights to her
without a fight. He never let anyone read his papers except the
assigning teacher, but there she was curled up in his bed. It
seemed to Wes that he had exchanged more emotional intimacies with Lucy in the past twelve hours than he had with Delia
in the past twelve months. It didn't seem right, somehow; a little too easy, somehow. What was he supposed to do—just
throw all that hard work out the window? He tried to imagine
the situation if it were Delia on the bed instead of Lucy—but
then, Delia never would be on the bed reading his paper
because she was not the type to just come around and flop on
people's beds and invade their personal space. Delia was dignified and aloof and cerebral, everything that Lucy was not,
which was everything he loved about her. And now that he
thought about it, Lucy had been that way with him from the
very first last night, lulling him with her open, uninhibited
manner into all sorts of personal revelations. Wes couldn't
remember everything they had talked about as they wandered
the apartment together, especially after his third Bloody Mary.
There was a kind of broad outline of the topics they had
touched on—parents, school, the election, his Nantucket bay
scallop risotto, of course; nothing too close to the borderline of
taboo—but very few details remained. More precisely, Wes was
able to recall the issues he had been trying to avoid, most particularly boyfriends, girlfriends and sex, because, even though
the entire set-up was artificial, he imagined that there must be
a right way to go about it, in which everyone, including all the
other guests at the party, played the role of people who had no
idea what the immediate future would bring. His role, he
believed, should be that of the innocent boy interested only in
the quality of mind of a girl he had met by chance. If they
talked about sex, or about the kinds of people who attracted
them, or who were attracted to them, it would feel like a
mechanical device, an ill-executed plot twist designed to move

the characters to a predestined development, whereas Wes had hoped that they would find themselves on that threshold without quite knowing how they had got there, or at least in the plausible pretence that it had come as a surprise to both of them. Wes had a very clear memory of all this fretting, which was probably why he had such trouble calling up the least detail of their conversations. One thing, certainly, was that she was not at all what he had expected, or been led to expect. She was nicer, smarter, sweeter, funnier. And he remembered, too, being struck by the irony that, even as he struggled to avoid the mildest sexual innuendo, all he could think about was that this girl, this very pretty girl fully clothed right beside him, fully intended to be lying fully naked beneath him before the end of the evening. He would try to listen to what she was saying, but then his gaze would lock on her mouth, and on the little pink tongue fluttering inside it and occasionally running along the rims of her glossy lips, and his mind would be immediately buffeted by stormy images of that tongue inside his own mouth and all the points at which their bodies would need to be in close contact in order for that to come about. Or he would be making a heroic effort to admire her hair as a Renaissance poet might, with the transcendent view to a delicate metaphor, when his eyes would stray to her ears, and then he was lost in an imaginary exchange in which he asked her, in all innocence, what perfume she was wearing, and she would tilt her head to the side and pull her hair back and invite him to sample it, and then suddenly they would find themselves naked with her ankles locked around the small of his back and his lips tenderly kissing the soft skin of her neck. And yet, she had behaved with such consistent modesty and passivity all evening that it was almost as if she'd been taken in by her own act. A good part of Wes's jitters was frustrated curiosity; he'd expected her to be far more direct and aggressive. Trying to read her game plan was like enjoying a well-written thriller in which the murder is announced on the first page and the mystery involves not the outcome but the process. You already know how it's all going to end, you just don't know how you're going to get there. Lucy was a very convincing ingénue, but of course Wes was not a big reader of murder mysteries.

Eventually, having roamed the entire apartment except for Lucy's bedroom, they'd ended up back in the bathroom doorway, facing each other cross-legged on the floor, each with a full drink in hand. At some point, Wes noticed that he'd completely forgotten that Delia was still at the party and waiting for him; a few minutes later, he had realized that it really didn't bother him one way or another. And then, odder still, it occurred to him that it had been some time, perhaps a whole Bloody Mary earlier, since he'd stopped picturing Lucy naked and had started really listening to what she was saying, mostly because she seemed interested only in asking him about himself. Wes was only seventeen, but it had been a very long time since anyone had asked him what he wanted to be when he grew up.

"What do you want to be when you grow up?"

Wes didn't even have to think about his answer, because he had rehearsed it in his mind on many occasions, although in this fantasy it had always been Delia who would be asking, in just the same benevolent earnest in which Lucy had spoken, and with just the same clear-eyed fascination in her eyes.

"A good person."

"Why wait? Can't you be a good person now?"

"I've been trying, but I'm not very good at it yet."

"What's holding you back?"

"I seem to be paralyzed by the challenge of doing the right thing. It's not like it's straightforward, the way you might think. There seems to be a trick to it, like a trick of the mind, or a trick of perspective, or something. It's like trying to look at something through a whole set of reflecting mirrors. You think you've identified it, but when you reach for it it's not there, it's just a reflection."

"What's the problem? It's not that hard being nice."

"But there you see, being nice isn't the same thing as being good. Anybody can be nice. My problem is figuring out how to do the right thing, the one right thing."

"Maybe there is no one right thing."

"Maybe. But you still have to try. At least I do. You know what it's like? You know when you're writing a paper, and you run it through the spell-checker? You'd think, right, that you'd catch every typo? But you don't, there's always typos left, because sometimes when you misspell a word it becomes another word, and the spell-checker misses it. A mistake like that is a lot harder to detect. There's nothing wrong with the new word, except that it's in the wrong place. It's out of context. That's me. There's nothing wrong with me, at least I don't think there is, but even so I appear to be some sort of a mistake. I don't fit in with the rest of the sentence, with the way everyone around me seems to think, or live their lives. Whatever it is that makes me out of place may be a tiny thing, one little letter transposed, but it makes all the difference. Maybe I'm not even a spelling mistake, just the product of poor punctuation. I'm a question mark at the end of a declarative sentence. From now on, you should tell everybody that my new nickname is 'Typo.' Call me Typo."

His monologue had left Wes feeling maudlin and exhausted, as if he had called his new status into being just by naming it. He also knew that uninhibited expressions of self-pity were no way into a girl's heart, let alone her bed, which only compounded the gloom and colored the silence that suddenly seemed to envelop the two of them. Lucy put her drink down onto the carpet beside her and stared at him from under shadowed lids, her face bathed in a wash of ethereal blue from the night-light in the bathroom. Then she pushed herself onto her hands and knees and leaned in towards him.

"You are so adorable, Wes," she said.

"My name is Typo."

Then she kissed him, and it was really, really nice.

"Hey, where are you?" Lucy was standing right beside him in the window. "You were, like, a million miles away."

"What did you think of the paper?"

"Honestly? I thought it was brilliant. Like, you-could-get-it-published brilliant. Way too good for high school." She put her hand on his forearm.

"You know, you're not my girlfriend. I mean, just because of last night, you're not my girlfriend or anything."

Lucy stepped back, her hands out in front of her like a crossing guard, and Wes could actually see the color drain from her face.

"Whoa! Where's this coming from?"

"Isn't that why you came here, all part of your plan? To claim me?"

Lucy collapsed on the bed, her face in her hands. She took two or three deep breaths. "Oh you're a mean one," she said softly, and Wes knew instantly, beyond any doubt or rational calculus, that he had got it all wrong, and that it was too late to take it back. His heart started racing and the skin on his face felt all prickly, and he strode over to his desk and began leafing through his papers because he hadn't the slightest idea what to say or do next. He felt as if he were in a dream, the kind of dream where you suddenly remember that you did something horrible years earlier that you'd completely forgotten about until that very moment, like killing one of your parents and burying them under the floorboards. He heard Lucy rise from the bed and cross the room slowly, and waited for the sound of the opening door. But then he felt her hand in his, and he turned and she was right in front of him, not even crying, but her eyes were all crinkled up as if she were trying to see him through a dense fog.

"Let me ask you something Wes."

Wes nodded.

"Would you describe yourself as 'bookish'?"

"'Bookish?'"

"I mean, you seem to have a lot of these preconceived notions about people, like you don't know how real people think, like everything you've ever learned is from books. Bookish."

"I guess. Maybe. I don't know."

"I told you last night, don't you remember? Don't you remember anything about last night?"

Wes shrugged, too traumatized to dare to try to speak.

"I had a really fun time last night, Wes. You were super cool. And yes, I thought it would be nice to come over and talk about it with you. But the real reason I came over here was to tell you something else, something really simple that I thought maybe I could just kind of slip in to the casual conversation. And that thing is, if you ever, ever want that to happen again you've got to bring condoms."

"Condoms?"

"Protection. I mean, I think it'll be fine, but never again."

"I thought . . . I figured . . . "

"I know what you figured. But I wasn't planning on losing my virginity last night either."

"*Your* virginity?"

The door opened, and Wes's father was standing in the doorway.

"Dad, for fuck's sake, don't you . . . ?"

"You forget something, Wesbo?"

"Dad! I'm . . . "

"You forget someone? Like your sister, maybe? Who just called me in tears from the movie theater?"

"Shit!"

"Shit is right."

"Hang on, I'll go right now."

"Never mind, I'm on it. I can see you're busy. But don't let it happen again, man." And his father was gone.

Lucy was standing by the window, looking out. Wes wondered what he should do. If it were a book, or even a movie, he would probably walk up behind her, put his arms around her and whisper "I'm sorry" in her ear. Is that what she would expect him to do, or like him to do? On the surface, it seemed like it would be the right thing to do: a sincere apology, a token of atonement, an invitation to emotional intimacy—an unbroken series of successful gestures. But the more he considered it, and the longer the silence between them was extended, the less appropriate, the less adequate, the gesture seemed to be. He was sorry, that much would be true and he believed Lucy would know that, probably without his having to say it, but because he was sorry for too many things, also things that had nothing to do with Lucy, apologizing to her would be sort of meaningless and the easy way out, putting all those problems in one box and labeling it the "Wes is a jerk" problem. It would be a kind of lie, too, because she wouldn't know what he was really apologizing about, and he didn't want his very next words to her to be a lie. And he didn't want her to be in any box with other problems that didn't have anything to do with her. She should be in a box all her own and remain the Lucy problem. Wes could deal with that problem, and he thought he might even be able to solve it.

"I like Elliot Smith, too. I also listen to Elliot Smith."

Lucy was silent for a moment before answering. "That's good. I like Elliot Smith. No secrets."

"And Lou Reed."

"That's good too."

"I didn't know you were a virgin. I'm sorry."

"You're sorry I was a virgin, or you're sorry you took it for granted that I wasn't?"

"I was one too. I didn't think."

"See, I knew that about you. The whole school knew it about you. Funny though—nobody's gonna be high-fiving me come Monday morning."

"Oh."

"I'm probably going to leave now. That would be the smart thing to do, don't you think?"

"Can you stay a little longer?"

"What, so you can find a thousand different ways to say you're sorry? Listen, Leslie, Wesley, Wesbo, Lczbo—I know you're sorry. I mean, look at you, you look like a puppy that somebody beat with a stick. It's okay, I know you're sorry. But I'd really like to hear you say something smart for a change, and I don't think that's gonna happen here right now. Why don't you think, I mean really think about what you want to say to me the next time we see each other, and make it count? Wouldn't that be better?"

"Maybe it would. Can I see you tomorrow?"

"Too soon. Anyways, I'm canvassing for Obama in Pennsylvania tomorrow."

"I could come with you."

"You've got a paper to write, remember? See, being a grown-up is all about priorities, Typo. It's all about deciding what's important to you, because it can't all be. You can't be a perfect person and a grown-up at the same time."

"What do you know about it? You're sixteen years old."

"I was raised by grown-ups. I know more about grown-ups than I ever wanted to know."

Wes's phone rang in his pocket, and he let it ring. Lucy came up to him, put one hand on his shoulder, rose up on her tiptoes and gave him a kiss on the cheek before she slipped out the door, and with the touch of her lips on his skin he felt something give way inside him, though he knew even as he felt it that he was too stupid to know what it was. And yet, the funny thing was that it didn't make him feel sad at all; in fact, the realization that he was too stupid to understand himself made him feel positively elated, the way he'd felt when Lucy had made fun of him. It was as if a great burden had been lifted off his shoulders—not the burden of struggle, but the burden of responsibility. It was as if someone had come along and anointed him, saying "This is too much for you. Shed this heavy burden, Wes, and begin to live," or something corny like that. Better, it was as if he were a Librarian of Babel who, after a lifetime's work, had finally found the exit. Wes thought for a moment that this must be what being in love felt like, but then he remembered that he had been in love and that it didn't feel anything like this at all. And then Wes remembered his dream of the godlike calf—*this* was exactly what it had felt like in the dream when he'd understood that he was in heaven and that he'd never have to do anything again for all eternity but brush the calf. And although she was not his girlfriend, he had Lucy to thank for this feeling, Lucy whom he'd kissed and kissed the night before.

They had necked seriously and tenderly for a long while, then Lucy had stood up and gone into the bathroom. Wes had risen to follow her, but she gently closed the door in his face. "I need to pee really badly." For some reason that he could no longer remember—the three industrial-power drinks inside him had something to do with it—Wes had wandered off. He had no idea what time it was, or what was happening in the rest of the apartment, and was surprised and a little irritated to find that the party was still going on full swing in the living room, although the lights were off and the music had been lowered and changed to slow dance numbers. A few couples bumbled around in tight clinches, and several more were closely entwined with each other on the sofas and behind the curtains. The place stank of cigarette smoke and sweat. A little wobbly on his legs, Wes leaned against the doorjamb and peered into the gloom, not quite sure what had brought him there except the vague need to clear his head or maybe to get another drink, and then his eyes fell on Delia, sitting by herself in the corner of a white couch, in the other corner of which some kid was all over some chick with his hand up her green polo shirt. It was so horrible to see Delia there like that—Delia, the most confident and self-possessed girl on the Upper East Side—that Wes felt that he should probably move away under cover of darkness, except that she was staring directly at him with an unreadable expression on her face. It was like finding yourself being watched by a ghost, or a cop. Wes raised his hand in an ambiguous gesture that, he understood even as he was doing it, could be interpreted either as a greeting or as a signal to cease and desist. Delia nodded solemnly, which Wes took as an invitation to join her, and one that was perfectly impossible to refuse.

"Hey. You're still here. What time is it?"

Delia shrugged indifferently, but shifted her weight in such a way as to make it clear that she expected Wes to sit close beside her. When he did, he felt the heat and even the imprint of her buttocks on the cushion beneath him. Wes left a slim gap between them, but Delia immediately pushed her left thigh against his right and reached across his lap for his hand, which she held in both of hers with a kind of peremptory, proprietary authority as they rubbed shoulders. The smell of her shampoo was still strong, but somehow cloying now instead of intoxicating. Wes turned his face away, moved and embarrassed by his own sense of shame and betrayal.

"I feel like you've been avoiding me."

"What? No, not at all. I just got, you know, caught up. Actually, I've been looking for you, now that you mention it."

"You know, Wes, I came to this party to hang out with you."

"You did?"

"It's not like there's anybody else interesting here, is it?"

"Guess not."

"I only agreed to come because I thought Jillian would be here."

"Who's Jillian?"

"Lucy's sister. I knew her at Dalton before she went to college. Then when she called to say she couldn't make it, it was too late to back out. I didn't want to hurt Lucy's feelings. So I asked her to invite you."

"No, that was James."

"That was me. You're here because of me. You were always here because of me."

At that moment, the phone in Wes's back pocket chimed a text message, and Wes, only too glad for the distraction, retrieved it with a trembling hand.

"want 2 dance?"

Even as he read it, Wes raised his eyes to see if Delia had noticed, and found himself looking straight at Lucy, who stood in precisely the same spot in the doorway where he had been standing only a minute earlier, leaning against the jamb with Blackberry in hand, smiling warmly and wiggling the fingers of her free hand in invitation. In a panic, Wes tried to click himself out of the text application, but managed instead to swipe the keyboard with his thumb and send a reply, signaled by an identical chime. Lucy looked down at her phone and frowned, then back at Wes with a quizzical, wounded tilt of the head. Wes had absolutely no idea what he must look like to Lucy at that moment, with Delia maintaining a firm grip on his left hand, their bodies pressed together from shin to shoulder. It can't have been encouraging, but Wes felt himself powerless to rise and follow as she slipped away into the darkness of the hallway. Delia nudged his shoulder.

"Where are you?"

"Sorry. What was it?"

"What was what?"

"What were you saying?"

"Jesus, Wes, what's the matter with you tonight? Can you focus, please? I'm trying to tell you something important."

"Right, sorry. You know what, though? It's so hot in here and I'm really, really thirsty. Can you just hold it for one second and I'll be right back, I promise. You want anything?"

"No, I don't want anything. But come right back, please."

Lucy was not in the kitchen, and she was not waiting for him by the bathroom. He thought she might be in her parents' room, where she had taken him earlier to heap scorn on her mother's collection of designer shoes and handbags in the walk-in closet, but the lights were out and there was a rumble of perfunctory grunting from the direction of the bed in there. There were a number of closed doors down a secondary hallway, but Wes did not feel emboldened or entitled to try his luck. Finally, his head spinning, he paused for breath in the dark, the sounds of the party a distant murmur, like a memory perched just over the borderline of awareness. Wes had no idea what he was doing. He tried to identify the remains of any rational thought to cling to, but all he could find were random snippets. When Delia had asked "Where are you?" he had, for the briefest instant, interpreted the question as literal, and even then he had been at a loss to answer it. Now, with the words echoing in what felt like a vast, empty chamber, all he could think of was Dorothy looking into the crystal ball. I'm here in Oz and I'm trying to get back home! But the crystal ball was his mind, all its infinite number of rooms now howling with wind-swept vapors and half-glimpsed visions—Elvira Gulch, Delia, Natasha, Lucy, Sonia, Prince André, Nora, Pierre, myriad pages torn from myriad books from all the world's libraries or one great universal library, all tossed and turned on the storm with nothing to grab on to. "Where are you?" had no meaning in a place like that, no meaning at all for a person like Wes, if there even were such a person. But even putting it that way had an immediate calming effect on Wes, because if there were no such person as Wes there was no need to get exercised over his struggles and travails. It could be like suddenly realizing that you were in the middle of a dream, it was all nothing but a dream. This had never actually happened to Wes in real life, but he could sense how liberating it might be in the face of a disaster or an impossible task, a plane crash or stealing a witch's broomstick. Say this were a dream, this standing in a darkened hallway with your heart pounding, your hair reeking of second-hand smoke, flying monkeys around every corner, and an iPhone suddenly materializes in your hand, its many-colored screen pulsing like a heart, like a soul, like your own soul in the night. You need not even be in your own dream. You could be a mysterious figure, unknown even to yourself, in the dream of a character in a novel that has not yet been written. Where are you now? Wes raised the device to his chest and began to type.

Yellow: "Where r u?"

White: "bdrm"

Yellow: "Too many. Which?"

White: "find me"

Wes had found Lucy, in a room dark like the rest, with just a slash of light from the half-open door of an en-suite bathroom. A pink toothbrush and a tube of toothpaste stood in a white shaving mug on the rim of the sink, beside a disk of pink soap. Everything else was in blackness.

"Lucy?"

"Typo?"

Wes turned towards the sound of Lucy's voice, and as his eyes adjusted he was just able to pick out her silhouette, sitting upright with crossed legs against the headboard of a twin bed. He crossed the room, aware of thick pile carpeting beneath his feet that absorbed all sound, and sat at the foot of the bed, straddling the corner.

"What's 'bnkdl'?"

"Bnkdl?"

"I said 'want 2 dance' and you said 'bnkdl.' I thought maybe it was some sort of code. Or maybe a joke, 'cause you were talking about typos before. Or maybe, just, you know, 'go away.'"

"It wasn't any of that. It was just a mistake. I didn't even mean to send it."

"It's okay. It was just a little confusing, you know, when I saw you sitting like that, after we . . . "

"I know, I'm really sorry. Delia's just having a hard time. She'll get over it."

Lucy sat there, unmoving, at the far end of the bed. Wes didn't know what to do. This here, now, was precisely the moment he had been imagining, and trying not to imagine, all day long, but now that it was happening he thought that maybe what he liked better was when they were kissing in the hallway. It had been so simple, and her neck had smelled not of perfume but of some simple, fresh-scented soap, as if she alone of everyone at the party had not been steeped in a smog of tobacco and alcohol fumes. Somehow, her simply being fresh and clean had made her seem even younger than she was, and Wes had not been able to help himself—even as they were kissing and he felt her cool hand on the back of his neck, he had opened his eyes and seen her as Natasha, with her tank-top and jeans transformed into some vast crinoline ball gown and a black velvet choker around her throat, layer upon layer of fabric concealing and guarding her nudity. And because she was Natasha, he was Prince André, a fallen, middle-aged creep who lusted after teenage girls, and suddenly he had lost all desire to go any further. It wasn't that he was not aroused, but she was clearly not the voracious carnivore of his fantasies, so his fantasies changed to accommodate her. He wanted to protect her, and kissing her in the dark seemed like the best way to do that. All the lurid imagery of the day had evaporated in the puff of sweet warm breath from her nostrils on his cheek. And now that he was here in her room, all he wanted was for her to invite him to kiss her again. It made Wes wish he was twelve again, and that he didn't know everything he knew.

"Can I ask you something, Lucy?"

"Okay?"

"Why did you invite me to your party? I mean, we didn't even know each other."

"I didn't invite you."

"You didn't?"

"You're a gatecrasher, buddy."

"I'm a gatecrasher? But James said you . . . "

"So is James a gatecrasher. I mean, I don't care. You're welcome and all. I mean, obviously I'm glad you're here and everything. But I didn't invite any of you. I only invited my friends."

"What about Delia?"

"She's a friend of my sister. I have no idea what she's doing here."

"Huh."

"But since you're already here, I suppose you might as well stay."

Wes had stayed, only to wake up in an existential panic at four in the morning and walk home crying in the dark.

Wes stretched himself out on his bed with the song of the oriole in his ear. To Wes, that song had always sounded like an elaborate question spoken in a very terse language, and it did so now, except that he had no interest in trying to answer it because it clearly wasn't intended for him. Rather, he intended for the first time that day to luxuriate in the memories of last night's adventure that he had been so assiduously avoiding all day, but he fell into a deep sleep instead, dramatically dream-free, from which he awoke only because the phone had some-how worked its way up the bedsheets and was ringing almost directly into his ear. Just to shut it up, he grabbed the phone and answered.

"Yeah what?"

"Wezbo, it's James."

"Okay."

"Listen, I've got something to tell you, I'm not sure how you're gonna take it."

"So?"

"So I just got off the phone with Jillian. She was really . . . "

"Who's Jillian?"

"Your new sister-in-law, only."

"What the fuck?"

"She's Lucy's sister. Lucy's older sister."

"Go on."

"Well Jillian's really good friends with Delia, and she told me that Delia's really pissed at you."

"Oh yeah?"

"Well, see, it turns out that Delia had dibs on you last night."

"*Dibs?*"

"Well, see, it turns out that Delia had something planned to happen between you and her last night, and that's why she asked Jillian to ask Lucy to invite you."

"I thought Lucy asked you to invite me."

"Well, I kind of made that up. I just wanted to get you away from Delia. I figured if you thought it was going to happen you'd make it happen, and you did. How was I to know Delia was plan-ning to jump your bones? I mean, she waits a whole year, and then that's the night she chooses? So anyway, she's mad as fuck that you ditched her. I thought you'd want to know that."

"Thanks, fuckhead. Except you just happen to have got it all ass-backwards, as usual. See, Lucy told me that nobody invited us. She said you and me were gatecrashing, so Delia never could have asked Jillian to ask Lucy to ask me."

"And you believe Lucy?"

"Why shouldn't I?"

"'Cause how else would Jillian know you went to the party? Why else would she call me? She must've spoken to Lucy, right?"

"So you think Lucy knew why Delia was at the party?"

"Maybe. I think so."

"And you think Delia knows I slept with Lucy?"

"Maybe. Delia's pretty tight with Jillian."

"All right. All right. I'm gonna hang up now. I've got to think this through."

"Listen, Wezbo, I . . . " But Wes had already disconnected.

Wes lay there, not moving; even shifting an inch in any direction, even breathing too hard, could crack a bone or rupture some internal organ. Thinking, too, was a delicate endeavor; in circumstances like these, an uncontrolled attack of deep thinking could well prove fatal. Simple, baby steps were in order, the kind that could inch him away from the precipice without disturbing the frangible ground beneath him. If this were a book—but there was no such book, at least none that came to mind, unless maybe *Les Liaisons dangereuses*, but Wes could no more recall the plot, or which characters were the villains and which the dupes, than he could make sense of whether Lucy had lied to him, or of what part he himself had played in the deception, or even if any of that mattered anymore. There must be somewhere such a book, the book with the story that had just unfolded, or the book with a stupid boy like him, just like him—a book that disintegrates at the very instant you become aware of it. That was Wes—a boy who vanishes the moment you look at him. And even as this thought occurred to him, he realized that it was not true, because there was a book, and it was sitting on his desk. He rose to retrieve it, then returned to his bed and began to read intently, flipping randomly through the pages.

"By order of the Secretary of the Army: CARL E. VUONO, General, United States Army Chief of Staff."

"Page 2-7. Change the fourth sentence from 'Release the trigger.' to 'Slowly release the trigger.' Add the following NOTE: For the purpose of this test, 'SLOW' is defined as 1/4 to 1/2 the normal ratio of trigger release."

*"**Warning**: With the bolt carrier assembly locked to the rear or in its forward position, if the weapon is dropped or jarred with a loaded magazine in place, it could chamber a round."*

"Do not expose ammunition to the direct rays of the sun. If the powder is hot, excessive pressure may develop when the rifle is fired."

"The radioactive material used in these instruments is tritium gas (H-3) sealed in pyrex tubes. It poses no significant hazard to the repairman when intact."

"If there's water in the barrel, don't fire the rifle. It could explode."

"Squeeze the trigger and fire."

"Hot, dry climates are usually dusty and sandy areas. They are hot during daylight hours and cool during the night hours."

"If your rifle needs improvement, let us know. Send us an EIR. You, the user, are the only one who can tell us what you don't like about your equipment. Put it on an SF 368 (Quality

Deficiency Report). Mail it to us at Commander, US Army Armament, Munitions and Communications Command, ATTN: AMSMC-QAD, Rock Island, IL 61299-6000. We'll send you a reply."

Wes wondered if the address were still active, and then he began to cry, and at that moment Nora entered the room.

"Oh Jesus not again," she said in Bobby's voice, and sat herself down on the edge of the bed besides Wes, who rolled onto his side facing the wall. Wes was immediately mindful of the need to control himself in Nora's presence, but her hand on his shoulder only made it harder. At least he was good at crying without blubbering or heaving; he didn't even sniffle, though that would have to happen eventually. He decided it would be best if he didn't say anything for the moment; instead he emitted a low, croaking groan, as if Nora could be convinced that he was both suffering some sort of gastric event and that he was enduring it stoically. It was at such moments, Wes recalled, that the Buddhist visualization techniques that Delia had attempted to teach him came in most handy, and he closed his eyes and tried to recreate in his mind's eye the calf-brushing scene from his dream. He felt it wavering into coherence; he saw the calf, and his own hand on the calf's shoulder, clasping the toothbrush, and the toppling verdant landscape; but he felt nothing, and he realized that the singular critical element of the dream—its sense of endless, unfettered serenity—was entirely absent from his visualization, and that without it the calf was just a dumb animal, the poor suffering mute that had exploded in outer space to provide him with its sweetbreads. But now a different vision emerged, more promising, and he followed it with interest and nascent detachment.

"What's Leslie thinking?" Bobby asked.

"I'm thinking about a river in a book I read once."

"Fascinating."

"In this book, a woman is chosen to be the devil's consort at his annual ball. She's given a magic cream that makes her invisible, and a broom that flies her half way across Russia. She flies high above the silent forests and grassy plains. And finally, the broom slows down and leaves her on the edge of a bluff over a black river somewhere in the middle of nowhere. On the other side there's an encampment of frogs playing flutes and drums. And she dives off the bluff into the river, and the spray leaps into the sky and sparkles in the moonlight. For some reason I always remember that—the water flying up and glowing in the moonlight, and swimming naked in the black river in the wilderness in the middle of the night. Just imagine that—all alone in a cool river in the middle of the nowhere under a full moon, and feeling completely safe and happy."

Nora was quiet, and Wes could feel her behind him visualizing the scene of Margarita in the river and creating all her own details, because that was the way her mind worked. One day, he hoped, she would read that book and love it as much as he did and it would be one more thing they had in common; but then again, Nora wasn't bookish.

"How many fingers does a frog have?"

"I don't know."

"I don't think a frog can play the flute, because of the webs."

"They're magic frogs."

"Okay."

"I'm just going to lie here for a while until I feel better?"

"You want Bobby to sit with you?"

"That's alright. I'll be down in a few minutes."

"Okay."

"How was the movie?"

"Bullshit."

"Sorry for forgetting about you."

"Jive turkey."

"What time is it?"

"I don't know. Six? Six thirty?"

"I'll get dinner started soon. Want to help?"

"Groovy."

When Nora had left, Wes didn't move. Not moving definitely seemed the right way to proceed. He tried to recapture the vision of the placid midnight river, but now all that came to mind was the scene from his dream in the Rose Reading Room where the jet liner banked over Bryant Park as it screamed towards the library windows. Wes had no interest in the occult, but he was beginning to see the dream, with its series of cascading enigmas, as a premonition of disaster. The question was— was his current situation the disaster it predicted, or was there worse to come? It didn't bear contemplating.

Something else was wrong, too, but it lingered just beyond Wes's peripheral understanding. He lay there and listened to hear if it would pipe up, like an unseen bird calling from the upper branches of a tree, so that he might at least focus his attention in the right general direction. It was silent; in fact, all the sounds of the world had gone oddly muted, or muffled, as if a great wet sheet had been draped over the city, and Wes opened his eyes and saw that the sun had set, somehow, and he was lying in darkness. When had it happened? Had he slept without realizing? Had it already been dark when James had called, when Nora had stopped in? Wes listened: a truck ground its gears on Hudson Street; two drivers angrily exchanged horn-fire; a pair of stilettos made its way uncertainly up Perry, stopped for a few moments as if they were aware of being listened to, then continued on their way. They sounded as if they were alone, but of course there was no way to tell; a pair of soft-soled shoes could just as well have been walking beside them, exchanging intimacies, but there was nothing in the pace or rhythm of the footfall that indicated such a companion. That, of course, was the problem with listening to footsteps in the night—for some reason, they always sounded lonely, no matter the reality. It was almost as if you wanted them to be lonely, because there was something sympathetic to the heartbeat in the sound of lonely steps echoing on a quiet cobblestoned street, the heart just sort of fell into step naturally beside them. The phone rang, lost somewhere in the tangled sheets, but Wes did not bother to look for it. The ringtone, mimicking the metallic bell that dial telephones had had before Wes was born, was oddly consonant with the disembodied message of loneliness sent by the stilettos. Wes could imagine the wearer of those stilettos pausing in the street to the distant sound of an unanswered telephone. She would stop just as she had done, look around in confusion, and wonder why she felt as if she were being watched; then she would shake her head—it was just an illusion, a trick of the lamplight through the breeze-laden branches—and be on her way. Wes wondered what the chances were that Lucy was feeling that way at this very moment, if perhaps the image of the woman in stilettos was a message that she had sent him telepathically, like the message of love that the alien Mrs. Fielding had sent him in room 405; although Lucy seemed the more practical sort, it might have been an inadvertent message, like the kind Obi-Wan Kenobi received upon the destruction of Alderaan. Wes felt as if he knew precisely what it would be like to hear a million voices cry out and suddenly be silenced—it seemed as if it happened to him a dozen times a day.

He sighed and sat up, feeling the iPhone slip and bump against his thigh. He reached for it and activated the screen. It was 6.47 P.M. on November 1 2008. There was one missed call, no message. The missed call was from Lucy, but Wes could face no further news, good or bad. He felt like André on his death bed, sickened by the prospect of another course of legless optimism. In a situation such as that in which he now found himself, the only possible course of action was one of blind duty. There were sweetbreads to be made, a mother to feed.

On his way downstairs, Wes pressed his ear against his mother's bedroom door and, detecting the sedate drone of a news broadcast, peeked in. She turned towards him with a crooked smile and the blank, open gaze of one who could not recognize an intruder at fifteen feet. Wes crossed the room and sat himself gently on the bed alongside her; she patted the back of his hand and returned her attention to the television.

"Can I get you anything, mom?"

"I am hungry."

"I'm just getting dinner started. You want something to drink?"

"Just some pudding, Leslie honey."

"No pudding tonight, mom. I'm making a real dinner.

"What are you making?"

"Mom! I'm making sweetbreads?"

She turned to him with a look of astonished horror, made all the more grotesque by the lazy eye that seemed to focus on something beyond Wes' left shoulder. She gagged and cleared her throat of her first attempt to speak, but managed on the second to emit a kind of croaky, froggy gasp. "Sweetbreads? Whatever for are you making sweetbreads?"

"Whatever for am I . . . ? Mom, you asked me to make sweetbreads, remember? Paris? Handbag?"

"I don't know what you're talking about, Leslie. I hate sweetbreads. I would never have asked you to make sweetbreads."

"You've never eaten sweetbreads, so how would you know if you like them or not?"

"I certainly have eaten sweetbreads. I ate sweetbreads on my honeymoon, as it so happens. Do I have to tell you I don't like them, goddamnit?"

Defeated, Wes hung his head as he held on to his mother's hand, cool and pulpy and inert. Outside, he knew, beyond the heavy curtains and sealed windows, the evening, too, was soft and cool, maybe fragrant as the dawn had been with a breeze that had flowed across the autumnal woods of the Catskills, the Berkshires, the Hudson valley, and further north the vast whispering darkness of the Adirondacks, dappled with deep, cold, slumbering lakes and ponds. And above it all a silver moon, waxing gibbous, under which to swim—to swim ever so gently, without a sound, without breaking the surface, to the center of a lake, and there to roll onto his back and float, and there to invite this breeze to wash this taste of clinging decay from the inside of his mouth and lungs. Wes closed his eyes and felt it penetrate, purest water, purest sky, for the briefest moment the impossible, dreamlike state of non-longing that had enveloped him as he draped himself across the calf's neck. No people, no phones, no books, no disease, no roads, no lyrics, no sex, no sensation but eternal, ineluctable cleanliness. Wes felt himself overcome by an almost messianic sense of kinship and sorrow for the tragic fate of Bob Ross, who had also yearned for impossible purity and had been condemned to spend countless hours and decades under hot studio lights, groping clumsily to communicate his vision to a congregation of the insensible blind. Wes opened his eyes to find that his mother's attention had wandered back to the television.

"If you don't like your dinner, I'll bring you some pudding. How's that, mom?"

"That sounds just fine, Leslie honey."

In the kitchen, as he began to assemble the ingredients for the sweetbread dish, Wes realized that for the past few seconds or minutes—he wasn't sure which—a phrase had been revolving around and around in his head. "What is the meaning of *anything*?" With the stress on "anything," it sounded as if it was the answer to a question, as if someone had asked him "What is the meaning of 'circumnavigate?'" or "What is the meaning of all this?" It kept repeating itself, meaninglessly, with that deeply irritating and equally meaningless emphasis on the last word, without any apparent expectation of being answered. In Wes's experience, when a phrase got stuck in his head this way, it was because it was the lyric of a song or a snippet of a conversation overheard without necessarily having been noticed, but in this case that was not possible, as no music was playing and there had been no conversation to overhear but his own with his mother, in the course of which nothing even vaguely resembling the phrase "What is the meaning of *anything*?" had been uttered. Where, then, had it come from, and what was he supposed to make of it? Wes could only suppose it was a message from his own subconscious, sent from some subterranean communications command post to alert his conscious self to a compelling task of analysis, but the phrase was so vague and portentous that one could only laugh at it. Who could ever answer such a question? It's hard enough identifying the meaning of something.

With all of the ingredients assembled on the counter before him, Wes found that he'd forgotten to provide for a starch. Noodles or polenta or rice would do just fine, but a cursory exploration of the overhead cupboards revealed none of these. The only plausible option available, short of another trip to the store, was a box of freeze-dried potato flakes and a quarter pound of sweet gorgonzola, which Wes' father liked to eat for breakfast with a glass of dry vermouth. Wes hoped that the blue cheese crumbled into the instant mash potatoes could, in theory, work as a credible substitute for risotto. He thought of Bobby and his love of all pungent cheeses, and that reminded him that he had promised Nora that she could participate in the preparation of dinner. He found her in the back yard, sitting under the light of a single flood with their father, bent over a Mastermind board perched on an upended cable-drum between them. Crispy sprawled on the cracked bluestone, panting.

"This dog get walked?"

"Sit down and shut up, daddy-o."

Wes found a chair and sat, facing the back of the yard. The sky was quite dark now, a deep purple, but under the sycamore very little of it was visible. The oriole had fallen silent. Wes felt a kind of serenity descend upon him, not a pleasant serenity like that of his dream but a contingent resignation. He looked at his dad, his face cramped in concentration over the Mastermind board. It occurred to him that his father's only winning quality was his willingness to continue playing against Nora, who never lost. It does not take many qualities—patience, consistency, fairness, one or two others maybe—to allow a son to worship his father, and the time when Wes had worshipped him seemed both impossibly recent and irretrievably lost. Wes could still remember himself at that age, the issues that had obsessed or preoccupied him, the way he had thought and felt, the hungry boy's self-serving contortions of logic. The terrible thing about losing faith in one's father is not watching him change and falter, Wes considered, but watching oneself grow into stronger understanding, an understanding that gradually but inexorably reveals that the father has not changed at all but has always been like this, even in those days when it had seemed that he was perfect in every way. Wes could still recall a moment, back around the time of 9/11, when he had been emotionally overwhelmed in school by the feeling of how beautiful and lucky it was to be born in the United States, the greatest country in the world. The teacher must have said something inspirational, or maybe some class parent had been killed in the attack, because the entire class had erupted in enthusiastic response. Wes had felt that way about his father, too. It had been more than a mere emotion, that certainty that he was the luckiest, happiest boy in the world to have such a dad. His love for his father—his pride in having such a brilliant, handsome, funny, sophisticated, loving and universally beloved father—

had been a whole emotional republic in which he had been blessed to be born, live and cavort. And although Nora was too young to remember those happy times, she had felt the same way, Wes knew. Children know where to draw the line, but if Wes and Nora had ever dared to set the choice between mom and dad when they played the game of who would have to be killed by the kidnappers, both of them would certainly have selected their mother. It was odd, looking at his father, to think that he had been the same person then that he was now.

Wes remembered a guy he had seen in the street on his way home from school a few days earlier. He was an older guy, with thinning, graying hair and a pot belly, in a blue polyester baseball jacket with the Yankee's logo. There was a pretty-ish secretary-type woman, trim and put together, walking towards him, and when she passed the fat guy had slowed and turned to watch her go. It was only an instant, the kind you see a hundred times a day on the street, but for some reason Wes had had a flash of clear, if not exactly blinding insight. He knew with absolute certainty that, at that moment, the guy had forgotten who he was and imagined himself as he may once have been, young and hopeful with a full head of hair and a future, the kind of person who might have stood a chance with a woman like that. This vision had made Wes feel bad for the guy, at least momentarily until the next distraction came along, and he'd forgotten all about it. But now that he looked at his father it came back to him. Wes had no idea why he should have any particular insight into the souls of middle-aged men, but he did seem to. James was always telling him that he acted too much like an old guy. It was probably because he'd had a lifetime to observe someone who was a master at seeing himself as something he was not. Despite all the evidence, his father still looked in the mirror and saw his younger self, but to do it convincingly he had to lie and lie and lie to himself. And Wes suddenly felt how tired he was of all the lying; it was an exhausting, all-consuming habit with no upside of any kind. His mother had a solid chance of recovering. His father really would finish that novel one day and return his attention to those who needed him. Nora would survive, beautiful and intact, the years of neglect and self-reliance. Delia loved him, but just didn't know it yet. Wes himself was strong and dependable, the moral compass and binding agent that would hold it all together for everyone. It would be scary, vertiginous even, to let them go, all these lies, but if he didn't want to end up the kind of guy who doesn't recognize himself in the mirror, he would have to find a way to do it.

His dad looked up and they locked eyes, staring at one another in abstracted curiosity for a few moments. Wes wondered whether his father would try to smile at him. Instead, he spoke as if resuming a conversation that had been interrupted only moments earlier.

"I've come to a great breakthrough."

"Oh yeah? What's that?"

"After nearly 40 years, I've decided to forgive Paul McCartney for breaking up the Beatles."

"What's that supposed to mean?"

Wes's father returned his gaze to the board. "It was just a joke."

"Jokes are supposed to be funny."

His father frowned, apparently in response to the logical challenge of the game, but more obviously to the challenge of responding to Wes' hostility. Wes was interested in what he would say. The floodlight was not kind to his face—the pouched, rheumy eyes, the smears of gray at his temples, the lower lip that seemed to grow more pendulous and glistening with every passing day, the broken shadow of his nose across melting cheeks, the trembling dewlaps below his chin—and Wes focused on each in turn as if in critical self-examination in a mirror. Although his father was several inches shorter than him, he had resembled Wes to a marked degree when he was young, but Wes knew that he would never look like his father when he was his age because these were the effects not of age but of lack of character. Nothing is thrown away; the mind is vast, and those rooms where the deeds and feelings of the past are stored may be in distant, forgotten wings, but they are never lost or sealed. The miasma that seeps from them will ultimately infect the entire edifice, Wes believed, and in his father's face he saw it oozing from every enlarged pore and smelled it on his breath with every banal utterance.

"I'm sorry if I fail to amuse you."

"Your failure to amuse me should be the least of your concerns."

"Wes, I'm trying to play a game here. If you have something to say to me please just say it."

"That's just it. I have nothing to say to you."

His father sighed, and Nora shot Wes an anxious look, but Wes didn't care.

"Did anybody walk the dog?"

"Why don't you do it, seeing as you've got nothing better to do?"

"What the fuck? I've been shopping and cleaning and taking care of mom all day, and now I've got to make your dinner."

"I won't be joining you for dinner."

"Dad! This is supposed to be a family night. I told you."

"I know, and I'm sorry, but I already had other plans and it's too late to break them."

"Must get lonely down in that basement all by yourself."

Nora got up and disappeared into a dark corner of the yard behind the sycamore.

"Wes, why do you have to come here and ruin a perfectly pleasant evening? Nora and I were just fine here without you."

"I'm sorry, am I disturbing your leisure activities?"

"You are. Please don't pick a fight for no reason."

"I'm not picking a fight, I'm just telling you how I feel."

"And how's that working for you?"

"I feel great. I got no sleep last night, I've had a miserable day, I'm doing all the work around here, and you don't give a shit."

"I do give a shit. Tell me about your day."

"I'm not telling you about my day."

"Then why are you busting my chops? Did I ask you to come here and spew venom? Why do you have to ruin it for everyone just because you're in a filthy mood?"

"I'm not in a filthy mood. I'm just sick of taking it up the ass for the entire world."

"Is that how you really feel? That the whole world is out to get you?"

"It's not?"

"No it's not. You're smart, you're handsome, you're healthy. You live in a beautiful home in a great city, surrounded by people who love you. You're in no danger of dying of cholera or starvation or diarrhea. You're getting the best education in the world and you have an incredible future ahead of you. How many people do you think can say that? Are they all out there feeling sorry for themselves and moaning and bitching? So you've had a bad day—it won't be the last. But for christ's sake get a grip, and stop making life miserable for the very people who only want you to be happy."

Wes stood up. "Put it on a post-it, dad. You don't understand a thing."

"You've got that right. Wes, I'm really, genuinely sorry you're having a hard time. I'm right here any time you want to talk about it, but I won't be your punching bag. And by the way, it's totally unfair to your sister."

"Nora, let's go. It's time to make dinner."

There was no answer from the bottom of the yard, so Wes turned and left.

Wes was feeling much, much better by the time he reached the kitchen—better, in fact, than he had felt all day, as if he'd had a long, restorative sleep, a cold shower and a productive writing session in quick sequence. He felt just the way he usually felt right after he'd signed off on an especially incisive homework assignment. He wasn't quite sure what he had done to make himself feel this way, but it probably had something to do with mouthing off to his father, which he thought he probably ought to try more often. If this was what people called speaking truth to power, he was all in favor of it. If this was what it would be like with Barack Obama in the White House, he was all for it. He reached into his back pocket and retrieved his phone. He texted.

"Pls. join us for dinner. Extra plate of extra crispy." He placed the phone on the counter where he would be sure to hear it.

From the kitchen window he glanced down into the back yard. His father and Nora had resumed their game; even from this height Wes could see that Nora was on the threshold of victory. He turned away. All the ingredients of the most ridiculous meal in the history of the world lay spread out before him on the kitchen counter like the keys of some improbable pipe organ. Wes removed the bricks from the plate covering the sweetbread, then swiped the plate away with a flourish, like a magician pulling a top hat off a rabbit. The sweetbread looked like a car that had been run through a metal compactor, only more brainlike, all its lobes and crevices smoothed into a flat, glistening surface the color of a battleship, laced with bluish filaments. Wes consulted the cookbook, which he had left open to the relevant page on the counter, then went to work.

He put a small pot of water on to boil, then turned to peeling and mincing the garlic and shallots, which made him think of Delia because of the several times he had caught himself crying that day. He wondered if all the crying indicated that he was emotionally immature or, on the contrary, that he was more emotionally advanced than almost everyone he knew. Certainly, neither James nor any of the seventeen-year-old boys he knew wept with such regularity, if at all, and they probably did not daydream about beatific calves and remote Siberian rivers. He thought that Delia would most likely approve, because crying revealed a kind of openness to and awareness of one's feelings that were necessary precursors to developing the ability to control them. On the other hand, she would probably find a way to take credit for it, and to make Wes feel small, that he was indebted to her in some way for this superior knowledge. That was how Delia always operated with him, and with her other friends and admirers—moving about in a kind of otherworldly aura that made you want to step inside and share in her transcendence, but when you were in it you found it was more of an electromagnetic pulse that rendered you powerless and without a will of your own. And maybe she had this power over you even if you didn't like her all that much, as Wes was beginning to suspect had been the case with him. He wondered why he hadn't seen it before. Because she really was a bit cold, wasn't she, and did anybody actually enjoy being made to feel that they were being led by the nose in a game of perpetual catch-up? Then again, maybe that was what Wes was looking for without knowing it; maybe he had been drawn to her precisely because the way he behaved in her presence and under her influence seemed to confirm all the bad things he thought about himself in his darkest moments. That he was cruel, narcissistic and ultimately allowed all his weakest impulses to drive him, and that only she could guide him through the minefield of his own soul? Wes had read enough books to know that it was perfectly possible to fall in love with someone who wasn't good for you, or wasn't the kind, generous person you would want to fall in love with when you thought about the kind of person you wanted to fall in love with. Even so, Wes was deeply disturbed by the idea that love was just as likely as not to turn out to be a destructive force, when all his life he had been taught and truly believed that it was the one thing that could save them all, that could save Nora and his mother and himself. But look at Nora—wasn't she the one person in the world that Wes loved with all his heart, and didn't he treat her like shit over and over again? Did that make Nora to Wes as Wes was to Delia? Did he make Nora feel like Delia made him feel—worthless and puny, yet too weak to break away because there was no one else to turn to? This was all too complicated; it made *War and Peace* feel like *The Runaway Bunny*.

The water on the stovetop was now boiling. Wes took his large tomato, scored it with an "x" at either end with a paring knife, and dropped it in the pot. For the twenty seconds or so that he allowed it to boil, he made a conscious effort to clear his head, not to think, but even as he brought the pot over to the sink and doused it in cold running water, the lingering idea of *The Runaway Bunny* reminded him of a book his mother had read to him frequently when he was little. In this book, a mother raises her son from a baby to a grown man, each stage represented by a page or two of drawings. At every phase of his life, the son is seen doing something to drive his mother crazy, but at the end of each she is seen tucking him in and singing him a lullaby. "I'll love you forever, I'll like you for always, as long as I'm living my baby you'll be." She does this to him as an infant, a toddler, a rowdy boy, and even as a grungy, rebellious teenager, and when he grows up and moves out she sneaks across town, climbs in through his bedroom window, crawls across the floor and rocks him in her arms, singing her song. Eventually, the mother grows old and lies dying in her bed, too weak to sing, and the son completes the cycle by cradling her in his arms and singing the song back to her. Even as a very little boy, as he must have been when his own mother had read him the book, Wes had felt that there was something deeply perverse about this story, that it was somehow not meant to be a book for children at all, and the drawing of the graying mother as she crept across the moonlit carpeting of her adult son's bedroom had unsettled him in nervous premonition of imminent catastrophe. Finally, Wes's mom had intuited that the book made him uncomfortable and stopped reading it to him. Much later he had learned that the author had written the book in memory of his own two babies who had died at birth, and this new information had recalled the odd, inchoate feelings of dread that the book had evoked in him long before. Although this back story had put the book in a new light—that it had been written to keep the memory of the dead babies alive forever—he had nevertheless been unable to reconcile his sympathy for the author with his sense that there was something very wrong about the book, that it was trying to say something about love and attachment that no child should be asked to understand. And now, as he stood over the chopping block, peeled and quartered the tomato, and reached into its atria to scoop out the seed pulp with his index finger, the book's he thought that he was no closer to grasping hidden message, or his own instinctive recoiling from it, than he had been as a four-year-old. Is it love and need that drive us to act perversely and against our own interests, or is it our own flaws that lead us to seek out love without understanding anything of its nature, the way a timid mouse is drawn to the smell of ripe cheese, not knowing if it is a rare treasure or a lethal trap? Worse yet, was it possible that there was nothing wrong with the book at all, and that it was Wes himself who had interpreted it in the most sinister possible light? And if that were the case, what did it say about his ability to understand anything that had happened to him today? Why did he always seem to be chasing his own tail? And then a little light seemed to go on in Wes' mind. What was it Lucy had said? "You're never talking about what you're talking about." What if—just *what if*—he had never actually been in love with Delia at all? What if it had all been some sick neurotic daydream? Maybe it was Wes who was groveling on the carpet in the moonlight. Maybe it was Wes who was plummeting like a meteor through the window of the Rose Reading Room. The iPhone chimed. It was a text reply from Lucy.

"bobross sweetbreds u charmr? C u soon"

Wes stared at the phone. And when, after thirty seconds or so, the screen went dark, he pressed the refresh button and stared at it for another thirty seconds. U charmr. No one had ever called him a charmer before. He wasn't quite sure what it meant, or what Lucy might mean by calling him one, but it had a nice ring to it. He couldn't remember Delia ever having said something so pleasantly mysterious to him, let alone about him. Still, given what a total basket case he'd been only a few hours earlier, Wes couldn't help wondering how easy it would be to just walk away from the whole Delia project. On the one hand, who ever gives a second thought to Rosaline, Romeo's infatuation before he meets Juliet? On the other hand, Romeo gets to sleep with Juliet the day after he meets her; it might have been a totally different story if she'd kept him at arm's length for a whole friggin' year. Wes sighed; maybe he was just being too sensitive. Maybe all the ungenerous thoughts he'd been having about Delia were just the result of exhaustion. He could stay friends with her, probably, maybe; he could let her continue to instruct him in the basics of Buddhism. But of course it would never be the same, and there was something sad about that. It wasn't even that it was an entire year of his life, a beautiful dream, that he would be putting behind him. It was a whole idea of himself, about who he was and the things that had once seemed so important, that he would have to leave behind. Those visions would now be part of his past, forever. Wes thought that this must be what it feels like to leave home for college—excited, hopeful, a little scared but a little grieving. Even if he ended up regretting it—even if it somehow turned out that he had given up on the better part of himself—he could never be that person again. But of course, he already knew that. He was sorry to think that it was a lesson that would have been useful for his dad to learn, and he felt a transient pang of compassion for the old jerk.

Wes had washed and dried the mushrooms, and was preparing to chop them when he sensed Nora's presence in the doorway. He turned and smiled at her, to show her that it was safe; she smiled back hesitantly but continued to hover on the threshold.

"Know how to chop mushrooms?"

She shook her head, and he beckoned her into the room.

"I'll show you."

He stood behind her, guiding her hands with his arms about her shoulders, and showed her how to trim the stems and quarter the mushrooms. With his face above her head, he could tell that she had not washed her hair in some time; it looked oily and smelled of bitter wax. When she had the hang of it, he returned to the tomato and diced it finely, then retrieved a half-empty bottle of Vernacchia from the refrigerator, its neck sealed with a crumpled scrap of tin foil. Through the open window, he heard a group of passers-by burst into sudden laughter, and one baritone laugh lingered longer than the rest, rolling like thunder. Wes paused to listen as the group receded towards Hudson Street, then looked down at Nora and gently stopped her hand with his. Nora looked up anxiously.

"Am I doing it wrong?"

"You know what?"

"What?"

"You're the greatest. I truly adore you."

Nora blushed with pleasure, although she seemed confused at the same time.

"You do?"

"I really, really do."

Nora and Wes stared at each other for a moment or two, and then she went back to chopping the mushrooms, the rhythm of her work subtly changed, or so it seemed to Wes. Wes tore off a sheet of paper towel and used it to dry the sweetbread on both sides, after which he seasoned it with salt and pepper. He poured a modest mound of flour into a shallow bowl and dredged the sweetbread through it, making sure that every shallow crevice and depression received a thorough coating. Then he sought out a heavy sauté pan from beneath the counter, placed it over a medium flame on the stovetop, allowed it to warm for a few moments, and added two tablespoons of vegetable oil. He tried to focus on the task at hand, to be in the moment, and not to allow himself to be distracted by wayward thoughts. As the oil heated, it thinned slightly and covered the bottom of the pan. When Wes deemed it to be sufficiently hot, he grasped the sweetbread between the thumbs and forefingers of both hands, shook the loose flour into the bowl, and gently laid it at the center of the pan. It sizzled briefly and emitted a thin cloud of steam. Wes grasped the pan by the handle and gave it a quick jolt to prevent the meat from sticking. Then he turned the oven on to warm to two hundred degrees, checked that the kettle was full, and turned the gas on high underneath it. Nora stood back from the counter—she had finished chopping the mushrooms and invited Wes to assess her work. She'd done a conscientious, workmanlike job, and Wes nodded his approval.

"See this blue cheese? I want you to get a small plate and crumble the cheese onto it, little pieces about the size of a pea. Can you do that?"

"What's this for?"

"The potatoes."

"Yum."

While Nora was occupied with the cheese, Wes chopped the parsley and cut the stems off the bok choy. He gave the pan another jolt. Wes wasn't sure that he believed, as he once had, that there was a right way and a wrong way to do anything, but it certainly felt that way when he was cooking. There was a precise, limited number of ingredients; they needed to be addressed in a particular order and handled and combined in a specific way; they were required, in theory, to undergo a pre-defined physical transformation through the application of the appropriate heat in a suitable crucible; the goal was that, by the end of the process, the disparate elements should have acted upon one another and melded into the single, ideal product that had been envisaged and desired even before the first step had been taken—even before the ingredients had been purchased and assembled. Wes could not think of any other activity in his life or the life of anyone else in which control, mastery and vision were applied to such satisfying, foreseeable ends. People said that writers were driven by the need to create a world over which they could exert total control, but Wes knew from his own experience and from observing his father that in writing you often ended up making something that was very different from what you had intended to make when you had started out. That was not and could not be true in cooking. If you start out with the idea of making a cake, you had damn well better end up making a cake—and exactly the same cake you had intended to make—because any other result is by definition a failure. If you start out with the idea of making seared sweetbreads with mushrooms and bok choy, and you end up with anything other than seared sweetbreads with mushrooms and bok choy, you have done something terribly wrong. But even if you do get it wrong, there is something reassuring and simple in the knowledge that certain rules and certain procedures, if followed, will and must yield certain results. If you understand what you want, and precisely what you need to do to get it, you ought not to end up with your heart broken or your thoughts confused. You can congratulate yourself and people will love and admire you for your ability to follow instructions. That was the theory.

Wes lifted one end of the sweetbread with a flexible spatula, considered the underside, then flipped the entire slab over. It was perfectly golden brown, crisp and glistening, just as called for in the recipe, and was enveloped in a steamy cloud that smelled of nuts, earth and something just on the right, sexy side of sweaty. He was briefly disturbed by a sense memory of his own lips on Lucy's inner thigh, but with Nora standing at his side, looking down into the pan like Macbeth seeking his destiny in the witches' cauldron, he chose not to indulge it.

"What's next?"

"Tear me off a square of tin foil, about yea big."

Wes thought there must be a way to make life more like cooking—a series of recipes that could be followed faithfully to predictable results. Why shouldn't he be able to line up all these ingredients on the counter and make perfect sense of them? What if he were just to come out and say to himself: "Okay, I loved Delia, or thought I loved her, but now I see that maybe I didn't, or don't anymore." Why shouldn't that come out just right? And yet it didn't. There was something missing. It was as if you were trying to bake a cake, say, but for every ingredient listed in the recipe there were three secret ingredients that you had to figure out for yourself. So, when you said "I loved Delia," the secret ingredients might be "I desired Delia," "I loved the idea of being in love with Delia," and "I invented Delia," or they might be three completely different things; when you said "I thought I loved her," the secret ingredients might be "you don't know what love is," "you would have loved anyone," and "you have never understood your own desires;" and when you said "I don't anymore," what you needed to add was "I will never love again," "I will never love" and "I love someone else." Or not. How the fuck did people do it? Did they just close their eyes and guess?

The kettle was now at full boil, and Wes turned off the heat underneath it. When Nora returned, Wes retrieved a baking sheet from the interior of the oven and lined it with the foil. Then he and Nora resumed their vigil over the pan. After a minute or two, Nora leaned her body against his, and he draped his arm over her shoulder.

"Still looks gross to me."

"It isn't."

"Stinks like a wet dog."

Another minute passed, and Wes again checked the underside of the sweetbread with the spatula, deciding that it was done. There was no getting around it—where earlier it had resembled a misshapen, metastatized, grayish and glistening turd, it now looked more like a beautifully golden, crispy, fragrant turd. He transferred it to the baking sheet, which he slid into the warming oven, along with a large, oval platter. He walked the sauté pan to the sink and poured off most of the fat, taking care to aim the stream directly into the drain so as not to create extra mess. Then he returned the pan to the burner, raised the flame a little, cut a one-tablespoon length from the stick of butter and dropped it into the pan, swirling it to make the butter melt a little faster. When the butter began to color, he reached across Nora for the chopping board and scraped the mushrooms into the pan, turning them with a wooden spoon.

"You want to stir?"

"'Kay."

Wes watched Nora stir the mushrooms as if they were precious, fragile jewels, and when they had given off most of their liquid and turned soft and light brown, he scraped in the shallots and garlic.

"Keep stirring."

Wes ground some pepper into the mixture and threw in a

light palmful of salt, then tipped the tomatoes into the pan along with a half cup of wine. Nora stepped away fearfully from the violently rising steam, but Wes stood behind her and gently nudged her towards the stove, showing her that she had nothing to fear. He raised the heat to high and the wine began to bubble vigorously, breaking down the tomatoes.

"Keep stirring."

Wes found an old wooden serving tray in the larder, brought it into the kitchen, and stacked it with four plates, four wine glasses, four knives, four forks and four paper napkins, then returned to Nora. With the tomatoes almost dissolved, he emptied the tub of veal stock into the pan, allowed it to come to a boil, then lowered the heat until the sauce loitered at a gentle simmer.

"Do me a favor, Cookie? Go make sure mom's awake?"

"'Kay."

Wes turned the gas on again beneath the kettle, and poured the potato flakes into a stainless steel bowl. The water in the kettle returned to the boil almost immediately; he measured out a full cup and poured it over the flakes, which instantly dissolved into a gluey pudding. Wes scraped the crumbled blue cheese into the mess and stirred until the cheese had fully melted into it. He sampled the potatoes, then added salt, pepper, butter and a dash of paprika from the spice rack. It was not, he considered, a dish that any reasonable person might identify as mashed potatoes, but it had a kind of perplexing uniqueness, a quiddity, that he hoped others would find intriguing. Back on the stove, the mushroom sauce had thickened appreciably, and Wes tested it for consistency against the back of a spoon, which it coated in a silken, coruscating unction the color of damp loam. Wes threw in the bok choy, parsley and a healthy pat of butter, swirled them into the sauce and turned the gas down to the lowest possible simmer while he retrieved the warming sweetbread from the oven. Using a pair of tongs,

he picked most of the bok choy leaves out of the sauce and created a bed of greens at the center of the platter, onto which he
transferred the sweetbread, then spooned the sauce directly
onto the meat. *Et voilà—ris de veau aux champignons sur lit vert.*
Bon appétit!

Nora appeared in the doorway. "Someone's here for you.
It's a girl. It's your girlfriend, I think." Lucy was lingering
behind her in the doorway. She stepped out of the shadows,
looking awfully beautiful, and smiled.

"'Allo, *Lez-lee*," she said in a cartoon French accent. "Ah
'ope you 'ave ze sweat breeds ah commanded? *Sacré bleu!*"

"Nora, this is Lucy. Lucy, Nora."

"I didn't even know Wes had a girlfriend until James told me."

"Leslie didn't know he had a girlfriend until James told him."

"She's not . . . "

"Don't say anything stupid, Leslie."

"He lets you call him Leslie?"

"I can call him anything I want. I'm his *girlfriend*. I usually
call him Typo."

"Typo? Can I call you Typo?"

"No. Think you can manage that tray, Cookie?"

"Maybe, but I better not."

"Okay. I'll take the plates and you take the food, Lucy.
Careful, the plate might be hot."

Wes conveyed the tray up the stairs, while behind him Nora
whispered something that made Lucy giggle. Outside the bedroom, Wes turned and entered the room backwards, opening
the door with his butt. Lucy followed close behind and gently
lowered her tray onto the corner of the bed, as there was no
other free horizontal space in the room. His mother was sitting
up in bed, hair newly combed and housecoat neatly draped
across her chest.

"Nora told me Lucy's here. Lucy honey."

Lucy planted a kiss on Wes's mother's cheek and sat beside

her at the edge of the bed. Only then did Wes notice that she had changed her clothes. She was now wearing a short black dress, made of some sort of shimmery material, with a kind of half-length purple cardigan.

"It was so nice of you to invite me to dinner, Marion. My mom and dad are away for the weekend, so when Wes said he was making sweetbreads . . . "

All four looked down upon the sweetbread, which swam in a pool of sauce the color of crude petroleum that shimmered and rippled in response to the vibrations of the mattress. Wes was put in mind of the raft of the Medusa, with the mushrooms, despairing of their lives, clinging to their pathetic vessel like starving, half-crazed seamen. On the television, Bob Ross enumerated the colors necessary to undertake the painting he was preparing to demonstrate: titanium white, phtalo blue, dark sienna, van dyke brown, alizarin crimson, sap green, yellow ochre, Indian yellow, and bright red. Wes took up a carving knife from his tray and proceeded to cut the sweetbread into four equal quarters, while Nora hovered anxiously at his back. The meat did not feel like steak beneath the blade, or even like brisket; barely resisting the lightest pressure and uniformly unctuous, it felt more like a heavy pudding. Each section was the size of a large burger.

"Your parents allow you to stay at home by yourself, Lucy?"

"My sister was supposed to come down from college, but she got stuck or something at the last minute, but I'm okay by myself."

"Well, I don't know about that but I'm glad you're here. Leslie works too hard, he never has anyone his own age around to keep him company."

"I'm only here for the grub."

"Did you hear what she said? You can sit a little closer if you like, Lucy."

"Thanks. I'll do that."

Wes took the top plate and laid down a shallow coating of sauce, upon which he placed a ragged bed of wilted bok choy to underlie the ration of sweetbread and mushrooms. At its side went a dollop of potato, which received a finishing drizzle of sauce. Wes thought it a reasonably professional presentation, in the context of lowered expectations, something that might perhaps be offered by an early loser on "Top Chef." He handed it on to Nora, who solemnly married it with a knife and fork rolled up in a linen napkin and sat it gingerly upon the breakfast tray that she had previously positioned on their mother's lap. It was the only such tray in the house—the rest of them would have to balance their plates on their knees. Nora proceeded to cut half their mother's portion into bite-size parcels while Wes repeated the plating exercise for Lucy, and handed it to her where she had stretched out beside his mother on the bed.

"Do you want me to hold the fork for you, mommy?"

"I think I can manage tonight."

"I think this needs the right wine, don't you? Would it be okay if we had a glass of wine, Marion?"

"I think one glass wouldn't do any harm, darling."

"I'll get it. Pause the tv."

Wes served Nora, who had claimed her mother's old wheelchair from the corner where it had sat unused these many months. He ran down the two flights of stairs to the garden floor, where his father kept the wine in a hallway closet. Wes didn't know a lot about wine; of the three dozen or so bottles most seemed like generic French table wines, but because many still had their price stickers he was able to select a Brunello that was at least five times as expensive as the rest. In his father's office across the narrow passageway The Band was playing "Up on Cripple Creek" at low volume; light shone through the crack below the closed door, but there was no way to know if his father was in there or not. Wes grabbed a corkscrew and took the stairs two by two to his mother's bedroom.

Nora had abandoned the wheelchair and was sitting on the bed with Lucy and his mother, who were doubled over with laughter. Bobby was apparently coming to the end of a typically breathless, elaborate shaggy dog story.

"Bobby paid for that cheese, Bobby waited for that cheese, Bobby suffered for that cheese, and Bobby wants that cheese NOW!"

Wes uncorked the bottle and filled three tumblers, reserving a thimbleful for Nora, which he handed to the girls on the bed, who toasted one another raucously. Nora drained her tumbler in one gulp and held it out brazenly for a refill, but Wes ignored her and grabbed the remote.

"We don't have to watch Bob tonight, Leslie, if you'd rather talk."

"Oh no, please Marion! Can't we watch one show?"

"That's fine with me, darling."

They settled down, adjusting their pillows and their clothing, and Wes resumed the program.

A plate of food had been set aside for Wes at the foot of the bed. Wes had forgotten to warm the plates, and the sauce had formed an unattractive skin across the bottom of his, which he dragged with the tine of his fork to the side, where it looked like a tiny pup tent collapsed by a strong wind. He brought his plate up to his nose—it did not smell of urine, the way sautéed kidneys did; nor of mild fish, as had his one and only taste of brains, rolled in egg and breadcrumbs and fried golden to resemble chicken nuggets as a prank at a Halloween party; nor yet of a stable, like tripe. It smelled unquestionably of rich, fertile soil, a good smell to Wes though he recognized that most people might find it a little ripe.

By now, Bob Ross was well into his painting. Wes recognized it immediately as an episode he had seen several times, one in which, before the start of the show, Bob had already covered most of the canvas in a very dark green, almost black paint with a white hole in the middle. Eventually, the hole would come to be seen as a distant clearing in a dark wood, with light streaming in from the upper right and a path meandering through the dark part of the woods towards the light. The prevailing color was lavender, and the feeling Bob seemed to want to evoke was one of quietude and serenity, like a romantic poem, as if the viewer were strolling deep in thought through a dim, pristine forest, when he was suddenly struck by a vision, or inspiration, or whatever. Bob never, ever talked about God, but Wes suspected that he was deeply pious, with an animist strain. This painting, for instance, Wes thought evoked a journey through danger towards salvation, or the experience of someone who has died and is following the light. The metaphor could only go so far, of course, because Bob would be finished with this painting in twenty-five minutes and move on to the next with barely a backward glance, but in his present mood Wes was feeling especially affable towards Bob and ready to parse his oeuvre in the most generous possible spirit of equanimity. Far better to be watching Bob Ross in the bosom of his family, howsoever fucked up, than upstairs in his bed trying to milk Tolstoy for pearls of wisdom about misguided love.

"This is a super painting for a young friend because it looks like something right out of a fairytale. You can add any kind of characters that you want to."

"I've seen this one."

"We've all seen this one."

Wes set his plate on the carpet and cut himself a heavy forkful of sweetbread, upon which he piled slices of mushroom. There was the briefest wave of nausea as he slotted it into his mouth and began to chew meditatively, but that was probably less to do with the aroma—which he had to admit was a little insistent—than with the size of the portion. Wes had read somewhere that the sense of taste was informed as much by the chemistry of scent as by the response of the buds on the tongue, and he made a deliberate effort to continue to breathe through his nostrils as he chewed. The sweetbread, he found, really did taste the way it looked and smelled—like a mouthful of liver mixed with a fistful of very rich loam or peat, but in a not altogether unpleasant way. There was a slight problem with the mouth-feel—somewhere between a boiled pudding and a ripe banana—but it was offset by the fattiness and mellow seasoning of the sauce. All in all he was inclined to believe that the sweetbread was quite palatable in its own way, and that no matter what you might say about it, at least it tasted better than it smelled.

"Isn't it fantastic that you can take a brush this big and make something that looks so delicate. And you can—you really can."

"I can, Bob! I really can!"

"Quiet. Can't you see he's in the zone?"

Wes glanced over his shoulder toward the bed, where Nora had insinuated herself between his mother and Lucy and was snuggled down in the crook of Lucy's elbow, her cheek resting lightly on her elbow. All of them were transfixed by Bob Ross's patter, and none had made much of a dent in her sweetbreads. Wes wondered what Delia would make of this scene—the sweetbread, the tv dinner, Bob Ross. In fact, Wes barely needed to think to know that she would hate everything about it. Delia, of course, was a vegetarian, so it went without saying that she would disapprove of the sweetbread. As he had heard her do often enough, she would lecture him about the wrongness of eating other animals, the cruelty of industrial farms and butchery, the bad karma accrued by consuming flesh, which was all fair and good, as far as Wes was concerned. But she would also feel the need to prove that she was broadminded because she was not a dogmatic vegan, she ate eggs and dairy products so long as they were produced humanely, as if Wes needed cajoling by someone he could "identify" with, as if he were unable to understand her arguments without being spoken down to. It was not so much what she said, because it all made a certain amount of sense, but the way in which she said it—that calm, authoritarian tone, the imperturbable patience, the steady gaze from her lofty perch, the implied condescension. In addition to all this, as if it weren't enough, Wes had the feeling that Delia would find something especially objectionable about sweetbreads, as opposed to "regular" meat, as if it were in a kind of hyper-fleshly category of its own. Delia probably wouldn't say any of these things, because she was quite political, but it would be hard to enjoy one's meal with Delia around, knowing what she was thinking.

"People will never believe you can paint this much detail using a big ol' crazy brush like this, but you can. You can do anything as long as you believe you can do it. It helps mentally, when you decide you're going to paint a picture, paint it mentally several times and get the strokes sort of worked out in your mind. Know what you want before you start, but do it mentally."

Lucy said: "Can we put it on pause a minute? I have a question." Wes paused the show. Lucy sat up and collected her thoughts for a moment while the others waited upon her expectantly. She cleared her throat.

"What the heck do you think he's getting at?"

"I don't follow you, Lucy."

"I mean, what makes Bob Ross tick? What's he trying to tell us, being the way he is? Who is Bob Ross?"

"Bob Ross is a runaway munchkin, obviously. Anybody knows that."

"What do you think he is?"

"I can't make him out at all. Sometimes I think it's all just an act—I mean, he made millions of dollars doing this, didn't he?—but then I think there's something else behind it, something dark, maybe even scary."

"You know, he spent years in the Air Force, and he always said that when he left the military he never wanted to yell at anybody ever again."

"So it's like a trauma? Like if he ever raised his voice again he would wake up this sleeping monster inside of him? So he spends his whole life whispering?"

"Maybe. My dad thinks he was a major scam artist, that he knew he was selling trash to suckers because he was so good at it, but I don't think that's it at all. I think he was totally sincere about his art and really believed in it, not just because he thought it was beautiful but because it was his gift to the world, like medicine. Something bad happened to him, and he was able to cure himself, and he wanted to share it. He didn't give a shit if real artists laughed at him because he knew he could help people. Does that make sense?"

Lucy was staring at him very intently, and Wes could not quite read the look in her eye, as if she were preparing some clever, sarcastic comeback. But then he saw the color rise in her cheeks, and it must have been a lot of color because she was already quite tan and the lighting was so poor in his mother's bedroom, and he knew then that she was thinking something really nice and warm about him, and he blushed in return, which she saw. And Nora was watching the whole thing with a look of such shock that it was clear she had grasped exactly what was going on. Lucy just shook her head and smiled.

"What do you think, Marion? Was Bob Ross a genius?"

Wes could tell that his mother had not quite been able to follow the conversation, that she was beginning to fade, as in some ways this had been quite an eventful day for her. She smiled, turning to each of them in turn with a shrug of the shoulders and a look of forlorn wistfulness, as if she were on the deck of a ship that was pulling away from the dock. But then she frowned, a frown of concentration, of remembering something that had bothered her long ago and that she'd meant to resolve but had put out of mind until just now.

"Bob Ross is the unknown. The unknowable."

"Cool."

Wes turned the show back on.

"I got a letter from somebody a while back, and they said 'Bob, everything in your world seems to be happy.' That's for sure. That's why I paint. It's because I can create the kind of world that I want, and I can make this world as happy as I want it. Shoot, if you want bad stuff, watch the news. This is a tranquil world here. We don't allow bad stuff in our paintings."

Bob had almost finished his painting. Wes had misremembered it—it was not a path meandering down the center of the canvas towards the clearing but a babbling brook. Bob Ross almost always had water in his paintings to show off his facility with reflections and ripples, which he was able to convey with startling realism with just one or two strokes of the brush or the edge of his paint knife. Bob's paintings were remarkable for their empty stillness—no animals grazing or hunting, and the clouds themselves always seemed to be suspended at a moment of dying wind, as if the earth were holding its breath and pausing to pose for the artist—so the water component was needed to give the scene a sense of movement and sound. Very occasionally, a painting might include an old cabin with sagging roof and darkened windows, but it always felt abandoned or, at the very most, lightly inhabited by woodsmen who spent days away in the wilderness. In any case, there were no people in Bob's pictures, and impossible to imagine that the world had such things as paved roads, power lines, contrails, four-by-fours or cities. That was part of what made him and his work so ineffably sad.

Wes glanced down at his plate and was surprised to find

that he had eaten almost everything, other than a few remnants of potato and greens. He couldn't remember eating any but the first mouthful. Nora, who was normally an adventurous eater, had made a game attempt, but the sweetbread had defeated her and more than three quarters of it remained on her plate. Her potatoes, on the other hand, were all gone. She caught Wes's eye and pointed with one hand to the emptiness where the potato had been, and mimed rubbing her tummy with the other. "Bobby like," she mouthed wordlessly, and returned her attention to the television.

"Now then, you have to start making some big decisions. Just sort of let your imagination go. Think if you were a tree where you'd like to live. This tree, he lives right here at the side of the brook. He has one of the prettiest views. He looks out over this brook and watches everything happen. This is your tree, so you make it any way that you want, any way that you want. In your world, you can have anything, anything."

Something had just happened, and now Wes thought he knew what it was. He had always imagined that if he could persuade Delia to look deep into this eyes, she would see herself in them the way he saw her, and that she would understand that she was being seen in a way that no one had ever seen her, and loved in a way that no one had ever loved her. He had been convinced of it, but what he had failed to grasp was how hard it is to persuade someone to look into your eyes with the confidence and patience to see what you wanted them to see. It wasn't the love that was difficult; it was the communication of love. It was the willingness of the other to be loved and to look for the love. And what had just happened to Wes was that he had looked into Lucy's eyes precisely the way he had always hoped Delia would look into his, and there had been a message waiting for him there. Its meaning had been far from obvious, its intention less explicit than what he had had in store for Delia, but it was clearly a message that was addressed to him alone. And it would also be a mirror of some sort, or a portrait, a painting of himself. That much he had been able to tell; he just hadn't been able to recognize himself in it in any way.

What exactly did she see when she looked at him? What if it were Wes instead of Lucy, stumbling upon a family scene like this one? He recalled a book or a movie, without remembering what it was, in which the dying hero floats disembodied over the battlefield where he has been mortally wounded, and looks down with infinite and equal compassion and understanding on the slayers and the slain alike. Wes imagined himself doing the same thing here, in this sickroom. What would he see? A frail, dying woman, half-crazed with suffering and ill-served by the indifference, confusion and horror of her children and absent husband; a perfect, beautiful little girl, born to be generous, kind and loving, but already firmly on the path towards a lifetime of myopic stumbling towards things that, from a distance, look like love but turn out to be anything but; a boy, angry and resentful, self-involved and self-pitying, a fly caught and struggling in a spider's web, a villain and a spy, a perennial shopper in the flea market of second-hand ideas and emotions, dressed in everyone's cast-offs yet with no style of his own, morose with offended vanity but covetous and envious of all and everything. If he were Delia or Lucy, what would he make of such a boy? If he were James, or Nora, or Mrs. Fielding, could he even like such a boy? Could he, like the dying soldier, ever summon up compassion and understanding for such a boy?

"And just remember, we don't make mistakes here. There are no mistakes, only happy little accidents."

Lucy slid off the bed and settled on the floor beside him, holding her finger to her lips and nodding towards Nora and his mother, entwined in sleep on the bed behind them. She pressed her shoulder against his and wrapped one hand around his bicep, but she kept her eyes firmly glued to the television, where Bob Ross was getting ready to sign his painting and call it a day. Whatever the message she had for him, she was going to hold it in store for a new day.

"This little piece of canvas is your world and on here you can do anything that your heart desires. You can create any illusion that you want here. You can find peace and tranquility here, or you can make big storms. It just depends on what your mood is that day. Painting is just a way of capturing a second of time and mood, and putting it on canvas. And maybe a hundred years from now somebody will look at your painting and know that you had a fantastic day, and that on this day you truly did experience the joy of painting. God bless."

The credits began to roll and the hokey electronic xylophone theme song to play, but Lucy didn't move. For a moment Wes thought that she, too, had fallen asleep, but then he felt her fingers tapping the beat against his arm. She smelled of the same soap she had smelled of at the party, and her nails were short, like a boy's, but shiny with clear polish. Wes turned to her and was about to try to kiss her when he thought better of it.

"Do you want to stay?" he whispered.

She hesitated a moment then shook her head. "I'm getting picked up at my place at six in the morning. Anyway."

"Yes we can."

"No, that's what I'm saying, we can't . . . "

"No, I mean Obama. Pennsylvania. Yes We Can."

She snorted and buried her laughter against his shoulder. "Yes. We. Can. But not tonight."

"Help me with this stuff?"

Together, they gathered up the dirty dishes and piled them on the tray as quietly as possible. His mother had not touched her food, but even Lucy had barely made it through half of hers.

"Not so crispy, eh?"

"They do it better in Paris."

"Not enough potato flakes."

He took the heavy tray from Lucy and handed her the empty one, and they went to the kitchen together. The wine bottle had been emptied. Wes was too tired to clean up, but since he knew that he would be the first awake in the morning, he was confident that the dirty dishes would be waiting for him the next day. Even in his exhaustion, he had enough presence of mind to rinse the dishes and fill the pots with water, in order to make his chore easier tomorrow. Nora appeared in the doorway, rubbing her eyes, and Lucy rubbed her back between the shoulder blades.

"I'd better be going, Typo."

"Don't go, Lucy. You can sleep in my room."

"Sorry Cookie."

"Leslie's usually a better cook than that."

"He'd better be if he wants me to eat at this restaurant again. Someone told me he makes a mean risotto."

"Who told you that?"

"He did."

"Chump."

"I'll see you when?"

"Monday morning, natch."

He leaned in to kiss her goodbye chastely. She whispered "Well done" in his ear, and was gone.

"Bobby like Lucy."

"Typo too."

"Are you going to bed?"

"Nah. I'd better try to make a little headway with my homework. Wanna come read in my room?"

"Sure."

Together, they plodded up the stairs in silence, Wes stopping off at their mother's room to tuck her under the covers and turn out the lights. At the top of the stairs, Nora branched off to her room. Even before he opened his bedroom door he felt a current of cold air on his bare toes, and upon opening it was met with a swirl of wind and the sound of rustling leaves. Without turning on the light, he walked to the window and leaned out. The night had turned autumnal, and there were even a few bright stars in the sky. The wind in the trees drowned out all other sounds of the city, and Wes enjoyed the feel of cold air on his face for a few moments before turning back into the room and shutting the window behind him. He grabbed his laptop and the copy of *War and* Peace from the desk. It had occurred to him that the scene of the dying soldier could well be out of *War and Peace*, and that if he could find it again it might provide sorely needed inspiration to the task at hand. But even as he leafed through the book he realized that the scene could not possibly be from *War and Peace*, because the soldier, whoever he is, dies on the battlefield, whereas Prince André is wounded at Borodino but does not die until much later. Even so, Wes continued to flick through the book, barely able to remember what the whole fuss was about. A thousand pages of nothing; even ten thousand would have been insufficient to describe one minute of a real person's life, he thought. But the paper had to get written, inspired or not. Wes came upon his scrawled notes at the back of the book, and his eyes fell on the paragraph about Petya.

- "Death of Petya. Manipulative to what end except pathos? Ultimately, P's death is necessary to get Natasha to focus on her mother and someone else's grief, but that is just a plot twist. Is a boy's life of so little value? Never identified with Petya, boyscout type, but angry on his behalf."

Maybe Wes could make something out of that? To show, by parsing the trajectory of a minor character like Petya, how Tolstoy manipulates character to further his programmatic novelistic ends—a kind of deconstructionist analysis that strips away the flesh of so-called "realism" to reveal the bare skeleton of ideology beneath? Wes was willing to bet that no one in Mrs. Fielding's class had ever written a paper about Petya before, or even given his character more than a passing consideration. It would be a very clever tour de force. But just as he was beginning to warm to the prospect, Wes felt his enthusiasm collapse like a punctured balloon. It wasn't so much that it was a bad idea, but Wes had had a sudden vision of himself—striving, conniving, intellectually dishonest and arrogant, too interested in making a mark and scoring a point— and it made him dizzy with exhaustion. He was exhausted by *War and Peace*, by the very idea of *War and Peace*, but most of all he was exhausted by himself, by the incredible amount of energy it took to keep this carnival on the road. It would be better just to dig in, like a road-weary donkey, than to maintain this charade. It would be more honest to resubmit the paper on the *Manual*, for all its flaws, and take the F he had coming to him, even if it meant ruining his college prospects, than it would be to try and find something interesting, original and engaging to say about *War and Peace*. Even as he thought these things Wes knew there was little chance that they would come to pass, that it was only the exhaustion speaking and that by tomorrow he would probably have some rescue plan figured out, but right now he was so heartily sick and tired of himself that the prospect of academic Armageddon filled him with a kind of ecstatic, mystic elation, like a medieval saint. He thought of the dream he'd had that morning, and the imagery of counting light bulbs and plummeting aircraft made a certain sense in light of the day's experience. He had been right, after all, to assume that the mind knew its own business and understood things that were difficult to communicate to the consciousness. Even when Wes came to despise his own mind and everything it put him through, it was out there working on his behalf. His thoughts were interrupted by a strange noise coming from the kitchen two floors below, and he paused to consider it just as Nora entered the room in pajamas and slippers, book in hand.

"What's that sound?"

"What sound?"

"Downstairs. Listen."

Nora halted in the doorway and cocked her head. She was in her old Paul Frank pjs, riddled with monkey-face logos, that she often wore in moments of stress, although now, of course, they were far too small for her and made her look a little like a circus freak. Wes considered her fondly, and smiled.

"It must be dad doing the dishes."

"Holy shit, I think you're right."

Nora threw herself down on the bed beside Wes and began to leaf through the pages of her book.

"Whatcha reading?"

"*I Capture the Castle.*"

"What's it about?"

"It's about a girl who lives in a falling-apart castle with her sister and her dad, who used to be a famous writer but isn't anymore, and she's sick of everything but she's super smart, and then she and her sister fall in love with some rich boys who move in next door, or something like that."

"Is it European?"

"I don't know? Is England European?"

"Is it a kid's book or an adult book? I mean, is it something you might read in a high school English class?"

"I don't know. It's by the same lady who wrote *A Hundred and One Dalmatians.*"

Wes sighed and closed his eyes. Whatever the solution was, it would have to wait until the next day, as he was too tired to think. He listened to Nora turning the pages of her book and breathing heavily through her nose, and he knew that he could fall asleep right then and there, but felt that there was something still to do that he had left undone. He opened his eyes, and his gaze happened to fall on the bookshelf above his desk. He pushed himself up heavily from the bed, crossed the room and reached out for the thin, ragged hard-cover novel sandwiched between two massive, glossy textbooks. It was *The Breadbaking District*. He took it back to the bed and examined it. Although he had never read it, this was not the first time he had held it in his hands, but he felt that in some way he was seeing it for the very first time. The cover was a kind of pastiche of a Dickensian novel, with a nineteenth-century lithograph of a baker sliding a paddle of dough into a brick oven, a daintily filigreed border and an ornate Victorian typeface that Wes thought made the book look cheap, as if the publisher could not afford a real designer. The paper stock, too, was clearly not of the best, and Wes wondered whether his father had been aware at the time of publication how little effort his publisher had put into making his book attractive. Wes turned the book over and read the captions on the back. "An impressive debut . . . captures the elation and sweet sorrow of first love." "The author shows promise beyond his years . . . someone to be watched." Even the blurbs—written not by real writers but by anonymous reviewers in professional journals— seemed half-hearted, hardly commendations at all, and Wes felt sad for his father. He was sure the book must at least be better than his publisher had made it look. When all this was over, Wes decided, he would finally sit down and read it.

Wes put his feet against the wall and stretched out his back, nestling his head against Nora's knees. She stroked his hair and perched her book on his forehead, saying "Good daddy-o" under her breath. Directly overhead was the crack in the ceiling. It really was a very modest crack, and certainly not big enough to stop his mind from wandering. He closed his eyes. Wes could feel himself drifting, but in a last moment of clarity he suddenly realized that he had always misunderstood the lyric. Because of the way Paul McCartney stressed the lines, Wes had always understood him to say: "And it really doesn't matter if I'm wrong, I'm right. Where I belong I'm right. Where I belong," as if he were implying that even when he was mistaken he had grasped something essential and unspoken. But in fact, the lyric made more sense if you parsed it another way. "And it really doesn't matter if I'm wrong. I'm right where I belong. I'm right where I belong." Wes thought it was more obvious and less interesting this second way, but it worked, and it rhymed better. Wes hoped that this insight wouldn't ruin his future enjoyment of the song, but how could it if the song now had two interpretations instead of one? It would be worth looking into. And then he remembered what it was he still needed to do before putting the day to bed.

"Want to go for a walk?"

Nora did not look up from her book. "I'm in my pjs."

"So? Throw on a coat. It's a beautiful night, and Crispy really needs her walk."

"Nah, I'm okay."

Wes sat up, found his sneakers under the bed, pulled them on and laced them up. He perched on the edge of his bed, gathered his strength, and stood with a muffled grunt, pushing with his palms against his knees like an old man. Then he gathered his hoodie from the floor and crossed the room to the door. On the bed, the iPhone emitted a crystalline chime. Nora lifted her head and looked at the phone, then at Wes, who waited with one hand on the doorknob. The iPhone chimed twice, three times, then with a delicate electronic burp sent the call to voice mail. Wes turned the knob and opened the door.

"I won't be long."

About the Author

Jesse Browner is an author, food writer and award-winning translator. He has written four previous books including the novels *Conglomeros* (Random House 1992), *Turnaway* (Random House 1996) and *The Uncertain Hour* (Bloomsbury 2007), and has translated works by Jean Cocteau, Paul Éluard and Rainer Maria Rilke. His writing has appeared in *The New York Times Book Review*, *New York* magazine, *Food & Wine* and *Gastronomica*, among others. He lives in Manhattan with his wife and two daughters.

Europa Editions publishes in the USA and in the UK. Not all titles are available in both countries. Availability of individual titles is indicated in the following list.

Carmine Abate
Between Two Seas
"A moving portrayal of generational continuity."
—*Kirkus*
224 pp • $14.95 • 978-1-933372-40-2 • Territories: World

Salwa Al Neimi
The Proof of the Honey
"Al Neimi announces the end of a taboo in the Arab world: that of *sex*!"
—*Reuters*
144 pp • $15.00 • 978-1-933372-68-6 • Territories: World

Alberto Angela
A Day in the Life of Ancient Rome
"Fascinating and accessible."
—*Il Giornale*
392 pp • $16.00 • 978-1-933372-71-6 • Territories: USA & Canada

Muriel Barbery
The Elegance of the Hedgehog
"Gently satirical, exceptionally winning and inevitably bittersweet."
—Michael Dirda, *The Washington Post*
336 pp • $15.00 • 978-1-933372-60-0 • Territories: USA & Canada

Gourmet Rhapsody
"In the pages of this book, Barbery shows off her finest gift: lightness."
—*La Repubblica*
176 pp • $15.00 • 978-1-933372-95-2 • Territories: World (except UK, EU)

Stefano Benni
Margherita Dolce Vita
"A modern fable…hilarious social commentary."—*People*
240 pp • $14.95 • 978-1-933372-20-4

Timeskipper
"Benni again unveils his Italian brand of magical realism."
—*Library Journal*
400 pp • $16.95 • 978-1-933372-44-0

Romano Bilenchi
The Chill
120 pp • $15.00 • 978-1-933372-90-7

Massimo Carlotto
The Goodbye Kiss
"A masterpiece of Italian noir."
—*Globe and Mail*
160 pp • $14.95 • 978-1-933372-05-1

Death's Dark Abyss
"A remarkable study of corruption and redemption."
—*Kirkus* (starred review)
160 pp • $14.95 • 978-1-933372-18-1

The Fugitive
"[Carlotto is] the reigning king of Mediterranean noir."
—*The Boston Phoenix*
176 pp • $14.95 • 978-1-933372-25-9

(with Marco Videtta)
Poisonville
"The business world as described by Carlotto and Videtta
in *Poisonville* is frightening as hell."
—*La Repubblica*
224 pp • $15.00 • 978-1-933372-91-4

Francisco Coloane
Tierra del Fuego
"Coloane is the Jack London of our times."—Alvaro Mutis
192 pp • $14.95 • 978-1-933372-63-1

Giancarlo De Cataldo
The Father and the Foreigner
"A slim but touching noir novel from one of Italy's best writers
in the genre."—*Quaderni Noir*
144 pp • $15.00 • 978-1-933372-72-3

Shashi Deshpande
The Dark Holds No Terrors
"[Deshpande is] an extremely talented storyteller."—*Hindustan Times*
272 pp • $15.00 • 978-1-933372-67-9

Helmut Dubiel
Deep In the Brain: Living with Parkinson's Disease
"A book that begs reflection."—*Die Zeit*
144 pp • $15.00 • 978 1 933372-70-9

Steve Erickson
Zeroville
"A funny, disturbing, daring and demanding novel—Erickson's best."
—The New York Times Book Review
352 pp • $14.95 • 978-1-933372-39-6 • Territories: USA & Canada

Elena Ferrante
The Days of Abandonment
"The raging, torrential voice of [this] author is something rare."
—The New York Times
192 pp • $14.95 • 978-1-933372-00-6 • Territories: World

Troubling Love
"Ferrante's polished language belies the rawness of her imagery."
—The New Yorker
144 pp • $14.95 • 978-1-933372-16-7 • Territories: World

The Lost Daughter
"So refined, almost translucent."*—The Boston Globe*
144 pp • $14.95 • 978-1-933372-42-6 • Territories: World

Jane Gardam
Old Filth
"Old Filth belongs in the Dickensian pantheon of memorable characters."
—The New York Times Book Review
304 pp • $14.95 • 978-1-933372-13-6 • Territories: USA

The Queen of the Tambourine
"A truly superb and moving novel."*—The Boston Globe*
272 pp • $14.95 • 978-1-933372-36-5 • Territories: USA

The People on Privilege Hill
"Engrossing stories of hilarity and heartbreak."—*Seattle Times*
208 pp • $15.95 • 978-1-933372-56-3 • Territories: USA

The Man in the Wooden Hat
"Here is a writer who delivers the world we live in...with memorable and moving skill."—*The Boston Globe*
240 pp • $15.00 • 978-1-933372-89 1 • Territories: USA

Alicia Giménez-Bartlett
Dog Day
"Delicado and Garzón prove to be one of the more engaging sleuth teams to debut in a long time."—*The Washington Post*
320 pp • $14.95 • 978-1-933372-14-3 • Territories: USA & Canada

Prime Time Suspect
"A gripping police procedural."—*The Washington Post*
320 pp • $14.95 • 978-1-933372-31-0 • Territories: USA & Canada

Death Rites
"Petra is developing into a good cop, and her earnest efforts to assert her authority...are worth cheering."—*The New York Times*
304 pp • $16.95 • 978-1-933372-54-9 • Territories: USA & Canada

Katharina Hacker
The Have-Nots
"Hacker's prose soars."—*Publishers Weekly*
352 pp • $14.95 • 978-1-933372-41-9 • Territories: USA & Canada

Patrick Hamilton
Hangover Square
"Patrick Hamilton's novels are dark tunnels of misery, loneliness, deceit, and sexual obsession."—*New York Review of Books*
336 pp • $14.95 • 978-1-933372-06-8 • Territories: USA & Canada

James Hamilton-Paterson
Cooking with Fernet Branca
"Irresistible!"—*The Washington Post*
288 pp • $14.95 • 978-1-933372-01-3 • Territories: USA & Canada

Amazing Disgrace
"It's loads of fun, light and dazzling as a peacock feather."
—*New York Magazine*
352 pp • $14.95 • 978-1-933372-19-8 • Territories: USA & Canada

Rancid Pansies
"Campy comic saga about hack writer and self-styled 'culinary genius' Gerald Samper."—*Seattle Times*
288 pp • $15.95 • 978-1-933372-62-4 • Territories: USA & Canada

Seven-Tenths: The Sea and Its Thresholds
"The kind of book that, were he alive now, Shelley might have written."
—*Charles Spawson*
416 pp • $16.00 • 978-1-933372-69-3 • Territories: USA & Canada

Alfred Hayes
The Girl on the Via Flaminia
"Immensely readable."—*The New York Times*
164 pp • $14.95 • 978-1-933372-24-2 • Territories: World